ETERNAL SIN

ARIANA NASH

Eternal Sin, Primal Sin #2

Ariana Nash - *Dark Fantasy Author*

Subscribe to Ariana's mailing list & get the exclusive story 'Sealed with a Kiss' free.

Join the Ariana Nash Facebook group for all the news, as it happens.

Copyright © 2020 Ariana Nash

Cover Design by Covers by Combs

Edited by Rascon Revisions / Proofreader Jennifer Griffin

ANTI-PIRACY WARNING

Long ago, a demon stole an angel's heart. He did not think the angel would miss his heart, because angels do not feel. But the demon was wrong. Without his heart, the angel became a monster. Where before, there had been compassion and trust in the angel, now he was hollow and hungry for vengeance.

The story of the demon who stole an angel's heart does not have a happy ending. If you steal ebooks, neither will you.

evern

HE DREAMED of kisses on a London rooftop. He dreamed of soft, black feathers shielding him from the rain. And he dreamed of falling in love with his enemy.

When he wasn't dreaming, pain ebbed and flowed, dragging his consciousness with it. He'd stopped feeling each cut long ago; now they were all one and the same. It hurt to breathe, to talk, to live.

He'd told them to stop, told them it was useless. He'd told them as they'd cut and cursed and tried to slice the illusion from his body. They did not listen.

Konstantin, Lost Lord of the Red Manor, had believed his own lies and made himself angel. It was impossible. But so was a demon falling in love with an angel.

Destiny had forsaken him.

If only his body would stop healing, so the pain would end.

And then it did end. But he'd been here before, forced back to consciousness by a break in the agony, and the pain always began again.

He blinked back into the moment, hearing his breaths, his heart desperately thumping, healing. The demons who did this to him—they were all gone, but they'd be back. Demons he knew. Demons of Red Manor who had once followed him. And the worst of it was, he knew why they hurt him. They'd bled for Konstantin, knelt to him, they'd die for him. And they'd do all that again to save him from himself, even if it meant breaking him into pieces before putting him back together.

Severn closed his eyes. A single, cool tear fell. He'd cried so many, this one had to be the last. He pulled his right arm, yanking the leather cuff holding him down. It didn't give. He hadn't expected it to. The restraints hadn't given an inch when he'd first been tied up, when he was stronger. Now, he was barely clinging to the pieces of himself.

A door rattled and swung open.

The demon who approached was the same one he'd seen in different dreams, older dreams—Konstantin's dreams. He still wasn't convinced the demon was real. Tawny skin radiated warmth and dazzling, golden eyes, the kind that arrested, shone. The demon wore a startling normal-looking pair of black trousers and a snug-fitting V-neck top. His wings were illusioned away, or they'd have filled the small room. Two horns curved like half-moons from his messy hairline. He didn't look over and instead pulled up a chair to the side of the table Severn was tied on. Then he sat and sighed.

Severn blinked at the ceiling. The demon wasn't here. His broken mind had dreamed him up.

"You gotta let go of the illusion," Samiel said.

He sounded real. Sounded like he'd lived in London his whole life. Severn remembered his laugh more than anything else. He'd loved to laugh. He'd laughed right up until the day he'd died, ten years ago.

Laughter tried to bubble out of Severn now. He swallowed it.

Another sigh. "Stantin, we're trying to help you."

Laughter choked him. Or maybe it was a sob. He couldn't tell. He turned his face away, afraid looking at Samiel might make him vanish. "Then let me go."

"We can't do that."

A warm, soft hand settled over Severn's. So real.

Samiel came and talked sometimes, but then he went away again, and the pain started. Severn didn't ask if his friend really survived all this time, fearing speaking it would vanish his ghost. So Samiel talked, filling the silence with updates on how Mikhail was tearing through demon forces, capturing and torturing demons. How he'd placed demon heads on spikes and lined them up along the killing fields. He spoke of how the demons didn't know Konstantin was alive. Rumors of his return had been quashed. Nobody knew he was in this little windowless room, having his skin cut from his bones over and over to make him less angel.

The warm hand traveled to Severn's damp thigh. He'd healed enough from the last round that his skin was smooth again. He healed like a fucking angel.

"We need to know you're still in there," Samiel said, and then whispered, "Konstantin."

The reverence in his name brought more useless tears to Severn's eyes. "Look at me! Fucking look, Sam!" He yanked at the restraints.

The door opened, and the demons were back, knives gleaming. Severn yanked again on the restraints, tried to thrash from the table, but it never worked. Hands held him down, a rod was forced between his teeth, and the blades dug in, carving flesh from bone.

The next time he came around, only Samiel was beside him, his hand hot on Severn's trembling, bloody thigh.

"You aren't feeding," he said, sadly.

Severn laughed. "Feeding?" His voice cracked and wheezed. He didn't care. What the fuck was he supposed to feed on? He looked over and found Samiel facing him, watching him, concern pinching his handsome face. "I'm tied here, they come, and they cut pieces off me, and you tell me I'm supposed to what... enjoy it?" He panted. Stringing words together took too much effort.

"You used to."

Severn thumped his head back down. It was true. He had enjoyed being restrained, but only with Samiel. And a little knife-play never bothered him. But this wasn't that. He could not harvest from those who cut him because they did not enjoy it. This whole situation was fucked up and wrong. "Free me or kill me. I can't..." His voice cracked again, coming apart like the rest of him. "I'll die here."

"Some think you're already dead," he said in the same soft voice he'd used to tell Konstantin he loved him.

Gods, that hurt. He'd known his kin either thought or

wished him dead, but hearing it made it real. "Then end it."

Samiel stood and leaned over Severn. His warm hand cupped Severn's cheek, turning his face toward him. This ghost looked just as Severn remembered Samiel. He had a gentle manner, always quick to smile. But he was no pushover. Too many made the mistake of thinking Samiel weak. He'd never been that. His glare bored into Severn's, drilling deep, seeking the truth. He smelled of warmth and heat and spices, like an open fire, and Severn suddenly ached to feel him close—to feel anyone close—just so the pain ended.

"They say you and Mikhail fucked. You're mated? Is that true?"

And there was the hardness Samiel revealed only to his enemies.

Severn swallowed. He was never getting off this table. He knew that now. They'd never let him go free, not while he looked like the enemy. If he wanted to live, to somehow get through this, and maybe... maybe make Mikhail see it hadn't all been lies, then he'd have to lie through his teeth. Again. Gods, it seemed lying was all he was good for. "The allyanse is an excuse for angels to fuck," he said, hearing the lies and hating them. "It's not a mystical bond or some shit. So yes, I fucked him, Sam. To feed. Because I could. Because ten years was a long time. Because angel tastes like a dream, and because afterward, he trusted me. I was going to ruin him. I just..."

"Then you're not bonded? It wasn't true?" he asked, eyebrows raised in hope. "We have to be sure."

"Fuck, no." He mustered a smile up from somewhere. They thought he'd turned completely angel. And well, he couldn't blame them because he had. Every word Samiel spoke of Mikhail made Severn's heart hurt. He wanted to go back to Whitechapel, to explain to Mikhail that everything had changed—they'd changed. He'd see, eventually. He just needed time to come around. But that couldn't happen while Severn was tied to a damn table.

Samiel withdrew his hand and dragged it over his mouth. "Shit, it's hard to look at you like this. You smell like *angel*." But there was no disgust in his words. Regret, perhaps.

"Try walking around inside this thin, pink skin for ten years." He'd grown to love this skin and remembered how sensitive it was beneath Mikhail's mouth, but that memory couldn't help him now. Neither could love.

"I missed you," Samiel said softly.

How... He wanted to ask. *How are you alive, Samiel?* He'd given up a memory to make this damned illusion stick. Had he given up the memory of Samiel surviving? It would have been powerful enough. He'd believed him dead. He'd used that to drive his passion for vengeance, to set him on the path of destroying Mikhail. But what if he'd been wrong all this time?

"They don't trust you," Samiel added.

Severn looked over and found Samiel's face full of concern. "If you're all afraid of one little angel, shit must have changed since I've been gone."

Samiel smiled, and Severn's heart skipped a beat to see it. He'd kissed that smile a thousand times. He'd loved Samiel. Loved him completely. But now... It was different. He was different. All of this... none of it made any sense. Samiel had died. Severn had fallen in love with an angel, and now he was here, his own kin butchering him while Samiel watched on.

Severn tore his gaze away and stared at the ceiling. He'd loved Samiel once, but felt none of that love now. He cared for him. He felt that inside, but not the breathless, soul-deep longing of love.

"I'll talk with Lord Jeseph," Samiel said, standing.

Jeseph? Well, that explained his extended stay having his skin ripped off. Jeseph had always despised Konstantin's meteoric rise through the demon ranks. He'd happily get off on having Konstantin tied to his table.

Demons... he'd forgotten what it was like to be among them, to have to fight for rank. They were fiercely loyal, hot-headed, and passionate. As Konstantin, he'd been among the most powerful. Now, he was, at best, a novelty, at worst, a threat. And if few knew he was here, Jeseph would take advantage of that secrecy. It was a wonder Severn wasn't already dead.

"Samiel?"

His name stopped him before he reached the door. He turned, and it didn't take much for Severn to imagine his glorious, leathery wings opening behind him. They'd once flown through the clouds together, darting, spiraling, racing, until his wings ached and the air burned his skin. And then Mikhail had ruined everything.

Severn wet his cracked lips. "You're really here?"

Samiel's soft lips lifted at their corners, but his eyes were sad. "I was always here for you."

He left, and Severn stared at the closed door, waiting for the others to return. Samiel was alive. That was good, amazing even. Why, then, did he feel so empty?

CHAPTER 2

$\mathcal{M}$ikhail

MIKHAIL WIPED AGAIN at the angelblade, where the vicious demon blood refused to let go. He'd tried everything to clean the blade back to its original spotless shine, but the thick, crusted layer of crimson had glued itself to the steel.

He threw the blade onto the desk by the window and waited for his heart to slow—the anger to pass. The filthy sword mocked him. He couldn't scrub the blood off like he couldn't scrub the demons from this earth or scrub Severn from his mind. No, not Severn. Severn was a lie. The demon lord *Konstantin*.

He couldn't think on him, or what they'd done, or the things they'd both said and how it had all been a cruel fabrication. Any time those thoughts crept into his head, he lost control, lost all reason and sense and composure.

He couldn't function when consumed with all the damned *emotion* Severn had awoken in him.

He swallowed hard and combed his fingers through his long hair, sweeping it back from his face.

Sunlight streamed in through the windows and over the desk, making the sword glow. A desk Severn had fucked him against. The entire house was full of memories. Severn sprawled in the bed, his smile a tantalizing question. Severn laughing on the rooftop in the rain. Severn's firm hips, his rounded ass, and the way he threw his head back, his loose golden locks aglow, when Mikhail...

Mikhail turned away with a snarl and soon found himself outside, walking the streets, needing to escape. He was a twitch away from spreading his wings and taking flight, returning to Aerie to stare at the horrid demon wings displayed on his wall. He always returned to the gallery, especially when his memories tried to convince him not everything about Severn had been a lie.

"I love you. That is no lie."

No, no, no... he could not listen, he could not fall under this insanity trying to bury him. His angels already mistrusted him. He'd... done things. Careless things. Killed angels in his haste to slay demons, killed... people, by accident, but still... it was a sin. He knew it. They all knew it. Vearn had covered up the worst of his mistakes, but it kept happening because the only way he could function was to turn everything off. All of it. And feel *nothing*. There was peace in nothing. A hollow coldness he welcomed, where only necessity pulled his strings. But it meant he forgot who he was supposed to be.

Whispers spoke of wanting him banished, of having a

guardian from another continent come in to *manage* him. Angels feared him. And they were right to, but he wasn't leaving London, and he would not be pushed from his home.

The only way for the madness to end would be for Severn to die. The allyanse remained, and maybe his death would kill Mikhail too, but at this stage, it would be for the best.

Demons had Severn hidden somewhere. In the two months since Tower Bridge had fallen, he'd caught demon after demon and wrung answers out of them. But the answers were always the same. Nobody knew where Severn —Konstantin was. Most thought he'd died a decade ago and knew nothing of his reappearance at the bridge. But some knew the rumors, some heard talk of Konstantin's survival.

There was one name the demons spoke of before the torture eventually killed them.

Samiel.

Konstantin's friend, *his lover.* The first time a demon had uttered those words, Mikhail had punched through his ribs and torn out his heart, then crushed that useless organ in his fist. The next time, he'd refrained from instantly killing him to merely breaking each of his wings to a cacophony of screams. And by the third mention of this *Samiel*, his importance as Konstantin's "lover" could not be ignored. This *Samiel* would know where Severn the angel was.

Mikhail had set about killing every demon and would continue, until this 'Samiel' stepped forward to stop the slaughter. In two weeks, he'd butchered thirty of the beasts, propped their heads on spikes, and left the gruesome display in the killing fields.

Still, nobody was talking, and Samiel remained elusive.

They should have given him up by now.

But Mikhail had a plan.

The demons had infiltrated angels. They'd destroyed Aerie and thousands of human lives in their act of terrorism. Mikhail was done following peace and order and Seraphim's archaic laws. No more rules. No more lines angels did not cross. No more killing fields. Mikhail would take the war to their streets, to their *homes*, and slaughter them in their beds.

London would witness the true power of a guardian. And Konstantin would die, watching everything he loved turn to dust.

He shoved through the church doorway. Inside the cavernous space, the angels tasked with guarding the prisoner straightened. Mikhail strode between them, toward the demon chained to the floor where the altar used to be. She was a hideous specimen, all purple skin and spiraling horns. So far, he'd allowed her to keep her wings, but if she didn't give him answers soon, they would be the first parts of her to go.

He stopped outside her lunging range and folded his arms. She kept her yellow eyes downcast. The defiance she'd arrived with had long ago faded into acceptance. He'd gone to great pains to find her, capture her, and bring her here to Whitechapel—the new angel stronghold while Aerie was being rebuilt.

"Do you wish to speak, or shall we begin again?"

She bared her jagged teeth.

They were stubborn, all of them. Torture had become

tiresome. They all screamed and begged and died. But few talked. One had, though. He'd had a great deal to say about *the madam*. She'd resided in the cauldron, ran a sex club, and she'd serviced Severn.

The very idea made Mikhail want to throw up what little he'd eaten that morning.

This... creature had met Severn's incubi needs for ether. Before he'd fucked Mikhail and fed from *him*.

Mikhail held out a hand, and the guard to his right deposited the coiled whip into his palm. The madam's gaze flicked to it and back to Mikhail's face.

Konstantin, the demon whose wings hung on Mikhail's wall, had lied and illusioned his way into Mikhail's heart and fed from him every time they'd lain together. Somehow, he'd made Mikhail feel things for him, manipulated him for years. That was why Mikhail had performed the allyanse. He'd been maneuvered into it. It wasn't love. It never had been. Guardians did not love.

And then, while Mikhail had been distracted, the demons had destroyed half of Aerie, killing angels, nephilim, and people.

Mikhail dropped the whip's tail.

Demons had crossed the line first. Now, Mikhail was done playing by the rules.

"Where is Konstantin?"

He didn't wait for an answer. Raising the whip, he looped the length of leather in the air and brought it down with a resounding snap. The tail tore at the demon's thigh, zipping her skin open. She gasped.

"Where is Konstantin?"

Again, the whip flew and cracked. The sound echoed about the church's vast space. And the madam gasped again, panting in pain. She curled tighter into herself, folding her wings around her as though they could shield her. The whip tore through their featherless membrane, making her cry out.

A smile twitched across Mikhail's lips. "Where is Konstantin?"

Crack.

She wouldn't speak.

He'd had her a week, and not a single coherent word had left her lips.

Crack.

Mikhail unfurled his wings, breathing out as he drew them back. The whip landed again and again and again until the polished marble floor ran red with demon blood.

She flung out a hand. "Stop!"

Mikhail lowered the whip. They both panted. His wings expanded with each breath and shrank again with each exhale.

She peeled her shredded wing back from her face and revealed a smile so broad it brightened her yellow eyes. "You took his wings and made him *stronger*."

Mikhail freed a growl and brought the whip down again, making the church ring with the crack.

Her skin glistened with blood, she shivered in a pool of it, but laughter still bubbled from her lips. "He'll come for you, *guardian*."

Crack.

Laughter filled the church now. Hers. "He's already taken your heart. Next, he'll take your wings!"

Mikhail threw the whip aside and snatched an angel-blade from the guard. He grabbed her torn, flailing wing by its ridge, yanked her chest-first into the church floor, and slammed a boot into her back, between her wings, holding her pinned. His own wings arched backward, shifting his weight and poise.

"Your Grace?"

The new voice hooked in, freezing him rigid. The demon squirmed beneath him, her wings flapping, spraying blood. He looked at the angelblade in his hand, and horror rolled over him, knocking him backward, away from the demon. The blade fell from his hand and clanged to the floor, ringing like this church's now-silent bells.

"Mikhail?"

The guard who had spoken looked back at him, his eyes a startling green and hair a deep red. He knew him. Solomon. One of the elite. Solomon knew. They all knew how Mikhail had *loved* a demon with all his heart and soul. Loved him so much he'd performed the allyanse. *Mated* them.

Mikhail's gut heaved.

"Sire?" Solo reached out a hand.

He batted him away and staggered for the door. "No food. No water. Until she talks."

"But she'll die?"

"Then let her die!" He tore from the church, spread his wings, and took to London's gray skies, beating higher, fueled by rage and pain and regret and shame and all the things no angel should ever feel. He flew into the clouds, numb to their damp kiss on his skin, and stumbled into Aerie—into his chamber and the gallery where the wings hung on the far wall. He almost made it to their great expanse before his legs gave out and dropped him to his knees.

It was too much.

All of it.

Everything.

He still loved him, even now. If he could rip out his own, treacherous heart, he would. He fell forward onto his hands and sobbed, unable to hold the immense pain inside. His wings, spread wide, shuddered, their feathers dislodging the moisture gathered from the clouds like tears.

Crossing his arms over his chest, he clenched his hands into fists and rocked back on the balls of his feet. The severed demon wings towered over him. Two great monuments to everything that was wrong in the world.

"I will find you. I will kill you, and that will be the end of this madness. For us both."

evern

THERE WERE voices and hands on him, but it was different this time. The pain faded and kept on fading, reducing to an ache he could ignore. He woke in a strange room, adrift from reality. The air smelled of demon, like home, but he hadn't been home in years. The room wasn't one he knew. No bright sunlight bouncing off sharp surfaces, no polished floors and glass walls. No echo of voices. Everything here, from the drapes to the bed he lay in, was soft and warm and dark. His memory told him this was a safe place, but why then was his pulse racing and his body strung so tightly, readying to flee?

He threw off the sheets and ran a hand down his smooth arm, across his naked chest, and over a thigh. No wounds. No scars. Like the torture had never happened.

He'd been trapped in a nightmare for so long, he no longer knew if this was real or fantasy.

The effort of walking to the shower almost dropped him to his knees. He propped himself against the tiled wall as warm water patted against his cool skin. Like rain.

Kisses in the rain on a London rooftop...

He rested his forehead against tiles and withstood the onslaught of memories. Mikhail on his knees, weeping. The soft, protective touch of feathers. Mikhail's cock between Severn's soft lips. How the angel would sigh and shudder and come undone beneath Severn's hands.

"You're up?"

Severn gasped out of the daydream and fell against the tiles. "Shit." Through the fogged glass, he saw how Samiel's concerned smile slipped sideways.

Samiel folded his arms and leaned against the door-frame. "Sorry. Didn't mean to startle you."

Severn turned off the shower and wiped the glass clear.

Samiel.

Real.

Here.

But different.

No, Severn was different...

Samiel handed over a towel as Severn stepped out of the shower. He muttered his thanks and patted himself dry, aware of Samiel's heated, curious gaze. As Konstantin, Samiel had always been the smaller demon. But now Severn was smaller, his skin peachy white where it should have been obsidian black, his muscles lean instead of broad. With the way Samiel was watching him now, Konstantin would have answered that questioning look by devouring the smaller demon in all the ways. They would have laughed and made love and spent hours, with wings and limbs tangled together.

"It's remarkable," Samiel began, gaze dropping suggestively.

"So I've heard." He tried a smile, found it stayed, and saw Samiel's smile grow. This was... strange. He knew Samiel, but as Konstantin. Looking at him through angel eyes, everything was all at once the same and unfamiliar.

He tucked the towel around his waist, breaking Samiel's study of his anatomy and drawing the demon's gaze back to his face.

"You truly fucked a guardian?" Samiel asked.

Severn hid the wince by turning away to examine his reflection in the fogged mirror. He swept a hand across its cold surface, revealing the blue-eyed, blonde-haired angel he'd so thoroughly become.

"What does he taste like?" Samiel's reflection appeared behind Severn's. Hot hands claimed Severn's hips, their warmth seeping through the damp towel. Samiel's smile turned predatory, as did the gleam in his golden eyes. His gaze fixed with Severn, and slowly, he bowed his head and placed a soft, open-mouthed kiss on Severn's neck.

Severn let his eyes flutter closed. The gentle touch after so much brutal agony made his skin burn for more. "Like sunshine," he whispered.

Samiel drew Severn back against him. The hard press of muscle pushed against Severn's back. Severn's ass fit snuggly against Samiel's crotch, the hard press of the demon's cock difficult to ignore.

Severn opened his eyes and watched Samiel trail kisses over his shoulder, his dark hair contrasting against Severn's. There was something beautiful in that contrast, something... poetic. Samiel's hand slid down Severn's thigh. His fingers spread, claiming, and he pulled Severn tighter against himself.

"I never thought I'd fuck an angel," Samiel purred.

Severn swallowed hard. Unfortunately, it was the only hard thing about him. Because for all Samiel's allure, the spark of lust—usually alive and racing through his veins at the first thought of sex—hadn't ignited. His cock lay limp and uninterested, and within himself, where his incubus soul resided, a yawning hollowness consumed any sexual need.

"Samiel..."

Samiel opened his eyes. They glowed bright and intense with hunger.

"I can't..."

His brow pinched, but he instantly backed off. And while Severn might not have wanted sex, he still mourned the loss of his ex-lover's hands. Concubi needed contact. Touch. He'd been without it for so long, and then was drowned in it with Mikhail, only to have it wrenched away and replaced by torture. Right now, he desperately needed Samiel's softness more than anything else.

Samiel was turning away, silently leaving, shutting down, rejected. And that wasn't right either. Ten years he'd been without Konstantin. Much must have happened in that time. He'd have had dozens of lovers, he'd have moved on, but had he missed Konstantin?

Severn snagged his hand and reeled him into an awkward embrace. Before, he'd have thrown his wings around the smaller demon and kissed him hard until he groaned and gasped for more. But this time, Severn was forced to rise onto his toes just to brush his lips against

Samiel's. The warm, spicy scent of demon summoned a familiar purr from the back of his throat—a sound all Konstantin's —and while Samiel resisted at first, at the rumbling purr, he opened and carefully, slowly brushed lips-to-lips, tongue-to-tongue, re-exploring, relearning. Tasting angel. Tasting his enemy.

Samiel withdrew first, licking his lips, eyes sad. "You don't taste like Konstantin." He stepped back and let Severn's hand fall from his. "You don't look like him." He swallowed, and his sadness turned darker, more determined. "But you still need to feed, don't you?"

Severn leaned a hip against the basin, using it to shore him up. "I do." The chances of him being able to harvest ether off any kind of sexual high were slim. His body wasn't willing and his mind was fixed far, far away, in a glass city, on an angel who despised him. "I will. But not now." He'd have to, eventually. And maybe then his body would be more willing. "I've been away a long time. Tell me what's changed. The lords, do they still squabble?"

Samiel tilted his head. "Why?"

"So I can..." What? Fit in again? Become a lord again? Walk freely among demons? That wasn't ever going to happen while he looked like an angel. "...figure out a way to fix this." He swept a gesture at himself.

"How does knowing about the lords fix *that*?"

Fuck. Why couldn't he just obey, like he had before? Like they *all* had. "Beneath this skin, I am Konstantin of the Red Manor. Tell me everything I've missed."

Samiel raised an eyebrow. "Jeseph allowed me to bring you here under the condition you don't leave," he replied, ignoring the order. Typical demon.

"I'm your prisoner?"

"You are. And if you're truly Konstantin, you'd understand why."

Severn huffed a laugh and ran a hand through his wet hair. "This wretched body will be the death of me. So, what... I'm supposed to stay here, in this room. We fuck, and I feed, and then what?"

Samiel's glare darkened. "Maybe you'd have preferred execution?"

Severn laughed harder, shoved by Samiel, and strode out of the small shower room, needing space to breathe. He tried the main door, found it frustratingly locked, and glanced at the window. Samiel emerged from the shower room as Severn threw open the window and peered down some fifteen floors to the street below. London's scattering of office blocks and houses, old and new, sprawled into the distance, toward the cloud-clad, imposing, half-broken disks of Aerie.

If he'd had his wings, he could have climbed from the window and simply taken flight.

But without wings, he was trapped.

Mikhail was out there somewhere, beyond the gray clouds, fixing his city and systematically killing demons. Eventually, he'd find one who talked. But only Jeseph knew he was here, holed up with Samiel. Severn was safe, for now.

"I almost had him," he whispered into the brisk wind. It wasn't entirely true. He *had* had him. His heart, anyway. And then he'd lost it. He could get it back. But not like this... not while wrapped in weak angel-skin and wingless. He'd get him back with the truth. It was the only way. He had to make Mikhail see that even as demon, Severn still fucking loved him. As wrong as it was, in the end, the love hadn't been a lie. And for that, he needed his wings.

Wings that were hanging on Mikhail's chamber wall. Impossible to reach. Almost.

Weak, wingless, and broken, he was of no use to anyone. He had to become useful again. Indispensable. He had to become Konstantin so thoroughly that his angel-skin didn't matter to the demons. He had to make them see through the blue eyes and golden hair.

He had to feed.

And he had to fuck.

And he had to be incubi.

To have any chance at making Mikhail see the truth, he had to be the very thing the guardian hated. And they'd stand as equals. If it ended there, with the truth, then so be it. Severn was willing to die for love. Destiny would have it no other way.

He'd spent ten years as a demon, trying to convince the angels he was one of them, and now he was an angel trying to convince demons he belonged with them. It would have been hilarious if it weren't so fucking painful.

THE NEXT DAY and physically recovered, Severn had his target fixed. Before leaving that morning, Samiel had lain out some clothes for him. None of which he had any intention of wearing. Samiel was right. He did need to feed. Tower Bridge and then being tortured for a few weeks had exhausted his reserves. Until he was stronger, there would be no escape, no reclaiming his title, and certainly no retrieving his wings.

What happened next was necessary, even if it did feel like he was betraying Mikhail.

Naked, he stood at the window, arm braced against the frame, and watched London's shifting moods. Bright sunshine had turned to torrential rain, then to a soft drizzle, the suffocating kind that soaked every surface. He was tracing the distant line of the Thames when Samiel entered the room. In the window's reflection, he saw Samiel lock the door behind him and slip the key into his pocket.

Samiel's gaze roamed Severn's back, fixing on the wing stumps. Severn hadn't spared the energy to illusion those away, and in fact, he'd hoped they might trigger something more familiar in Samiel. It worked. The demon's gaze trailed lower, down his back, to his ass, heating all the way.

Severn could do this. He was a fucking incubus, despite appearances. He knew sex better than he knew how to breathe.

"You don't like the clothes?" Samiel asked, heading toward the cupboards. "I struggled to find a shirt small enough—"

"They're fine." Just a little longer. The tingling, warm scent of desire had entered the room with Samiel. Whatever problems he had with Severn's current appearance, he still wanted to fuck it. Maybe he'd always had an angel kink and was just now discovering it. Or maybe he saw more of Konstantin in Severn's new body than Severn had realized. Either way, Samiel's arousal was sweet enough to awaken Severn's. Yesterday, fresh from torture, he'd been floundering. Today, he had a purpose. Fuck, feed, get stronger.

Severn summoned to mind the memory of Mikhail

braced over him, the angel's face lost to rapture as he'd buried himself hilt deep inside Severn. Lust woke the single part of his anatomy that really needed to quit fucking around and play along. Or rather, absolutely fuck around. With Samiel.

The scent of desire and need spiked, and Severn turned to find Samiel standing on the other side of the bed, staring. He knew from the demon's expression the kind of picture he made. Angel, at the window, stark naked and erect as the day an incubus was born.

"Come here," Severn said, adding a familiar demon tone. He'd deliberately lost the grating rumble from his voice when he'd chosen this illusion, but it was back now.

Samiel stiffened, in more ways than one, and Severn's lips twitched to see the effect the order had on him. Oh, Samiel wanted to fuck all right, but he was also confused because demons fucking angels was one of those taboo subjects even concubi didn't touch. Humans, yes. They were fair game. But not the enemy.

Severn took his invested cock in hand and gave it a few leisurely strokes, imagining Mikhail's firm hand working him over. There had been nothing like the feel of Mikhail's fingers sliding over his erection. So firm, yet yielding, just like Mikhail.

"I said... *come here.*"

Samiel started to move around the end of the bed, unbuttoning his shirt, revealing his dark bronze rack of abs. Then he tore the shirt off with jagged tugs and tossed it aside. His hand locked around Severn's throat, fingers choking.

Severn's back struck the window, making the glass rattle.

"You dare order me, *angel?*" Sharp teeth glinted.

Severn bared blunt teeth in return. If Samiel truly wanted to hold him, he couldn't escape. But this wasn't about force. Samiel wasn't concubi. He couldn't smell emotions, but he saw how Severn's cock leaked in eagerness. Samiel was demon, and in his mind, this was wrong. Samiel needed the power here, or he'd never get over his mental barriers enough to enjoy what was to come. Severn needed him lost to pleasure. He needed that moment of abandonment peaking into a crescendo of ecstasy so he could drink his ether down. Gods, his mouth watered just thinking on it. He really was starved.

Samiel's grip eased. His hand spread around Severn's collarbone and down his chest, sweeping, exploring the new angel body.

"What do you want?" Severn asked.

Samiel looked up. Golden eyes blazed. "Konstantin."

"Close your eyes."

His lashes fluttered closed.

Severn dropped to his knees, quickly unbuttoned the trouser fly, and grasped Samiel's thick length. The demon's breath stuttered. Severn's hands weren't Konstantin's. He didn't possess long, sharp nails. His skin wasn't as warm and as rough. But he remembered exactly how Samiel liked to be pleasured. He sealed his lips over Samiel's crown and tongued the tiny, sensitive slit, then licked hard and swallowed him deep.

Samiel's hips tilted, cock sinking deeper. He made a strangled sound and thrust his hands into Severn's hair, grasping for horns that weren't there, but it didn't matter, Severn had him now. Ether smoked off his skin, sweet and light and everything Severn needed after the exhaustion of the last few weeks.

Samiel thrust harder, his cock far larger than an angel's throat was designed to take. Severn winced around the thickness, fighting for air, but it didn't fucking matter because Samiel's ether was flowing now, thickening, luring Severn into its embrace while filling him up.

Samiel's panting breaths turned to heavy grunting, each one ending as his cock beat the back of Severn's throat. *Not yet...* Severn pulled free and smiled up into Samiel's glassy-eyed, questioning gaze. Samiel yanked him straight and slammed a kiss over his mouth, then plunged his tongue in. His hand wrapped firmly around Severn's cock and pumped frantically.

Samiel gasped from the kiss. "I've missed you."

Gods, no, don't talk. Memories of Konstantin's hand in Samiel's, of sunbaked grass beneath them, Samiel's beautiful wings spread, and Konstantin above him, wings arched high, the two of them so lost to lovemaking there was nothing else in this world. No war, no angels. That was before Samiel never returned from battle, before Konstantin lost his wings to the horror that was Mikhail. Before destiny claimed him for her own purpose.

Memories clogged Severn's thoughts, stuttering him from the moment.

A new memory. A fragmented one. One that faded as soon as it flashed, like lightning, there and gone again— Samiel watching, smiling, and pain, so much pain. Of the heart and the body. On and on, it went—

Samiel's hands gripped him, turning Severn to face the window. The heavy press of male smothered Severn's back, pinning him still, fingers probed. Ether stuttered, Severn's diminishing pleasure choking off the flow. *Think of Mikhail.* It was Mikhail's touch stretching him open, Mikhail's cock pushed against his hole, then filling him up. He clung to that thought because if he let it go, he'd have to stop Samiel, and the demons would never believe he was still Konstantin.

"You smell sweet." Samiel's weight slammed Severn against the window. "Missed you so much." The pounding began, rhythmic and quickening. Skin slapped skin. Ether swirled, plucking on Severn's strings, teasing him toward his own climax even as his mind tried to sabotage it all. Samiel's sharp teeth clamped down on Severn's shoulder, wrenching a cry from his lips. Fuck, it hurt, it all hurt, but the ether was bright and all-consuming.

Samiel thrust, grunting hard. Ether stole away the pain, and then Samiel arched, growled low in Severn's ear, and buried his pulsing cock so damn deep, Severn bit his own lip to keep from crying out. The climax struck at Severn's incubus soul, slamming strength through his veins where before there'd been only hollowness. On and on, it pulsed, spilling power into Severn's veins, making them blaze. His own cock—almost forgotten—spent its load over the windowpane. He took more ether, took it all, reminding his body how he was demon too. *The best bits of both.*

Samiel slumped against him and moaned, weakened by the climax, and by Severn's gorging on his freely given sexual energy. All the times they had laughed and loved together simmered between them.

Samiel's hand caught Severn's and drew him around, turning him to face Samiel. His fingers ran the length of Severn's jaw, golden eyes full of post-sex wonder. He threaded his fingers through Severn's silky hair and brought it to his nose, breathing in. "Sunshine..." he purred.

Severn grabbed him by the back of the head and kissed him hard before the mad laugh that had begun to crawl up his throat had a chance of bursting free.

He could do this.

He had to do this.

He was Konstantin, Lost Lord of the Red Manor, and the new power in his veins meant he was going to get his fucking wings back.

CHAPTER 4

Mikhail

His war council reported on how the demons were unusually quiet. A few skirmishes had bubbled up around London's backstreets, but nothing of any real concern. The killing fields were now in angel territory. Mikhail had ordered the setting of fires along the boundary line as a warning to any demon watching on.

For now, the demons were hanging back. Probably rocked by the death of Argothun and Mikhail ripping the stars from the skies at Tower Bridge. It had to be difficult to argue you were in the right in the face of such power.

He wasn't entirely sure where that power had come from, or if he'd be able to summon the same again. No angel had dared ask him about the display, or the fact he'd sprouted two extra pairs of wings. A good thing they hadn't asked because he had no idea how to answer them.

Guardians always had access to more power than most angels. But it was restrained, always controlled. What he'd summoned at Tower Bridge had been wild and devastating.

The angels around the table fell silent.

He looked up.

They'd asked something of him and waited for his reply. He hadn't heard a word of it. "Council adjourned," he said. They glanced at each other, open faces full of doubt. They judged him as out of control, as emotionally broken. They thought him tainted by Konstantin's cock, and it was all Mikhail could do not to roar out his frustration at them.

Sensing he was about to snap, they hurried out of the old church, leaving just Solo and Vearn behind.

Neither spoke. They just waited, like good angels.

"Well?" Mikhail snapped.

"The demon is refusing to speak," Solo reported. "Soon she'll be too weak to be of any use."

Mikhail stared at the red-haired angel. Severn's *friend*.

Konstantin had fooled them all. All but Vearn.

"Take her wings," he said.

Solo glanced at Vearn, querying Mikhail's order. They'd all been glancing at Vearn a lot more of late. Should he ever be *removed*, it would be Vearn who would lead them. She'd make a fine guardian. But it would be over his dead body.

"If I may suggest another way, Your Grace?" Vearn asked.

He nodded, teeth gritted to keep from unleashing his increasing ire.

"Send her back to them. With this." She placed a small square on the table in front of her. Human technology, it had to be. Angels didn't need human technology. It was beneath them. But humans surrounded themselves with it. They always had something shining and electronic on them. "Place it somewhere beneath her skin without her knowing. She'll return to the demons, and probably to Severn, considering how... close they were. She'll lead you and your forces straight to him."

Human tech. It seemed so... crude. But, he was prepared to try anything. Another dead demon was no good to him, but one who unknowingly revealed Severn's location was worth some meddling with technology.

He nodded again. "See it done." If he went near that demon, he'd rip her wings off and tear out her heart while it still beat. By Haven, this anger was a force all its own, like a living thing on his back, growing and feeding and consuming him.

"Your Grace?"

"What?!"

Vearn lifted her chin. "I merely asked if you were well?"

"Well?" He stood, scraping the chair across the floor behind him. "No, I'm not *well*. Demons broke our city. They killed thousands. I won't be well until Aerie is rebuilt and Konstantin is found so I can mount his head alongside the wings on my wall." His own wings spread, set free by the great surge of emotion. "I won't be well until London is free of the demon infestation. Until their kind is eradicated from my land and the rest of the world. They were Seraphim's foul mistake, and it's our duty to make it right."

"I agree," Vearn replied, withstanding his lashing voice without a single wince. "But perhaps, Your Grace, it would be wise for you to visit Haven, where they know how to deal with the kind of emotions you're wrestling with." She'd said the last few words in a breathless rush.

Solo visibly shrank into his chair.

The last time he'd been shipped off to Haven, he'd been forced to shatter his own wings to escape the cage, resulting in them turning all-black. He'd healed, but only because of *Severn*. But he wasn't completely blind to his own out-of-control behavior. He knew he was falling apart. He saw it every time he witnessed the fury on the face of his own reflection.

Mikhail fixed his unblinking gaze on Vearn. "I'll go when every last demon is dead."

Vearn sighed. "Guardian Remiel is on his way. You should prepare for his judgment."

"Guardian Remiel can go—" He stopped, hearing the finishing words in his head but not speaking them because they sounded too much like something Severn would say. "Remiel's journey will be a wasted one."

"*Mikhail,*" she pleaded. "None of us want to see you suffer."

Remiel was well-known for his battle prowess. He'd remove Mikhail by force if he had to. But Remiel had never sprouted three pairs of wings. "I will thoroughly defend Aerie and my place within it. You might want to make sure he's aware of that before he arrives."

"Please, be reasonable." The plea only went as deep as the word. She didn't care. Not really. Because she wasn't capable. Did any of them actually care?

"This is reasonable. The alternative is what you saw at Tower Bridge. You're both dismissed. See to it the human technology finds its way onto the demon." He watched them go and then dropped his gaze to the table, seeing the ghost of Severn. *I want you... right here on this pretty table.*

Enter me.

Like this?

He groaned into the silence and tore himself from the table before he could break the damn thing in two. If he didn't find Severn soon, he'd lose what little he had left of his sanity.

CHAPTER 5

evern

IT HAD BEEN a week since the torture sessions had ended. And in that week, Samiel had proven in multiple ways how he'd taken to the taste of angel. Which was all well and good, but if Severn didn't escape Samiel's room soon, he'd lose his damn mind to frustration.

Samiel's mention of the madam's return was all the persuasion he needed.

"She helped me feed for years." He hastily dressed in a shirt and trousers while watching Samiel reluctantly peel himself from the bed and throw on a hooded, gray top and loose, black jeans. So understated. He looked like a large human. One of those substantial types who tried to build muscle to emulate demons. Of course, no human could grow horns. His wings were still tightly illusioned out of sight.

"I have to see her."

"I'm not convinced meeting her is a good idea," Samiel mumbled, flicking his hood up to tent over his horns.

"What harm is there? You said she's waiting. Besides, as much as I enjoy spending all my spare time with my tongue wrapped around your cock, my dear, I need to get out of these four walls before I lose my fucking mind."

Having been reminded of Severn's tongue and with the addition of "my dear"—a pet name from before—the tension instantly drained from Samiel's body, and a smile propped his lips up. He drew Severn into his arms and nuzzled his neck. "Hm... A minute in those clothes and I want you out of them again. Even as an angel, you're fucking irresistible."

Severn kissed him hard and plunged a hand into his pocket. He snagged the key and pulled it free with a grin. "It's mine now. Like you're all mine, demon."

Samiel frowned, then playfully lunged. His solid arm caught Severn around the waist and reeled him into a long, deep kiss. There was no doubt in Severn's mind that he'd once adored this, adored Samiel, but the only thing he got from this now was ether. Ten years had changed more than his body. It had changed his heart too. He'd moved on.

Gods, this was wrong.

Severn pried himself from Samiel's grip before the kiss turned to more and unlocked the door, flinging it open to get a good look at the corridor. Basic, old, some sort of human high-rise built long ago to house people without the means to buy their own homes. Wallpaper peeled from the walls, and a musty smell tickled Severn's nose. The building sounded empty. No slamming doors, no distant laughter. This wasn't Samiel's real den, just a temporary one. Severn had no right to be offended that Samiel hadn't trusted him enough to take him home, but he was all the same.

"You don't even know where you're going." Samiel laughed, jogging behind to keep up.

"Outside. Outside is good enough."

The elevator worked, and as they waited for the carriage to rumble to the correct floor, Samiel gently shoved Severn back against the control panel and braced his arms beside him, trapping him under the full force of warrior-demon. Samiel was handsome. The curved horns made his height impressive. He hadn't revealed his wings yet, probably assuming the sight of them would only remind Severn of how he'd lost his, but Severn remembered them well. Lightly tanned, almost fawny, and velvety smooth.

Samiel sucked gently on his neck as the elevator pinged a countdown. Severn didn't need the ether, he was brimming with it, and while this was nice, it wasn't Mikhail. But pushing Samiel away wasn't an option. No other demon would let an angel feed off them.

"You were right, you know?" Samiel mumbled, hands claiming Severn's hips. "Angel tastes fucking amazing."

He tried not to think of Mikhail, or his silken hair and how it had trailed over Severn's naked chest. "Right?" He cleared his throat. "Who knew we've been missing out all this time."

The elevator doors rumbled open, and Severn twisted from Samiel's grip to duck inside the car.

"Do you miss it, the taste?" Samiel asked, leaning against the side of the car, his desire waning as talk turned to angels.

"No," Severn answered quickly.

"Liar."

"Yeah, all right... Fine. Yes, I miss the taste of angel."

"Do you miss *him*?" Asked so casually, but Samiel's face was sincere.

"No." And Severn made that single word convincing this time.

"What was he like?" Samiel spoke carefully, too, hiding his thoughts from his face.

Severn stared at the control panel, watching the numbers count down the floors. "Like the rest of them. Cold. Hollow. Emotionless. Brittle. It's like they're not even alive. They follow their own rules with single-minded dedication, like machines. It's... sad."

"Sad?" Samiel growled low. "What's fucking sad is that they're still killing us and breeding and taking over London like they think it belongs to them. I don't agree with what Djall did, killing all those people in the cauldron, but maybe it was time."

Djall was someone else he'd have to contend with soon. The last time he'd seen her, on the Thames's muddy bank, he'd tried to kill her, so their reunion would be interesting. She'd have to wait. First, he needed out of this building and to check in with the madam. She'd have news about Mikhail.

The elevator doors pinged open, revealing an unfamiliar trash-strewn foyer. "Where is the madam?"

Samiel jogged ahead. "Follow me, and keep your hood up and your head down. We don't need word getting out that I have a pet angel at my heels." He threw a smirk over his shoulder.

Pet angel? Severn chuckled and tagged behind, head down.

Mist clogged the street and muffled the noises from the occupants of nearby buildings. Snippets of conversation drifted on the breeze. A laugh here and there. A demon swooped in over their heads and landed in a jog on the street. As soon as they touched down, their wings folded away and vanished, and they ducked into the doorway of a brick-faced building. Another smoked in a doorway, the tip aglow. He flicked the ash away and eyed Severn warily.

This area was unfamiliar, too, and nothing like Dagenham's old streets where Severn had grown up. Perhaps it was the fog, but the damp air carried with it a heavy, somber feel.

"Here." Samiel passed through a doorway into a huge, brick warehouse. The enormous space echoed with the sounds of their boots, and ahead, waited the madam.

She whirled at their approach, came forward a few steps, and then went down to her knee and bowed her head. "Konstantin, my lord."

Finally, someone knew how to greet him properly. Severn touched her head between her horns, and she rose. "My lord, he's tearing the city apart looking for you. Where have you been?"

"Having my skin systematically ripped off." He flicked a hand at Samiel. "And feeding."

She blinked, piecing the bits together.

"I'm stuck as an angel. Hence the secrecy. My kin have already made it clear an angel among them is a fucking travesty. But I'm working on it..."

"I see." Her wings shuddered open, their membranes torn to strips.

Severn winced in sympathy and fought off the urge to reach out. "Gods, what happened?"

She tried to stretch their arches wide but failed and panted in pain. "He thinks he's a god. *Mikhail* happened."

Mikhail's rage was getting worse. "He did *that*?"

"And worse."

"Butcher," Samiel growled. "He took Konstantin's wings, and now he shreds yours. Have the medics take a look at you." He approached the madam, looking over her expanse of wrecked wing membrane, his face guarded.

"I will." She eyed Samiel warily.

"Samiel won't hurt you," Severn assured.

"Konstantin, while in Whitechapel, I overheard the guards talking. Mikhail has summoned reinforcements. Another guardian is on his way to London. One called Remiel. He's a cruel bastard, or so the angels say... in their dull words. He's bringing with him hundreds of angels."

One guardian was bad enough, but two? If they could both pull the stars from the skies, then London would no longer be safe for any demon. "When?"

"A few weeks."

Two guardians. Guardians rarely worked together. Their enormous egos didn't allow it. The extra guardian's arrival had to be for the final push to clear all demons out of London. "How many numbers are in our forces?" he asked Samiel.

"All in, three thousand, maybe? We've been recruiting more, but they're untested. Bluster and balls, but no brains. It'll take a month to organize our full forces."

It wasn't anywhere near enough. Even after Aerie's

collapse, angels were better equipped, and now they had to contend with guardians. By the fucking gods, if the angels learned the demons' numbers were so low, they'd plow right over them.

"Mikhail has slaughtered dozens of us just these past weeks," Samiel explained.

Severn took a step back and pinched his lips closed. The words still burst free anyway. "He murdered demons while I was tied to a table?" Mikhail had lost his mind, or was close to it, that much had been obvious at Tower Bridge, but Severn could have tried to stop him before now, if the demons hadn't been so fixated on trying to rid him of the wretched illusion. "Fuck!" He backed up some more and began to pace. How many more demons had to die before his kin would allow him to take back his squads? Before he could get to Mikhail and talk with him?

"Who leads us?" he snapped.

Samiel glanced at the madam and back to Severn. "There have been some developments on that."

Severn jolted to a stop. "Developments?"

"It's been ten years. A lot has changed."

"Samiel—"

"Lux."

"Wait... what?" Lux wasn't a warrior. A brilliant strategist, but not a warrior. How had he risen to the level of High Lord in ten years? Lux was a concubi, one like Djall, who had learned to lurk in the shadows rather than fight in plain sight. Djall and Lux had always hated each other. But what if Djall had whispered in his ear and together they'd hatched the plan to destroy Aerie. Oh, it was all beginning to fall into place. Djall and Lux would absolutely kill humans to get to the angels. They'd even invite this carnage as proof the war needed escalating. Lux couldn't rise alone, but he'd whisper in the ears of any demon stronger than him and manipulate them. He'd always been a slippery one.

"I need to see Lux."

Samiel cleared his throat. "I don't think that's a good idea."

"You didn't think coming here was a good idea either, and here we are... The madam has told me more in minutes than you have in days. Samiel, I need to know what's going on."

Samiel's laugh cut short. "You really don't."

"How can I stop Mikhail if I don't know the facts?"

"Stop Mikhail?" Samiel echoed, his voice rising to match Severn's. "You can't stop him. You can't just walk back into angel towers. You had ten years, Stantin. You failed!"

"No." He strode toward Samiel and pointed a finger. "No, I didn't fail. I rose through their ranks to stand beside him. I learned everything there is to know about angels."

"By becoming one?"

"Yes, fuck yes! I know how they work. I know what makes them tick. While you and your kin had me tied to that fucking table, Mikhail kept on killing, worse than ever. I could have stopped him. We've wasted weeks. Lives lost. Lives we can't afford—"

Samiel's leathery wings burst open. "He killed them because of you!" He was in Severn's face suddenly, his wings arching, his snarl so close Severn felt the brush of his breath on his face. "He put their heads on stakes, and he burned their bodies, *because of you*. You're not fucking

Konstantin. Look at yourself. You're an angel, and you failed, *Severn the Wingless*. You can't go back, and you can't command our kin, because you're the enemy. If you walk out that door alone now, you won't get ten paces without someone killing you. Konstantin is dead. The sooner you get that into your angel-head, the better it will be for everyone." He strode back the way they'd arrived but paused at the door, sighed, making his wings sag, and turned. "I can't damn well leave without you. I have to babysit you like a fucking pup. Are we done here?"

Gods, this was hell. He was trapped in hell, in a useless angel body without wings, with nothing to his name, just the memories in his head of being someone better, someone who could take control and turn the battle around.

"There could be a way," the madam said.

Severn rubbed at his face. "Go on."

"The guardian angel Remiel, it'll be weeks before he gets here. Unless he arrives early."

"And?" Severn asked. Remiel arriving early would surely be the death of them all.

"You want your wings back?"

He glared at her. "I hope that's rhetorical."

"Just walk right in and grab them, as a guardian."

"Absolutely not," Samiel growled out. "I've just gotten used to his face, and you want him to change it again?"

"It doesn't matter what he looks like. He's Konstantin inside. Whether he wears the body of Severn or this Remiel, it'll all be dust when he gets his wings back."

"He can't go back in there." Samiel's face turned to thunder. "We don't even know if getting his wings will break this illusion. It's too risky. No, Konstantin." He met Severn's gaze. "No."

The madam drew her wings back in, briefly closing her eyes to their pain. "We need him. We need Konstantin. After Argothun's death, there's only Lux, Djall, and Jeseph left. We have no reinforcements to call upon. We are disorganized and fractured. The old manors are collapsing. Konstantin back from the dead would change everything. He has to go back for his wings, for us. It only needs to be a few days, at most. Do you know where Mikhail keeps the wings?" she asked him.

"I have a good idea."

Samiel visibly recoiled. "You've known all this time?"

"I only recently suspected I'd found them," he replied grimly, thinking of the crack in Mikhail's chamber wall.

"Good." The madam nodded. "I have a feather. The feather you gave me, Konstantin. Mikhail's feather. I paid off a nephilim to confirm he uses feathers to lock his chamber door. If he has his rumored gallery of wings, then you'll need a feather to get in."

"You took that feather off me all those weeks ago to get inside his gallery?"

She straightened proudly. "I dreamed of breaking in and tearing them all down. Stupid, perhaps. But it's not right that he keeps them."

He liked the madam more and more. "That feather I gave you, I found it on the killing fields. I..." He glanced at Samiel and felt a twinge of regret for things that never came to pass. "I kept it all this time to give to Samiel."

Samiel's eyes widened, and his lips shaped a silent O.

He'd kept the feather for Samiel for so long. "I don't think it's Mikhail's... it's just an angel feather."

"Well then..." She pulled the tatty feather from inside her tightly wrapped clothing and handed it out. "Whoever it belongs to, you'd better have it back, but you'll need one to unlock his gallery, and you'll need to wear another illusion to do it."

He took the feather. She was right. Gods, he had to summon another illusion, this time one belonging to a guardian. It wouldn't be easy, and it would require another sacrifice, but it could be done. As to whether retrieving his wings would finally rid him of the illusion? It could. Besides, they were running out of options. "I've never seen this Remiel. I need to know what he looks like. I won't be able to imitate his voice. And if Mikhail has met him before, he could easily see my lies."

The madam smiled. "I'm sure some human images can be found. They love photographing those feathered freaks. And it won't need to be for long. A day or two, just to get you inside Aerie."

"No." Samiel folded his arms. "Jeseph will never allow it. And if Luxen finds out you're even here—"

"Jeseph can go fuck himself," Severn said.

The madam's smile turned into a grin. "No one else will."

"Exactly." She was getting it. He knew there was a reason he liked her. "Lux doesn't need to know."

"You're both insane," Samiel exclaimed. "It's not going to happen... It can't happen."

Severn's grin grew. He sidled up to Samiel and eased a hand down his back, where his muscles were bunched in tension. Severn knew exactly how to relax him. He'd make him say yes to anything. "I'm going to need a great deal of power to pull this off."

"No, Stantin." His eyes flashed.

Severn took his hand and pressed the feather into it. "Ten years ago, I took this feather from the killing fields and brought it back for you. You dared me to get one. Do you remember?"

Samiel's big eyes glistened. He wrapped his fingers around the feather, crushing it in his palm. "I wasn't there the last time, when you created this illusion you wear now," he said softly. "If I had been, I'd have stopped you then. Mikhail will kill you for real this time, and you'll be gone again."

Severn clutched Samiel's face. For all his sharp teeth and demon eyes, the emotions were right there, mapped in the worry and fear, and by the gods, he wished he could feel it too. Feel for Samiel, because clearly the demon felt deeply for him. "You weren't there because I thought you dead. I wore this illusion and got close to Mikhail *for you*. What happened, Samiel? You went into battle and never returned."

A single tear gathered at his lashes and fell. "You don't remember?"

"No, I..." The memory he'd sacrificed. The moment he'd given up to wear this damned illusion. That was it. *Something* had happened during the battle. Something to do with Samiel. Something terrible. And he'd given it up as the price to wear an angel's skin. He could feel the truth now. Like a beast lurking in the dark, waiting to strike. "Tell me."

A thump sounded on the roof, followed by another. Then silence.

The madam's wings splayed. She narrowed her eyes and hissed, "*Angels!*"

"Here?!" Samiel hissed, tearing from Severn's grasp.

A section of roof splintered and exploded inward. An angel in full battle armor plunged inside, her wings spreading behind her to slow her descent. Her angelblade flashed in her hand.

Another section of roof collapsed.

"Run!" The madam whirled, but without a weapon, she'd last seconds.

"Konstantin!" Samiel's cry rose. "Run!"

Severn bolted *toward* the angel. The beat of her wings kicked up dust and trash, whipping it about the warehouse. He caught a glimpse of more angels pouring in. So many. Fuck. But angels... they were predictable. This one with her silver-white hair and gleaming armor looked like something from nightmares, but she had a weakness.

She pointed her blade at Severn as he made his charge, tucked her wings in, and dove forward.

There was a moment when he looked her in her silvery eyes and she knew, the same as he did, that only one would survive what came next.

Severn deliberately dropped, skidding across the smooth warehouse floor. Her blade slashed inches from his face. He reached up, sank his fingers into the joint of her armor, and yanked her out of the air.

She tumbled, struck the floor in an explosion of silver feathers, and briefly lay, stunned.

Severn stamped on her wrist, making her fingers burst open, and snatched up the blade. She saw her death in his eyes seconds before he plunged the blade through the slit in her helmet and through her skull. Maybe he'd known her, maybe he'd fought with her, but she would have killed him now as surely as she'd kill every demon here.

Samiel hauled Severn into a run. Outside, the gray streets churned with angels.

"Get down!" Samiel shoved Severn forward, almost sending him sprawling.

An angel soared over their heads, dipped his left wing, and circled back. A demon-blur shot from the clouds above and slammed into the angel, punching it into the road, where it lay still but for its twitching wings.

Angels tore unarmed demons from their houses and cut their throats. Blood ran in the gutters.

This wasn't a battle; it was a fucking massacre.

A demon lunged for Severn—mistaking him for the enemy—but Samiel caught him and swung him around before shoving him back into the fray. "That angel is mine!" He grabbed for Severn's arm. "We have to get you out of here."

An angel slammed into Samiel's side, knocking him clean off his feet. The warrior-angel roared and lunged to finish his attack.

In the confusion, the angel had mistaken Severn for an ally, thinking he was saving Severn from Samiel.

Severn plunged his stolen blade into the angel's back. The angel's wings flew out, and he fell to his knees.

Violence sang in Severn's veins, ether from the killing lust lifting his soul up, making his hungry heart sing, but the chaos on the street sickened him. He knew both sides, had fought for both sides, *loved* both sides. A chilling sense of wrongness wrapped around his heart.

An angel tripped into Severn, recoiling from an attacking demon—the madam. She thrust a short dagger up, under the angel's armor, sinking the blade into his gut. Severn stumbled backward, into the reach of another enemy. He whirled and cut them down, panting around the taste of blood on his tongue.

It wasn't supposed to be like this. This was demon ground. Their ground, their *home*. These demons were unarmed and unprepared.

He lost himself to the melee, drinking ether, breathing in its heady mix, until the attacking angels suddenly, as though by some silent command, retreated into the fog.

Severn stood, panting and dripping blood among dead and dying.

Angels lay at his feet, wings broken and bloody. He hadn't wanted this. If he looked too closely, he'd probably recognized the fallen. Spilled angel and demon blood mixed. It all ran red in the end.

Samiel wiped blood from his face with his sleeve. He staggered over a fallen angel, raising his lips in a snarl. The two short blades in his grip dripped gore.

A jagged memory flashed inside Severn's mind; Samiel beside him, his prowess on the killing fields both lethal and precise. He'd been a vision of killing, and next to Konstantin, they'd been unstoppable. Until Mikhail. And then, in the memory, Samiel had turned to Severn and smiled, but the smile seemed twisted.

The memory shattered, fragments ripping through him, surrendered years ago. He clutched his head and staggered on the spot.

"We need to go..." Samiel pulled on Severn's arm. "Now."

Go. Yes. He blinked, clearing his vision and his head.

Demons had begun to leave the safety of their homes to attend the wounded, but some saw him—an angel standing among dead angels, covered in *angel* blood. Snarls burbled. Teeth were bared.

Severn pulled his hood up with trembling hands and stepped around the dead. Instinct demanded he stay and help, but the crowd would soon turn. He glanced back at the madam. Her wings sagged behind her. Blood glistened on her thighs and chest, where the angels' blades had caught her.

"Get to the medics," he told her. She nodded, and Severn let Samiel lead him away.

This couldn't continue. Angels had never attacked in such a manner. They didn't ambush demons in their homes. That wasn't how the war should be fought. Mikhail needed to be stopped. And if Severn couldn't reason with him, this would have to end the way battles did. With blood.

CHAPTER 6

Mikhail

AERIE RANG with the sound of saws and hammers and the weighty beat of angel wings in flight. The missing residential disk had been replaced with scaffolding. There was still a long way to go before angels would once again be living in Aerie, but the city would rise again.

He strode along the suspended platforms, silently observing the construction. A smudge of red burned against the brilliant blue sky. Mikhail's heartbeat stuttered. Solomon. He'd be reporting on the attack behind enemy lines. Had they found Severn? It seemed unlikely the human technology would result in capturing Severn so soon, but hope swelled inside him. Hope that this would all be over soon, that he'd have Severn knelt before him in chains.

Solo alighted on the end of the platform and strode

forward, tucking his red wings in behind him to keep them from tangling in the scaffolding. His face was grim, lips thin. Dark freckles stood out against his pale face.

He dropped to a knee and bowed his head. "Your Grace."

He almost didn't want to hear it. The wind tossed Solo's long red hair and pushed at Mikhail. The sound of hammers ringing matched Mikhail's beating heart.

"How bad was it?"

Solomon looked up. "Severn is alive. He was seen, but," he wet his lips, "they fought back."

Anger crushed the bright light of hope. "Did you expect them to welcome you? They're demons!"

Solo winced. "The ambush would have been a success, Your Grace. The rank I sent in was one of our finest. The demons were caught unawares. They took heavy casualties."

"Then why are you not here with Severn in chains?"

"He disabled—" Solo's voice hitched. "He stole an angelblade and... Severn is a formidable warrior, and he was not alone." Solo straightened slowly, his gaze meeting Mikhail's. He was full of pride, this one. "He fought alongside a demon—the one they call Samiel."

Mikhail closed his eyes and clenched his jaw so hard its pain subdued some of the rage burning through his veins. But not all.

"We're regrouping and intend to launch a more substantial force. He will not escape a second time."

He opened his eyes to find Solo staring back, his chin up and eyes fierce.

They'd lost the element of surprise. Severn would be ready for a second attack, and so would his demons. He wasn't a novice angel. He was a battle-hardened demon warrior. As Konstantin, he'd led thousands of charges against angels, leaving the killing fields strewn with their dead. Solo had underestimated him. "Solomon, Severn was your friend," Mikhail began, keeping his voice level, controlled, calm—very different from the maelstrom in his head.

Solomon swallowed. "He was." The male blinked quickly, trying to hold on to his composure. In many ways, Solomon shared the same betrayal as Mikhail. There was no allyanse tying Solo and Severn together, but there had been betrayal. He should not feel anything, but the fire in Solo's eyes suggested he did.

"You asked to be charged with retrieving him, and I granted that request. Never forget who he really is. Konstantin is a demon lord. He has slain countless angels. He adopted our ways, lied and manipulated his way into our ranks, for years. Do not underestimate him because of your past together."

"No, Your Grace," Solo replied stiffly.

"Your friend does not exist. Only Konstantin exists. Whatever forces you plan to send in, double them. He must be in our custody by Remiel's arrival, or you will personally suffer the consequences."

Solo thumped a fist to his chest. "It will be so, Your Grace."

Mikhail watched him take to the air and disappear inside glaring sunlight. Solo had always been sensitive. He'd understand more than the others why Severn needed to be caught, not just out of necessity, but because he'd been used too. Solo would capture Severn.

Mikhail dropped off the platform, beat his wings, and

soared, circling high above Aerie, where the air was thinner and from where the city he loved didn't look so damaged. The world was a simpler, quieter place when riding the winds high above it. But for all the peace flying afforded him, he still found himself returning to the gallery, to stand in front of Konstantin's wings, staring at the lightning pattern of veins latticing the gruesome but elegant arches.

He should cut them down and burn them. His angels all knew he had them, knew he came here for hours. He didn't care how they all thought him mad or how Remiel was coming to unseat him. He didn't care about the angels who had died in his pursuit of Severn. Nothing mattered. Just Severn, on his knees, begging for mercy.

He freed his angelblade from his back, between his wings, and approached the splay of demon wings on the wall. He reached up and spread his left hand on the broad bone, the bone that bore all the weight of the right wing. By Haven, the wing was *warm*, like it had been cut from Konstantin hours ago, not years.

Raising the blade in his right hand, he aimed the tip at the top of the first arch. He just had to plunge it in and tear downward, slicing the membrane in two. It would make a fitting demonstration of how Severn had cleaved Mikhail's heart in two.

The shining blade's tip dented the leathery skin. *Just sink it in and pull.* The wings were a reminder, a risk, a curse. Mikhail almost wished he'd never taken them on that fateful day. He wasn't entirely sure why he had. He recalled he hadn't been alone. Someone else had sparked the idea in his head. But blaming another was a cowardly act. He should have killed Konstantin. If he had, Mikhail never would have learned to love, and the agony of its loss wouldn't haunt him now. He'd still be the guardian angel Aerie needed, but now, he was a curse upon them all.

Warmth throbbed under his hand. The wings were alive like Konstantin was alive. Wherever he was, did he feel the ghost of Mikhail's touch? He slowly, almost tenderly, stroked his hand along the arch, as far as he could reach. The thick, dappled leather was harder along the bone, protecting it, but almost velvety soft beneath. Did Severn feel that too? Did he think of Mikhail in this moment as Mikhail thought of him?

With a cry, Mikhail plunged the blade in and ripped its edge down the membrane until the blade pulled free. Blood ran down the wall and pooled on the floor, so red against white marble. He pushed himself from the horrible sight. Instead of hurting Severn, the pain of his actions struck at Mikhail's heart. Guilt... It choked him, dropped him to his knees, beneath his own limp wings. By Haven, it wasn't even a real pain, but it hurt like one. He couldn't survive this, survive *him*. Severn, with his lopsided smile, his bright laugh, and his beautiful blue eyes. Severn, the angel he'd turned to in his time of need and vulnerability. The angel he'd turned to for answers and comfort. The angel who had touched him in ways no other being ever had. The angel he loved. Why couldn't he stop loving him, why wouldn't the torture end, why did he feel so alone? He'd only ever tried to do the right thing. Why was he being punished?! *Why-why-why!*

Numb, thoughts a whirl, emotions turning him inside out, he staggered from the gallery, from Aerie, and descended through the clouds, wings aching, then landed with a stumble on the roof of Whitechapel's Royal

London Hospital. A nephilim rushed over to aid him, but he swept them back with a snarl. He could do this, he could stand... These emotions did not control him! He climbed to his feet only to fall again. This was the allyanse, surely. What else could cripple him so? The rooftop door seemed too far away. Was love supposed to hurt so?

"Sire?"

The nephilim.

"Saphia," he hissed. "Get Saphia."

The wait went on for an eternity, but then Saphia's reassuring tones settled around him, even if he couldn't make out the words beyond the throbbing in his head and body.

"Retract your wings."

He heard that but fought to organize his thoughts enough to pull himself and his wings together.

Soft hands cupped his face. "Mikhail... Listen to me." Her eyes were soft, like the eyes of a mother he'd never known.

His vision swam, but he saw her face, wracked with concern—for him.

"Listen... You must retract your wings. I can't treat you on the rooftop."

His wings. Yes, his wings. He tried to pull them in and tuck them away, but their weight dragged, and the wings flapped chaotically, raining black feathers. "What is... wrong with me?"

Her thumb stroked his cheek. So soft, like she used to when he'd been just a fledgling. Just an angel. Not a guardian. Just Mikhail. He wanted to be that young angel again. No more pain, no more blood, or war, or anything, just the wind beneath his wings.

"It's all right... I'll help you." Tears glistened in her eyes. "Focus on your wings. Can you do that?"

He buried his head against her chest and wanted to crawl into her lap. It was insanity, for sure, but he could not stop the madness from clawing at him. He focused on his wings, on their suddenly terrible weight, and tried to fend off the onslaught of emotions. Finally, breathlessly, he pulled his wings in and illusioned them away, feeling small and lost without them. *Nothing* felt right.

"Little Mikhail," Saphia whispered, "I have you, darling. It's going to be all right."

He wasn't sure he believed her, or that he cared, but the pain was fading, and so was the guilt. Wordlessly, she helped lift him to his feet and guided him inside into a room set aside from the rest, so he wasn't seen. The nephilim was given strict instructions not to speak a word of what he'd seen and sent out of the room. Mikhail collapsed onto the bed and succumbed to fluttering his eyes closed, to the sounds of chinking bottles and Saphia's comforting whispers.

CHAPTER 7

M ikhail

HE WOKE TUCKED into a small human bed, wearing only his undergarments. A brief few moments of panic clutched at his breath, but then Saphia was at his bedside, her hand on his arm.

"By Haven, what happened?" he croaked, shifting upright to lean against the headboard. His body felt heavy and abused, muscles aching as though he'd just returned from battle.

She smiled sympathetically and drew up a chair, but instead of taking it, she slipped her hand into Mikhail's and squeezed. "How do you feel?" Her aging face with its soft smiles was a ray of sunshine in what had otherwise become his dark existence. He should have come sooner.

"Battered."

"Yes, well... That's not a surprise. Did anyone see you descend from Aerie?"

"No, I don't think so..."

"Be sure."

He'd spiraled from Aerie, lost to pain, but nobody had seen. "Just the nephilim on the roof."

She nodded. "That's good. I've spoken with him. He won't talk." She took a breath and asked, "Mikhail, are you aware you had six wings?"

He rubbed at his aching shoulder. That would explain the weight. "No."

"How many times has it happened?"

"Once before, at Tower Bridge."

"Ah. I heard the rumors. Didn't believe them. Clearly, I should have." She released his hand and settled in the chair beside the bed.

Whenever he thought of Tower Bridge, shame sickened him. Guardians did not lose control. Tower Bridge had been a travesty. "Have you seen anything like it before?" he asked quietly.

"Not in my lifetime. I've never known of an angel with more than one pair of wings. Well, apart from..." She waited, letting him fill in the obvious.

"Seraphim." The resemblance had crossed his mind, but it didn't mean anything. Tower Bridge had been an isolated incident... until last night.

"The substance the demon coated your wings in, I suspect it did more than heal them."

His thoughts tripped. "That crone healed my wings?"

"Yes, I believe so. After analyzing the concoction, I found no traces of poison. The salve was remarkable, actually." He frowned, and Saphia tutted. "Don't give me that look. You said yourself your wings were broken. You'd have healed them eventually, but the salve clearly made a difference."

"It's just, I thought..." *Kisses on a rooftop in the rain...* Severn in his arms. He'd thought Severn had healed his wings.

Saphia's brows lifted in inquiry.

But, of course, Severn healing him was ridiculous, considering he wasn't even an angel and demons don't heal. By Haven, he'd wept on the rooftop with Severn in his arms and *thanked* him. "Nothing." He rubbed at his chest, over his heart.

"Tell me more about this crone?"

He tossed his memories back to that moment in the hut when everything had hurt and he'd had to suffer the wretched company of a demon. "She had a pet rayvern. Damn thing was the size of a dog. Jasper, she called it. Treated it like kin. I'm sure she was quite insane."

"How did you come to be captured by her?"

He told her how the crone had taken advantage of his weakness and trapped him right after he'd broken out of the train carriage, then proceeded to lecture him on some demon fairytale and paint his wings black with her hideous concoction. "Did she do this to me? Make my wings so different?"

"It's possible. Your wings are changing, and not just their color. Clearly, Tower Bridge was not an isolated incident."

"Tower Bridge was..." He sighed and let his head fall back against the headboard. "It's the allyanse. We were supposed to be fated, and he... He's a demon lord, Saphia." He hated how his voice trembled, how a chill raised the fine hairs on his arms, betraying all the hurt. He couldn't look at her. Her face would be full of pity and sadness and shame, for him. As a guardian, he'd vowed to be good, to do what was right, to lead the angels to victory, and instead, he'd fallen in love with the enemy. "I've tried to fight it... It shouldn't have worked, knowing what he is. Why did it work? Why do I feel these things?"

She patted his hand. "I really don't know, Mikhail. I wish I did. And I wish you would go to Haven where they can treat this."

He groaned and rolled his eyes. "No. And don't suggest it again. If I go there, it'll be over, and I'm not ready to surrender to Konstantin. He did this to me. I have to destroy him."

"Yes, well..." she sighed. "You always succeed in whatever you put your mind to, that much is true. But sometimes, when the problems are within ourselves, we need some help to see them."

"Severn is my problem. When he is dead, everything will return to normal, perhaps including my wings."

She nodded in that way that suggested she was just agreeing with him to prevent an argument. "It would help if you could find this crone again, so I can talk with her."

"I wouldn't know where to begin. Her hut was destroyed when Aerie's disk fell. She's cambion, she told me that much, and she has a foul sense of humor." He shuddered at the thought of her touching his wings. But if she truly had made him change, what was her reasoning? "She said she didn't want to hurt me."

"Well, that seems true."

"She also said she wasn't finished."

"Hm. She sounds intriguing, for a demon," Saphia mused.

"Intriguing is not a word that crossed my mind at the time."

Saphia chuckled, "No, I imagine not. You mentioned she told you some demon tales?"

He waved the question away. "Nonsense, it's not relevant." Stories of how Seraphim and Aerius had been lovers, like Mikhail and Konstantin—He had no intention of repeating her disgusting stories to anyone. Not even Saphia. Just the thought of such a union was blasphemy. The crone's very existence—cambion, half demon and half human—was blasphemy too. It was more likely her salve did nothing, and he'd healed his own wings.

"I don't think her paste did this," Mikhail said, with sudden confidence. "I am a guardian. Perhaps this is some natural evolution."

"If it is, it hasn't been documented in living memory."

"It's more likely to be natural than by the hand of some cambion crone living in the cauldron with her pet rayvern." He threw back the sheets and tested his balance. His shoulders burned a little, but otherwise, he was fine. *Everything* was fine. The wings were troublesome, but he could manage it. Just so long as he didn't lose control again. They might even help him stamp out some of the rumors of his madness circulating. "Clearly, my issues of late are to do with this evolution and nothing to do with the allyanse."

Saphia glowered. "Your spin doesn't work with me, Mikhail."

"I know that, but that is the official explanation should anyone ask you. Do you understand?"

"If you have an episode in public, like the one you had last night, your lies won't save you."

Anger ignited like it always did of late. "I do not lie."

"Only to yourself."

Mikhail straightened and regarded the healer he'd known all his life. "In what way do I lie to myself?"

"You loved. A true, honest love. There is no shame in that."

He barked a laugh and picked up the folded pair of trousers waiting at the foot of the bed, hastily dressing. "Be that as it may, the love was based on a lie. I was weak. He exploited that weakness. He will never have such an opportunity again, and neither will anyone else. Love is a curse. One I'll be glad to be free of." This conversation was over. He had angels to attend to. He headed for the door.

I love you... That is no lie.

"Mikhail," Saphia said, pulling him to a stop. "Seraphim was more than our creator. In the end, he was a terrifying force, feared by all, demons and angels. Don't forget that."

"Seraphim is little more than a myth." He left, feeling stronger and more focused than he had since Severn's betrayal. Every day brought him closer to capturing his enemy. Soon, it would be over, angels would rule supreme, and everything would be right again with the world.

evern

BACK INSIDE SAMIEL'S ROOM, Severn watched the fog swirl below his window, obscuring most of London from view. But Aerie loomed in the distance, rising out of a broken city like a sword thrust into the earth.

He knew angels. Arguably, he was one. And they could change. He'd witnessed the beginnings of it in Mikhail. He would have listened to Severn about the war, about how the correctioners clearing the streets of misbehaving cambion lied to Mikhail every day about speaking with demons instead of killing them. Severn was no fool. These things couldn't change overnight, but he'd been close to making change happen before Vearn had revealed his lies to the world.

What had begun as a mission of vengeance had turned to one of love. Of course, he'd known it wasn't going to last, but he'd hoped, perhaps foolishly, that Mikhail would never learn who he was, and together they could have changed the world.

Well, all that had gone to shit. Now, Mikhail was off the rails, murdering demons in their homes and rallying his angels behind him.

He had to be stopped.

"Your angel lover is fucking insane," Samiel said, snaking his arms around Severn's waist from behind. He breathed in, his chest expanding against Severn's back, and Severn closed his eyes, leaning into the touch. A touch that was becoming more comforting with every day.

"I can stop him, Sam."

"With a blade through his cold heart." The words brushed Severn's neck.

He had no intention of telling Samiel or any demon that he intended to *talk* with Mikhail. They'd strap Severn to a table and continue to try and torture his angelness out of him. No, he had to play this carefully. As carefully as he'd played the angels.

Severn twisted in Samiel's arms and looked up into the demon's eyes. In their youth, they'd once tossed around ideas on how to kill Mikhail. Ideas about how they'd stop all the angels. None of those ideas had involved *talking* with the enemy.

In many ways, his demonkind were just as guilty as Mikhail. Djall's attack on Aerie was a heinous act, and she hadn't been alone in planning it. Fighting was all anyone seemed to focus on.

Samiel stroked his thumb across Severn's cheek. His sharp nail left a sensitive trail. He leaned in, his warm, soft lips brushed Severn's, and Severn opened, accepting him, needing him. It wasn't enough. The sex, these moments, they were nothing like the blinding intensity of being with Mikhail, but as incubi, he needed to absorb any freely given ether. To abstain was to weaken himself. But it still felt wrong. Like every kiss, every touch, was a betrayal.

Samiel withdrew and bumped his forehead against Severn's. "It's not the same. Between us, I mean. You're Konstantin, but you're not my Konstantin."

His instinct was to lie, to tell Samiel everything was fine, that of course he was the same inside and nothing had changed, but he was so damned tired of lies. "I'm sorry." It was the truth, but not all of it. *I'm sorry I love the enemy*.

Samiel's playful mouth quirked at the corners. "I've waited ten years to have you back, what's a few more months?"

Only, he wasn't ever getting his Konstantin back. Even if Severn had his wings again, too much had changed. He pressed a hand to Samiel's cheek and smiled, hating the lie of that smile on his lips. He needed Samiel. Without him, he'd still be strapped to that table, might even be dead already. The best he could hope for was for them to slowly grow apart. But not yet. He had to use Samiel, and that thought truly sickened him. But the alternative—telling him he was going to save Mikhail to save them all—was worse.

"I have to go back. I have to wear another illusion, and I have to try to make everything right before more demons die."

"I know." Samiel's dark lashes fell. His hands fell, too, softly landing on Severn's hips. "I know, and it hurts to think of you leaving again." He eased Severn back against the wall beside the window.

The feel of him, pressed close, brought all the memories bubbling to the surface. His touch, the taste of him, how he arched beneath Konstantin, taking and giving, and so fucking beautiful.

"I didn't leave you before. *You* left me, Sam."

"I..." Samiel pushed away suddenly and marched to the middle of the room. He ran a hand over his right horn and through his hair. "What happened... out there. I couldn't stay. I thought, I thought you'd despise me."

Severn's brow pinched. No matter how hard he tried, he couldn't remember anything like what Samiel suggested. He only knew Samiel didn't return from battle. "When I made this illusion, I gave up a memory. A powerful one. The one you're speaking of. Tell me what happened."

Samiel bit into his lip and grimaced. "I can't."

A few quick knocks at the door pulled Samiel from the moment and farther away from Severn. Samiel opened the door to find a young demon in torn jeans and a patched-up jacket, waiting. His deep blue skin reminded Severn of a twilight sky, that moment right before day turns into night. The stubby horns would one day be brutally efficient weapons. "Jeseph wants to see the angel."

"Now?" Samiel asked.

The demon shrugged. "He just said to come." He lifted his gaze to Severn and stared. "Is it true then? Is he really Konstantin?"

Samiel glanced over his shoulder. "Sounds like the cat's out of the bag."

Severn approached the pair, collecting the angelblade

from the end of the bed on the way. The demon—barely more than a pup—gawked at the blade and flicked his big brown eyes up to Severn's face. "I heard about an angel killing angels. You killed all 'em angels on the street last night. That was you."

The admiration in the pup's eyes was difficult to ignore. So many dead angels would normally have brightened Severn's day once too. Not anymore. "Yeah." He managed a small smile, enough to make the pup grin.

"You were brutal. Took 'em down like, one, two, three." He punctuated each with a punch into his palm, suddenly becoming animated.

"I don't know about that." He followed the pup out of the room with Samiel trailing silently behind. "What's your name?"

The pup almost fell over his own feet as he skipped ahead and walked backward in front of them. "Ernas of Blue Manor."

"Blue, huh?" Argothun's manor. Manors were a demon's home, their territory, and their family. "How many of you are there?"

"Not many," his mouth twisted, "after Mikhail took out Lord Argothun. We're pretty much scattered all over Dagenham, right?" His eyes widened as an idea occurred to him. "Maybe we could join Red, huh? If you're back? Are you really back? You look so... angel, it's pretty weird, but dayam, you fooled 'em all."

"How many of Red Manor are left?" Severn asked, trying to keep him focused.

"Maybe, like... er, three?"

Severn tried not to wince. The Red Manor had been in

decline for years, even before Severn had left. "No leader, huh?"

"Nah. Not enough of them. The other manors just kind of absorbed 'em." Ernas grinned and jogged ahead to jab the elevator button. "This is so fucking awesome. Konstantin is back, *bee-atches!*"

"Not yet," Samiel grumbled, earning a scolding look from Ernas that almost had Severn laughing aloud. A look like that from a pup was the same as some fledgling angel trying to pick a fight with Mikhail.

Severn ruffled Ernas's spikey hair between his short horns as they stepped into the elevator car. "Red Manor would be honored to have you."

Ernas beamed, visibly swelling with pride. "Best. Day. Ever."

The pup chatted about how he'd lost his family—all but one younger sister—to the war as he led Severn and Samiel across an old, junk-metal scrapper's yard and between rows of tall, empty warehouses. The building they approached appeared to look the same as the other struc-tures, clad in rusted metal sheeting, but on opening the small side door, the building revealed its true purpose as a meeting house—or lord's court, though that term had been fading out of use in Konstantin's time.

Severn tripped at the sight of so many demons under one roof. They gathered in groups, propped against the old rusted car chassis or metal drums. The height of the structure amplified their murmuring. A metal walkway clung to the inside of the building a floor up but was open, so all the demons gathered above could see into the central stage area. The area Ernas was leading Severn to now.

The murmuring ebbed to silence, punctured only by the occasional cough or rustle of wings.

Djall stood at the back of the stage, whip coiled at her hip and wings clamped closed. Others stood alongside her, too, faces Severn only vaguely remembered, who appeared to have risen in power. But one face he knew well. The stern, narrow face of the concubi lord Luxen.

Samiel gently took the angelblade from Severn's hand and veered off to one side. It was probably a good idea not to appear as an angel *and* armed in front of the lords.

Djall's eyes narrowed on seeing Severn climb a set of steps onto the stage. Ernas bowed his head to the demon court and hastily jogged off-stage, leaving Severn alone, surrounded by hundreds of demons. Their collective stares made his skin tingle and tighten. Every single demon here saw an angel.

Even Jayke was here—the hard-ass demon who had helped Severn first get inside the cauldron, and thus Aerie, a decade ago.

Ah, this was a trial.

Jayke was here to give evidence.

They were all here to condemn Severn.

He searched for any sign of the madam but couldn't see her. She was likely with the medics. He had few allies here. Even as Konstantin, he hadn't been universally accepted as a lord. Too young, too brash, some said too compulsive to be a lord.

In hindsight, they had a point.

"Konstantin, Lost Lord of the Red Manor," High Lord Lux began, voice booming, "you stand before the demon lords, accused of defection. We have heard the testimony of those you employed in your subterfuge. You were not made available to voice your defense, but it seems clear you went willingly to the angels, wearing your... new skin."

As High Lord, he was the closest thing demons ever had to a king, and it was a testament to how far the demons had fallen that a sly, political-game player like Luxen ruled them now. As concubi, he stood taller than most others here, with a wingspan (currently folded) that rivaled Konstantin's. And clearly, leadership agreed with him. He might not have been the most muscular demon here, but adorned in fitted leather punctuated with buckles and clips, his physique radiated the kind of undeniable *fuck-me-feed-me-worship-me* aura that all mature concubi possessed. Lux was the epitome of everything Mikhail had tried to eradicate, and in Konstantin's absence, he'd risen to lofty heights.

Jeseph leered from among the lords, enjoying the shock on Severn's face at having been denied a chance to speak at his own trial.

"High Lord," Severn began, "that's not—"

"How do you plead?" Lux asked.

"I did not know this trial was ongoing, or I would have presented myself."

If Lux cared, his stern face showed no sign of it. "How do you plead?" he repeated.

"I did not go willingly." How was he supposed to explain how he had technically defected, but only because of vengeance for the death of a demon who stood very much alive in the crowd.

"Then, you were captured?" Lux asked.

To be captured and held for so many years by Mikhail would be just as much a disgrace as defecting. "No, I wasn't captured. That's not—"

"Then you were there by choice?"

"Yes, but—"

Lux's thin lips stretched into a grin as Severn dug his own grave with every word.

How could he deny it, standing before them as an angel? The demon court had always been fair, but much had changed, and the faces of the lords looking back at him were not sympathetic.

Severn dropped to a knee and bowed his head. "I plead not guilty."

Furor erupted, a cacophony of descent. Lux's cries for order initially fell on deaf ears, but eventually, the crowd settled again.

Severn lifted his head to see Lux had moved forward. He'd never felt so small as he did in that moment. Even if he'd knelt as Konstantin, Lux still would have wielded all the power in the court.

And for the first time in ten years, he regretted his decision to leave, to chase after vengeance. In leaving, he'd abandoned Red Manor, his home, his people. A snake like Luxen becoming High Lord? That fuckup was on him.

He'd be lucky to survive whatever judgment happened next.

Lux bared his sharp teeth. "You kneel there, as angel, in this court and have the balls to plead not guilty?"

"It is not what it seems." Severn raised his voice, unable to stop the tremors every demon here must have heard. "This illusion is fixed. I cannot—"

"We're aware. Jeseph has been attempting to have it removed, but you insist on clinging to it. Why is that?" Lux asked, like any of this was Severn's choice.

"No. I'm not—that's not... If I could get rid of it, I would."

"Is that really the truth?" Lux's brow lifted, clearly disbelieving.

"Why would I stay as angel among you, my kin? I sacrificed my life, my title, to defeat Mikhail. I almost succeeded, but Argothun acted too soon. We had an agreement. He was to wait for my signal, but he blustered in. What happened after..." Severn wet his dry lips. The allyanse had happened after. Mikhail had saved Severn and bonded with him, and no doubt, every demon here knew it. The thought of it sickened him again, like it had when he'd first learned of it, because he knew all those here would see him and his love as monstrous.

"Argothun and his manor suffered for your mistake," Lux declared. "Demons have died for your mistakes, Konstantin. You killed demons in battle, alongside Mikhail. You went to him *willingly*. What defense can you possibly have?"

He glanced at his sister. Her brow was pinched, but not by much. Would she stay silent, or had she already spoken up? They'd always disagreed as pups, but she didn't hate him. Severn had only tried to hurt her—kill her—to protect the outcome of his relationship with Mikhail, to protect the change he could have implemented. It would have been worth it, but, of course, she wouldn't see it that way. Had she spoken, she'd have told them all how he tried to kill her on the banks of the Thames.

"I made mistakes," he admitted, setting off another round of dissent from the crowd. But he stared at Lux, at the demon's proud face and striking, curved horns, at the way his wings arched behind him, their tips reaching higher than any other demon's here. "I can stop him. Stop all of this. He trusted me. I was getting through to him. I can end his relentless attacks. You all think it's over, but it's not. I'm not finished. It's why I'm like I am." He slowly straightened, still having to look up at Lux, but at least he was on his feet. "Never in our entire history has a demon gotten so close to an angel. Years of work, a decade devoted to bringing him down—"

"But you failed."

"It wasn't done. We have an opportunity here to change things forever. We have to take it. Or the war will go on, and eventually, Mikhail or another guardian like him will wipe us out. Our numbers are too few. Despite Djall's attack, they will rally, and as we've seen— thanks to that very attack—they no longer care for the Law. Djall opened the way for dissent, and the angels have embraced it. They were deadly before, but now they'll stop at nothing. There are no laws, no rules. If I do not finish what I began, we will all die."

His last words rang through the silence. He let them hang there, let everyone hear them over and over, because it was the truth. "Put me on trial afterward, if there is an after. But let me finish what I started now. I stand before you as an angel because I'm the only weapon demonkind has left."

The mood among the crowd quickly shifted, signaling a change. His words were getting through. Lux heard it too. His dark eyes skimmed the demon masses until finally resting again on Severn. His lips ticked, and, almost lazily, he said so only Severn could hear, "You always did have their hearts."

Lifting his hand, the crowd fell silent, and he backed

up to his place among the lords. "Unlike angels, we are reasonable. We have heard Konstantin's words. Lords, it is time to decide Konstantin's fate. Do we acquit, or do we condemn?"

Severn's heart beat in his throat. This wasn't about his not being guilty, they all knew he was. This was about whether Lux could have him conveniently killed in the name of justice and get away with it. This was all a ceremony, but whatever happened, Lux would eventually make sure Konstantin was removed—Severn was sure of it.

"Acquit," Djall said.

Severn sighed. He hadn't been sure what side she'd fall on, but it seemed his sister did not want him dead even after the fiasco at Tower Bridge.

A few more "acquit" rang out from the lords. When it was Jeseph's turn, the big demon merely glared and growled, "Condemn."

Lux nodded and let the quiet stretch on. For all the lords' input, it was Lux who had the final say. "As High Lord, it is my duty to protect you all. I have heard the words of your lords. Konstantin, Lost Lord of the Red Manor, you are hereby acquitted, *but*"—he barked, bringing a verbal scythe down on what would have been an uproar—"you will report to me on your every move. Your reckless disregard for authority ends now." The gathered demons erupted, some in cheers but most in dissent.

Severn swallowed the hard, dry knot in his throat. Justice had been done, but there was another kind of justice, the kind that would likely see his end in a dark alley with a blade in his back.

Lux approached, his boots thunking heavily against the stage boards. He gripped Severn's chin, squeezing his jaw.

"You escape punishment only because of your name. Your reputation will not save you a second time." He tore his hand free.

"I understand."

"I don't think you do." The incubus's eyes flashed. "Attend my chamber, Lord Konstantin. We have much to discuss."

CHAPTER 9

evern

DJALL MANAGED to push her way through the demons escorting Severn through a back door in the warehouse. "Brother." Her face was full of pity, and it hurt to see. "Be careful. Luxen is slippery. He—"

The guards flanking Severn shoved him forward. "Move along," one grumbled.

Djall reached forward and managed to briefly touch Severn's shoulder. "Be strong," she said, but the guards had already swept Severn away, and the crowd swallowed Djall somewhere behind him.

Her words shook his core. Djall still cared after everything he'd done? He looked for Samiel among the crowd but saw only disapproving faces. Anxiety gnawed at his heart. He'd always avoided crossing horns with Lux. The demon gave the impression of someone who would rather stab his enemies in the shadows than fight them in daylight. Was Severn his enemy? On the outside, certainly. But there was a chance Lux had risen to power because he genuinely wanted to lead the demons to victory, and Severn wanted the same thing. They might disagree on how to get it, but surely it was common enough ground to warrant Severn's survival.

High Lord Luxen's chambers occupied the entire top floor of a five-story building. Demons bustled and drifted about, his staff perhaps. The deeper into the accommodation he went, the more the demons lost their air of authority, lounging on the mismatched furniture, clad in loose clothing. All unarmed. As a concubi High Lord, he'd have a harem on hand to top up his ether whenever he felt the need. His power was likely ten times that of Severn's. Whatever was about to happen, Severn would have to endure it.

"The High Lord will be with you soon," one of the guards said, leaving Severn in an overtly sumptuous bedroom. He frowned at the luxury being High Lord afforded. Angels would probably give their right wings for a chance at getting inside the High Lord's den. It would take a few of them to bring Lux down. Or Mikhail. After that show at Tower Bridge, he'd be able to kill Lux one-on-one, provided he didn't let his emotions distract him.

He drifted about the darkly lit room, breathing in the spiciness of demon, but his thoughts lingered on Mikhail. He'd sprouted six wings on the bridge and pulled the stars from the sky. That power was undeniable and indiscriminate. And dangerous. If Mikhail could wield that power again, it wouldn't take much for him to wipe out what remained of all demons.

Lux strode through the door, leaving it open behind him. The noisy hubbub from outside spilled into the room. He'd hidden his wings to move more freely from building to building,but revealed them now, adding a few settling flicks to shake out any stiffness. He'd always had a reptilian ambiance and a predator's grace. That hadn't changed.

"A drink?" the High Lord asked.

"Thank you."

He collected two glasses and a decanter from a cabinet and poured out the drinks, then strode forward and handed Severn's out. Severn took it, waiting for the trick, but when none came, he lifted the rich, woody whiskey to his lips and drank deeply.

Lux's wings drew his eye again. He remembered them being glorious. Not in the same as Mikhail's were glorious. Demon wings were displays of strength and virility. When Mikhail had taken Severn's, he might as well have severed his cock too. Socially, it amounted to the same thing. Lux's wings were a blatant advertisement of his incubi prowess, and Severn had a sinking feeling he'd be more than admiring that prowess soon.

Lux threw back a large gulp of whiskey and narrowed his glare, blatantly unimpressed with Severn. "You did me a favor in leaving."

What was he supposed to say to that?

"Left a vacuum in power," Lux continued. "We were already short on concubi, and you took off on some personal vendetta. I asked Djall where you were. She said you were dead, but from one liar to another, we all knew it was bullshit." His slanted smile tucked into his cheek. "You were a risk. Powerful, respected, rising as a lord in a blink. I'd had my eye on a lordship for a long time, but you took all the council's attention—good and bad. And then you were gone, and I didn't have to lift a finger to see it done." He chinked his glass with Severn's and drank deeply, before adding, "Thank you for fucking off."

"At least you're honest," Severn grumbled.

"Are you honest?"

"Not in the least."

"No, I didn't think so." The High Lord's expression turned calculating. "You love Mikhail."

Severn's internal emotional guard slammed down. "Love?" he laughed. "No, angels don't know the meaning of the word."

Lux gestured with the glass toward Severn. "But you, an incubus, loves passionately." He backed up, slanting his gaze, slithering it through Severn's armor. "Whenever Mikhail is mentioned, your pupils dilate. In your natural form, that wouldn't happen—you'd guard against it—but illusions are complex to manage."

Observant bastard. Severn played nonchalant while silently cursing his angel body. Just when he thought he'd gotten a handle on how to control being an angel, it threw up bullshit like that.

"I often thought of you," Lux continued, clearly enjoying the sound of his own voice. "Assuming you were this *Severn* who stood at Mikhail's right side. To do what you did for so long, it could not have been easy. The only way you could succeed was to fall in love with the lie."

Severn smiled, hoping it came off as sympathetic and not grief. "The act was flawless, but it was just an act. I no more love him than I do you, no offense."

Lux laughed loud and free. He put his glass down on a

sideboard near the bed and began to flick open all the buckles of the jacket wrapping his torso in leather. The zips went next, slipping it from his shoulders so he didn't have to pull it from his wings. "We'll test that theory." He laid the jacket over the back of a chair. "Incubus to incubus." Innate hunger widened his pupils.

Severn knew that need well and recognized this for exactly what it was. "You want to fuck to prove I'm not in love with an angel?"

Lux's smile was a slippery thing, there one moment, gone the next, leaving behind that radiating need in his eyes. "Of course. Or more accurately, to prove you're still demon under all that..." He gestured at Severn's body.

Severn laughed dryly and threw back the remainder of his drink. It was beginning to look as though he might need the whole bottle. Fucking Samiel was one thing. Fucking an incubus like Lux was entirely another. Sex was a language to concubi, a language almost impossible to lie in. Lux would scent his emotions. If he wasn't completely focused on the task, Lux would know.

"Been wanting to fuck an angel, have you, Lux?" he teased. "Some might consider that beyond grotesque, even for you."

Lux's fingers worked open the undershirt buttons. "Perhaps. But if we're to trust you, I know no other way of reading the truth."

"How about you just trust my word as a lord?"

Lux barked a laugh. "Says the demon who lied to the enemy for a decade. To be fair, I didn't know you had it in you, Konstantin. You always struck me as a blunt tool, not a precision instrument. I'm impressed... so long as it was all lies. If it wasn't, then there's an angel in my den, and we have a problem."

If Lux discovered his true feelings and the depth of them for Mikhail, he'd kill Severn. But if Severn fought, he'd never be able to return to his home. He really would be the traitor they all thought him to be.

It was beginning to look as though the only way out of this was to fuck Lux and make it damned good while keeping him from wringing the truth out of Severn's body.

He strode to the cabinet and refilled his glass. "Fine. But in case you hadn't noticed, we're hardly physically compatible." Severn propped his ass on the cabinet's edge and ran his incubus gaze over Lux in a more studious way. Compared to an angel, Lux was heavier, broader, stronger, with well-defined muscles. Seraphim hadn't been screwing around when he'd made demons to counter angels. Almost all demons were physically bigger than angels, in all ways.

Lux shrugged the shirt off in the same way as the jacket went. His wings twitched open a little, and his fingers dropped to his belt. "I'm sure we can work with what we have."

Severn dragged a half smile onto his lips, helped by the alcohol. "And what if you discover you like angel ass?"

Lux gave him a droll look. "Considering how fragile you are, it's highly unlikely."

"Samiel had no complaints."

"So he told me."

Severn winced at that. Samiel had been reporting everything back to Lux? He hadn't expected that but should have. The High Lord was within his rights to know everything. It might even be the case that Samiel had been working for Lux all along. Gods, he was out of his depth among these demons in the same way he'd once been out of his depth among angels. But that had changed, and this would too. He was going to seduce Lux until the demon begged for angel. Just so long as Lux didn't seduce him first. Fucking another incubus always had risks. Not least because it had little to do with plea-sure and everything to do with prowess. It wasn't unheard of for one partner to kill the other, and Severn was at a distinct physical disadvantage. This was not going to be easy.

His gaze dropped to the solid outline of the swelling cock filling out Lux's trousers. He'd seen bigger, but not often. He tried to swallow but found his mouth had dried. More whiskey went down.

Lux let his belt hang open but didn't touch his fly. He wasn't about to get his cock out this early on. They had a long way to go before Severn earned that feast.

Laughter from the other demons in the building sailed in through the open door, but it sounded as though it were another world away. Lux folded his arms, waiting for Severn's next move.

He set his drink aside and approached. The High Lord's wings ticked slightly. For all his restraint, he was curious. Severn had once wondered what angel tasted like too. He was beginning to wonder if lusting after angels wasn't as rare among demons as he'd been raised to believe.

He stopped close enough to reach out and touch Lux's face but held back, looking him in his dark eyes. "My pupils dilate at mention of Mikhail because fucking an angel is like nothing you've ever experienced."

"I've experienced much," he replied, trying to sound

nonplussed, but his tongue darted out to wet his lips in anticipation.

He probably had experienced a great deal. Older than Konstantin by several hundred years, Luxen knew all the tricks. But he'd never had *angel*. If Severn stood in front of him as Konstantin, they'd probably end up killing each other. But Lux wasn't aggressive now. He didn't think Severn a threat.

Severn stepped in and stroked his fingers down Lux's cheek to the upward tick of his lips. "When I'm done with you, you'll forever crave angel. Is that what you want?"

Lux caught Severn's wrist, holding it still. "A bold and unlikely claim."

Severn rose onto his toes and peered into Lux's eyes. He saw the reflection of himself in their dark coloring. Blue eyes, golden hair, the epitome of everything demons despised. "When I'm done..." Severn whispered against his lips, "you'll beg me to fuck you, again and again, because it'll never be enough."

Lux's gaze dropped to his mouth, thinking about claiming it. Tensions strummed through the demon, holding him back. Every word pulled on his strings, ramping up his desire from mild curiosity to focused need. And Severn, attuned to the moment, felt it all.

He dropped his free hand, cupped Lux's large cock through the trousers, and leaned so close his chest pressed against Luxen's. "Back out now, if you like. There'd be no shame in it." Lux's heat warmed Severn through, rousing the demon within, making his own cock finally pay attention. Overthinking this would get him in trouble. Better to throw himself into the task and get it done.

Lux caught Severn's chin in his firm grip, leaned for the

kiss, and hesitated, mouth so close to Severn's they shared breaths. And then his wings slowly unfurled, drawing Severn's gaze. Lux's mouth was on his, slowly at first, so achingly soft and full of demon potency. Ether began to shimmer off his shoulders and dance across his wings, and Severn groaned at the taste of it on his tongue. Lux's hand swooped around and clutched his ass, grinding him closer, smothering him in the hot, hard feel of demon.

Lux's sharp teeth drew blood. Severn swallowed it, sensing the lord coming undone in the moment. He knew how he tasted because Mikhail had tasted the same—like he was the air Lux needed to breathe, like he could bask inside him and drink him down and drown in everything angelic. Maybe it wasn't the same for all demons kissing angels, but considering how fucking hard Lux was, filling Severn's grip, he assumed he was angel enough to tempt this experienced incubus. Good. If he could distract him, Lux wouldn't go looking for the real emotions swamping Severn—like how this was a betrayal of the worse kind.

Lux backed Severn into the wall. His hands tugged his shirt free of his pants and rode up his bare chest, nails scraping. But Lux's overflowing ether was key, and Severn had a hold of it now, drinking it down, feeding, making his demon heart and soul sing. He freed the demon's cock and grasped the warm, veined shaft.

Breathless, Lux pulled back and nuzzled Severn's neck. "Hm... you do taste good *for an angel*."

Severn could feel just how good as he slowly stroked the demon off. He hopefully radiated his own ether now, evidence he was as into this as Lux was.

The demon's wings, now flung open, shuddered with every stroke of Severn's hand along Lux's eager cock. The member pulsed, and for all Lux's words about his experience, it wouldn't take much to push him over the edge. Severn could drop to his knees and suck him off to completion in seconds, but this wasn't about quick gratification. He needed Lux to believe he was still demon in his heart and soul. If the High Lord trusted him, the others would fall in line.

Severn sensed the lord's crackling energy, and also how there was a whole lot more of it to give. He wedged his free hand between the demon's hip and trousers waist and levered the garment down over his ass until it fell to the floor. The undergarments went next, and Lux stood in all his glorious nakedness, crowding Severn against the wall. He seemed the sort to like control, but often the most obvious kink hid some other, deep-seated desire. Severn sank his nails into the demon's thick ass and raked them down his leg. Lux's rumbling growl and the waves of ether revealed how he enjoyed pain.

Severn tipped his head back, and Lux's mouth immediately went to his throat, leaving Severn open to tilt his head and sink his teeth into Lux's shoulder. Lux grunted, and Severn abruptly stopped his stroking, instead pinching the base of the male's cock.

Lux threw his head back and his wings out and thrust blindly against Severn's waist. Precum cooled on Severn's belly. Gods, his mouth watered to take that piece of demon meat in and work him over, but not yet, not while he had Lux losing himself in his hands. It wouldn't be the same as Mikhail. Mikhail had been more delicate, even in his mad thrusts and—

Lux opened his eyes and tilted his head.

Fuck.

Severn grabbed him by the neck and smashed their mouths together, fending off all thoughts of Mikhail. He could do this, and drinking Lux's ether would make crafting a new illusion all the easier. He had to do this. Make them *believe* he was the Konstantin they knew and feared and loved. He had to do this... for Mikhail. Even as part of him ached to have Mikhail in his hands, Mikhail's mouth on his, his soft eyes and naïve questions about love and demons.

Oh gods. He couldn't stop circling back to his angel.

He dropped to his knees, grasped Lux's heated cock, and stroked his tongue from base to tip, gathering his balls in his free hand to crush them lightly, making Lux squirm. He braced an arm against the wall over Severn's head and looked down. "Fuck, yes... angel."

Severn heard himself saying those very words to Mikhail, later switched to *"Fuck me, Your Grace."* His own cock pulsed, the memories making it ache.

Lux's cock thrust over his tongue, not too deep, the incubus aware enough not to choke him. Then Lux's hand swept down, grabbed Severn by the throat, and hauled him to his feet. His other hand grasped both their cocks, Severn's notably smaller even fully erect, given his angel body, and Lux rocked, rubbing his cock against Severn's while his fingers rubbed them both.

Severn grabbed the demon's shoulder, needing to clutch on. He might have sworn. He was beginning to lose track of his body and mind. Ether buzzed through him, lighting him up. He wished for his wings, so he could throw them open like Lux's. Angel and demon. Light and dark. Bad and good. He ached to be Konstantin again in this moment, to have the power, to have his wings, to have

Lux on his fucking knees, his thin lips circled around his pounding dick.

"You going to come, angel?" Lux purred. "Hmm... so soon?"

"Fuck. No," he ground out through gritted teeth. *Maybe.* Shit. Lux tasted delicious. Tasted like power. Tasted like demon and everything Severn had forgotten he was. This had nothing to do with emotion and everything to do with asserting his control and strength over the powerful incubus High Lord.

The sound of his growling was nothing like an angel's. Lux grinned and quickened his jerking hand. "Come, little angel, spend for me."

His mind tried to grasp at the memory of Mikhail, but if it took hold, he would climax. Instead, he shoved both hands into Lux's shoulders with enough force to rock him backward. The demon began to laugh, but Severn wasn't done. He shoved again, this time fast and hard, slapping his palms against Lux's chest. The demon's slick, glistening cock jerked, and the demon himself lost his smile, his glare turning icy. Ether poured off him like heat haze rolling off concrete on a hot summer's day. It made Severn's head foggy, his cock rage, and his body want to crawl out of the illusion and back into the body it belonged to just so he could feel all this how it was supposed to be felt. Like he was the fucking king here and Luxen his subject.

"Kneel," Severn snarled. Any thought that Lux might argue quickly faded when he dropped to his knees. Severn wasted no time, stepped closer, and Lux's swollen lips parted, sliding him in. His hands came around Severn's ass, squeezing, separating, sharp fingernails stroking over the tight hole.

How many times had he dreamed of making Mikhail kneel, of demanding he spread himself for Severn? And Mikhail would have. He wanted to. He preferred it that way. His naïve, powerfully broken angel.

Ether rolled off Severn now too. He saw it in the way Lux had lost his focus, his eyes glazing, mind drowning. His cock leaked thin streams of precum, and he was going to come sucking an angel off—the wave of it approached, crashing in all around, and Severn gripped the bastard's horns, thrusting wildly, opening himself completely.

He was going to come, to shudder his release down Lux's throat and at the same time, absorb the demon's ether, and fuck it would be too much, but he didn't care. He was made for this.

The crescendo broke over them both. Lux moaned around Severn's cock as Severn's prick spent its load in short, sharp bursts, and pleasure rammed through Severn's body, down his spine, lighting him up. His cock pulsed, ejaculating hard, and Lux took him to the hilt, wings stretched, flushed with heat.

Ether tried to drag Severn's wrecked body into unconsciousness. He staggered, pulling himself free of Lux's grinning mouth. And then Lux caught him, wrapped thick arms around him, and folded him close, in the way demons did. Severn unashamedly clung to the superheated body, wishing it were Mikhail, but the demon High Lord would do for now. Shit, had he done it? Had he convinced Lux he wasn't just the angel he appeared to be on the outside. That he was still a thoroughly passionate incubus?

The High Lord growled, low in his chest, and practically carried Severn to the bed. Severn made no argument when Lux left him there, and watched mutely as the demon kicked his door closed and turned, rapture in his eyes.

Oh gods, he'd done it all right. Maybe a bit too thoroughly.

Lux climbed into the bed, his wings raised above him, and stalked up Severn's body, peeling off the remaining clothes, until he was eye-to-eye with Severn. He had the rabid look about him of pups who had abstained for too long, like forming words was too much effort and fucking was all he was good for.

"Lux—"

The demon pressed a finger to Severn's lips, then with a smile, removed his finger and kissed him deeply. "More," was all the incubus mustered, before trailing his mouth and tongue down Severn's chest to encircle a nipple.

Severn let his eyes close, and Lux ventured lower. This hadn't been part of his plan. But at least he'd be fully charged for the illusion, if Lux let him do it. Which seemed a whole lot more likely now the High Lord had his lips around Severn's reinvigorated cock again.

What would Mikhail say if he learned Severn was fucking the High Lord? Would he be jealous? Perhaps it was best not to think on those things, seeing as Mikhail's anger alone had the potential to be world-ending. He closed his eyes and pretended the mouth and tongue working him over was Mikhail's. Lux wouldn't know, too lost to the ether high to care. And Severn wasn't far behind him.

Mikhail

HE STOOD on the London terrace rooftop, the one Severn had brought him to, and regarded the chimney stack rubble strewn about. He'd destroyed it, along with much of the house they'd shared, including the desk Severn had fucked him against. Taking his anger out on inanimate objects was supposed to make him feel better, but all it had done was make him emptier. *Nothing* helped.

The heavy flap of wings signaled an angel's arrival behind him. He waited for whomever it was to speak, and when they didn't, he glanced behind him to find Solo patiently waiting to be acknowledged.

Mikhail sighed. At least it wasn't Vearn. He was sure she was in contact with Remiel. She'd probably been the one to summon him here to kill him or ship him off to

Haven, where he'd no doubt slowly go insane without his mate. Maybe insanity would be better than this.

"Is the second wave ready to attack?" Mikhail asked.

"Yes, Your Grace."

Will you fuck me, Your Grace?

Mikhail ruffled his wings and rolled his shoulders, shaking out the tension and the terrible memory of Severn's words. He stared at London's twinkling skyline, just like Severn had shown him. There were more lights farther afield now. The humans had moved away. But their lives continued, all because angels protected them, as it had always been since time began.

Solo drew up alongside Mikhail. "It's magical."

"Yes," Mikhail agreed reluctantly. "Angels, long ago, walked alongside humans. I wonder sometimes if we should again." Severn had said that... Told him to *get down to their level.* He'd said a lot of things, strange things, different things—like implying how the correctioners weren't saving cambions.

"Solo, I want you to visit the nearest correctioner facility, unannounced. Report if you find anything untoward."

"Sire? Is there a problem?"

"I hope not." He glanced over, and his thoughts stalled at the way the light softly touched Solo's gentle ripples in his red hair and how it highlighted his green eyes. Had he always been so enchanting to admire? He shook off the odd thought and stared at London instead, but soon found his gaze wandering back. The breeze teased at Solo's hair now and whispered its trailing edges across his red feathers.

Solo noticed the attention and turned his head. "Please, forgive me for asking this... but perhaps a few days away from the responsibility of all this"—he gestured at London—"might help?"

He'd snapped at Vearn for suggesting the same. "I'll go insane," he said, speaking the absolute truth. He barely clung to sanity now.

Solo turned toward him and tucked his wings in. "Your Grace, is there anything in your life besides war?"

"Like what?"

"Do you like to go anywhere, do anything, that isn't related to warfare?"

"I don't see how that's relevant."

"Well, no, I imagine you don't. But... even guardians need to step away sometimes."

"No, guardians don't *step away*. Ever. When I became a guardian, I gave up all things."

"Everything?" Solo asked in a small voice.

"Everything."

"There is no pleasure in your life at all?"

"There's pleasure..." he answered automatically, and had been about to mention how the battles brought him pleasure, how killing demons brought him pleasure, but none of those things ever had. He'd done them because it was what guardians did. But there had to be pleasure somewhere in his life, didn't there?

"What about a hobby?"

"A hobby?"

"You know... like..." he gestured at the air, clearly struggling, "fishing." Solo mimed an overarm throw, and Mikhail frowned.

"Fishing?" Mikhail echoed. "For fish?"

"Well, not demons," Solo laughed a low, melodic laughter, and the sound of it shot a dart of lust to Mikhail's useless member, making the damned thing begin to sit up and take notice.

Mikhail gasped at his body's own betrayal and staggered. He spread his wings, instinctively wanting to flee.

"Your Grace?" Solo reached for him. "I'm sorry, I had no idea fishing was so traumatic—"

And then he was close, so close, head tilted up, eyes bright and full, and his lips were the kind meant for kissing, weren't they? By Haven, Mikhail didn't know, but his body did, and before reason could regain control, his lips were on Solo's. Just a small skim, nothing really. But then Solo sighed, like he'd been holding his breath, waiting, and Mikhail tasted his mouth a second time, this time deliberately teasing the male's lips apart, waiting for resistance, but none came. He should resist. Why wasn't he?

Solo's soft, wet tongue brushed Mikhail's, seeking acceptance, or permission, or something that Mikhail didn't understand, like he didn't understand any of this. Severn was... Severn was special. The allyanse had made it so. But there was no allyanse in this moment, just two angels on a rooftop, each seeking the other in a way they shouldn't.

Mikhail jerked back, stumbling, falling over the fallen bricks. His wings flung out, losing feathers in his ungainly attempt to balance himself, only just succeeding.

Solo touched his own lips, as though not quite believing. His eyes widened, and he flung a panicked look at Mikhail. "What was that?"

Mikhail fought the fledgling-like urge to fly away. "A mistake. Nothing." His heart hammered.

"Was that *a kiss*?"

Oh, why wouldn't the Thames rise up and drown him? "I'm sorry. It was... wrong of me."

Solo touched his lips again and looked at his fingers. "I've never been kissed before."

"I'm ashamed, Solomon. I should never have touched you. It was wrong of me, and I apologize. I'm not entirely in my right mind, as you may have seen, and these emotions are—"

Solo launched himself skyward in a flurry of red feathers. Mikhail watched his silhouette slowly disappear among the nighttime clouds. Well, that was a fucking disaster, as Severn would have said. Kissing Solo was yet another crime he could add to his long list of vulgar and hideous acts of late. And the worst of it was, for a moment, it had felt *good*. He wanted him back, not like he needed Severn—because of the allyanse—he just needed someone, anyone, to hold him. He was so very alone, and before Severn, it hadn't mattered. But now, it seemed, the loneliness was the hollowness inside of him, and for a second or two, Solo's kiss had made him feel fuller, not as empty, not as cold. Did it mean anything, or was it just his broken mind desperately reaching for company, even if that company was so thoroughly wrong?

He didn't want to stand on this rooftop alone. He didn't want to be alone anywhere. It hurt, though, and he was cold, and empty. He folded his wings around himself.

It didn't matter.

Soon, he'd have Konstantin in custody. Remiel would come. He'd present the source of all these problems to the other guardian and then kill Konstantin, proving the allyanse was nothing and Mikhail was perfectly capable of leading London's angels in the battle against demons. All of this emotional nonsense would die with Konstantin.

~

THE RANK of angels flying above the shimmering clouds was several hundred strong. Each one was a capable warrior, and the sight of them made Mikhail's heart soar too. Severn would not escape them this time.

Solo had tracked his tagged demon to the same location, where she'd stayed for over a week. It had to be the demon stronghold. A scout had reported the warehouses looked empty, but the tagged demon was inside them, and so the angels would attack there first. There hadn't been any further sign of Severn, but he was sure to appear as soon as the fighting began.

Solo flew at Mikhail's right, his red wings stroking the air. His face had been hidden behind a helmet visor when Mikhail had arrived to lead the flight. Solo had simply obeyed Mikhail's orders, and now here they were. The angel gave no indication he was still disturbed by the kiss. So, nothing had changed. Nothing at all.

The clouds parted, revealing the long, narrow warehouses below, like squares on a patchwork quilt. Mikhail freed his blade and spiraled downward. All his angels fell into formation behind him. Solo's first attack on the demons' home ground had been chaotic and generally ineffective, resulting in more angry demons making a stand—like kicking a wasp's nest. But this time, Mikhail needed the chaos. It would shake Severn free from wherever he was hiding. It was time to face Konstantin.

He pulled his wings back, tipped his weight forward,

held his breath, and plunged silently toward the warehouses. Wind tore at his face, burning his skin. His wings ached at their awkward angle. The warehouses grew bigger and bigger, swelling to fill his vision.

A shadowy missile flew in fast from Mikhail's left. Mikhail tucked his wings in tighter—making them ache—and rolled. The missile sailed past. The demon banked for a second strike.

Mikhail caught the eye of a descending angel and nodded. The angel veered off to intercept, and Mikhail plunged ever downward, his rank tucked in close behind him.

More demons dotted the skies, like useless flies. His angels peeled off to attack.

The warehouses filled his vision.

Mikhail threw open his wings, banked hard, focusing on the dusty windows, and with his angels following his lead, he tucked his wings in and burst through the glass. Chaos erupted inside. He hovered, swirling up a storm of dust and debris, and saw them. Demons. Surprised. Unarmed. *Afraid*.

Angels poured in from all sides to the cacophony of raining glass and screams.

Wait.

The demons... they were laid up in cubicles.

They were... sick?

By Haven, this was a place of healing.

A demon in flight lunged at Mikhail. Their blades struck, but the demon was small—his horns barely even sprouted—and Mikhail's blow sent him reeling. Gallantly, or foolishly, perhaps, the pup rebounded off the wall and came at Mikhail a second time. Mikhail brought his blade down and kicked the pup in the back, sending him flapping and flailing through the air.

Mikhail's gaze fell to the unfolding scene below. Angels tore into the vulnerable demons, ripping them from their beds and slaughtering them in seconds. Acidic horror burned Mikhail's throat. This was a mistake.

A body slammed into Mikhail's side. Steel twanged against his armor, skipping off. Mikhail easily righted himself, grabbed the pup by the throat, and yanked him close. Brown eyes blazed with scorn. Two short horns declared him barely mature enough to hold that blade he wielded.

"Where's your honor?" the pup wheezed, leathery wings flapping uselessly.

A blade through the heart would end this one's young life. He wore only shabby clothing, no armor, and no training either, and yet, he'd attacked. No... not attacked. He was defending those below. Those Mikhail's forces had already slain.

"You think you're better than us," the pup growled. "Are you proud of what you've done?"

Mikhail flung him aside. "Go!"

The pup bared his teeth. "Never!" He drew his legs up, pulled his wings in, and charged. Mikhail backhanded him hard enough he felt the crack of it through his shoulder. The pup fell like a rock and slammed into a table, shattering it beneath him, then lay still.

"Withdraw!" Mikhail bellowed, and repeated it again when his angels barely responded. Finally, to the sound of beating wings, they took to the air and left the warehouse, retreating into the airborne fray. Demons filled the skies. Few wore any armor at all. Many weren't armed and fought with their bare hands and teeth. Mikhail dispatched those who dared tackle him, sickness swelling inside with every blow he landed.

This wasn't war.

It wasn't right.

What had he done?

"Withdraw!"

A demon horn sounded, and a fresh wave sailed in, this time led by a demon lord. His wings beat the air with a fierceness that reminded Mikhail of Konstantin, but Konstantin wasn't here. He wasn't in the streets below, and now the battle had turned sour. He climbed higher, rising out of the madness and into the sun. *"Withdraw!"*

The rank of angels receded, disengaging and flying higher, leaving the demons below. Those demons didn't pursue. They hovered as one blanket, protecting their home.

The demon lord fixed his glare on Mikhail, lifted his chin, and bared his teeth in warning.

Mikhail pulled back, drawing his force with him, until clouds swallowed them all.

Uncertainty, guilt, shame—these things wracked his body and soul. He hadn't known the warehouses were a healing center. But he should have. He should have checked. His angels had killed indiscriminately, like he had killed indiscriminately. It was wrong.

All of it.

Everything.

He no longer knew what was right.

The ranks of angels returned to the barracks in Aerie, but Mikhail descended to Whitechapel's wide main street. His armor faded and his wings sagged. He didn't care that he was seen. He wasn't even entirely sure where he was going, but the hospital was nearby, and Saphia would hear him. She'd listen. He needed someone to listen, to tell him he wasn't out of his mind.

A red-winged angel flapped to a hasty landing in front of Mikhail. "Your Grace..." Solo pulled his helmet off. "Remiel," he said breathlessly, face flushed. "He's here."

Mikhail pulled up short and instinctively retracted his wings. "What?"

"I've just received word. He's here. Arrived early. He's waiting for you at the church."

Remiel was here now? And Mikhail had failed to capture Konstantin. He'd just attacked a demon *hospital*, and *Remiel was here... now?!* He couldn't do this now. He wasn't ready. He didn't have control of anything, let alone himself.

"Shall I tell him you're waylaid?"

What good would that do? Nothing was going to change in a few hours. "No. It's fine. Is he alone, or did he bring forces?"

"He appears to be alone."

Perhaps that was a good sign. Remiel would have brought guards if he intended to detain Mikhail.

"Thank you. I'll see him now." He passed by Solo, aware of the male's steady, penetrating gaze and the weight of things unspoken between them. None of it would matter soon. Remiel was only here for one thing, to relieve Mikhail of his guardianship.

But he would not be surrendering London lightly.

He pushed open the door to the church and found the guardian standing beside the council table, arms crossed, face stern. Mikhail had only seen him from afar and thought him impressive then. He was no less formidable up close. Square jaw, hard eyes. In bone mass, they were similar, but Remiel carried a harsher presence that made lesser angels kneel without him speaking so much as a word. White-gold hair fell like silk to his shoulders. An angelblade hung at his waist, hitched to his belt.

Perhaps he didn't think he needed a force to bring Mikhail down? Perhaps he intended to take Mikhail alone?

Mikhail strained to keep his wings closed and not flare them wide in warning. He approached the guardian and offered his hand. "Welcome to Whitechapel."

Remiel peered down his nose at the hand as though considering not shaking. Was he so offended by Mikhail? But then the guardian gripped Mikhail's wrist in a familiar greeting between two warriors. Mikhail did the same, feeling a slight tingling in his fingers.

"I'm honored," the guardian said, wincing as he withdrew his hand. His voice was deep, the kind of voice most everyone would immediately obey.

"Are you wounded?"

Remiel cocked his head in question. "What?"

"You winced. We have excellent healers here. Saphia is especially attentive."

The guardian blinked. "I was recently wounded in battle. I'm somewhat sore, and between you and me, I'm grounded for a few days, but it's certainly nothing to be concerned over."

Grounded. That explained why he'd currently illusioned his wings out of sight. No angel liked to display bruised or battered wings.

"Do you have lodgings?" Mikhail asked stiffly. What he

really wanted to do was shove the guardian off his territory, but such things were not done.

"No, I've just arrived."

"You're early. And without your ranks?"

"Well, nothing says invading forces like a rank of angels landing on your doorstep." He smiled, and there was a softness in that smile that Mikhail hadn't expected. Remiel blinked, and the smile vanished like it had never been there.

"Indeed. I'll have Solo see to it your house is in suitable accommodation. Until then, I must debrief my ranks from battle." He turned away, keeping his wings clamped as tightly as his emotions.

"A battle?" Remiel asked, his tone oddly flat. "Who won?"

Mikhail answered before he could choke on the words. "They did."

evern

HIS ARM still tingled from where Mikhail had grabbed his wrist and threatened to unravel the illusion so soon after he'd built the damn thing. He slumped against the council table and sighed in relief.

The fresh illusion hadn't yet seated itself and felt like it wanted to peel off and turn to dust at Severn's feet. Had that happened, he was sure Mikhail would have taken up the blade he wore and plunged it through Severn's heart. Mikhail had certainly looked like he'd been looking for a fight. Clearly, there were no good feelings between him and Remiel.

Severn couldn't blame him. Every piece of human and demon intel on Remiel had revealed the angel was a dick, and not the good kind. He made Mikhail's leadership—before his meltdown—look tame. Ruthless, brutal, and as cold as ice. At least Severn only had to play him for a few days while he got his wings back.

"Your Grace." Solo entered the church, adorned in armor but missing his helmet.

Severn straightened. His demon heart skittered some to see an old friend, but he kept the urge to grin from his lips and nodded instead, like the cold slab of ice he was supposed to be. He'd screwed up earlier by smiling at Mikhail. But it could have been a whole lot worse. He'd wanted to do a lot more than smile when Mikhail had greeted him, looking rigid and ragged all at once. He'd aged in the weeks since Tower Bridge and wore the strain around his tired eyes and tight mouth. It had hurt deeply to see Mikhail hurting too.

"I'm to escort you to your lodgings," Solo said, professionally distant.

Severn followed the warrior from the church and kept his eyes forward, even as angels and nephilim—who had all thoroughly taken over this part of London it seemed— watched them pass by. Another guardian was sure to have the nephilim gossiping. Severn's skin itched. He'd forgotten how uncomfortable new illusions were, and crafting a guardian had been exhausting. He'd sacrificed a few memories, none of which he recalled—of course. But only small ones. The illusion this time was weak and would last mere days.

He still didn't know what had transpired on the day Samiel had left him on the battlefield. Lux had been intense, barely letting Severn out of his sights for three entire days and nights. There had been no time to see Samiel, which was probably for the best. They did not have the greatest history when it came to goodbyes.

At least Lux's unexpected attention had lavished Severn in ether. He was beginning to think angel ass really was addictive. Lux had certainly and thoroughly enjoyed his.

"Here you are." Solo opened the door of a handsome Georgian period, terraced house. Impressive railings framed the front steps, and large sash windows looked out over the street of similarly designed houses. Inside, the human who had decorated and furnished the dwelling had done a grand job of echoing the house's exterior with the use of period chandeliers, wooden floors, and fireplaces. He or she must have been pissed when the angels descended from Aerie and stole it.

After receiving a brief tour, which ended back in the hallway, Severn considered how Remiel would react and scowled at all the mundane humanity.

"Is it not to your liking?" Solo asked.

"It's adequate. I don't intend to stay long."

Solo grimaced and straightened, standing rigid, as though expecting to have to defend himself. "Sire... If I may be so bold?"

Severn regarded his old friend behind the calculating eyes of an asshole angel. "Yes?"

"Mikhail is... He's had his challenges of late. But..." Solo wet his lips. "He is the light who guides us. We'd be at a loss without him."

Severn's frown turned real. "Is he going somewhere?"

"Aren't you... I mean, your forces... We assumed you were going to..." Solo gulped, "replace him?"

"What?" Shit, the angels were ousting Mikhail? "No. I mean, yes. Right. Yes, well, his behavior is unacceptable." The real Remiel wasn't bringing reinforcements to help fight the demons, he was kicking Mikhail out of London. Angels were fucking epic bastards to themselves as well as demons.

The corners of Solo's mouth tipped downward. "He had his heart broken, Your Grace."

Severn swallowed, trying to clear the painful knot in his throat and failing. "As I said, unacceptable. Guardians do not possess hearts to break." That sounded suitably dickish.

"I can see that." Solo's green eyes darkened in a wholly disgusted way.

A guardian would not appreciate that look from a lowly angel such as Solo. "You seem very concerned for Mikhail's wellbeing. Almost like you care?"

"What?" Solo blinked quickly, regaining his lofty composure. "No." He laughed, but the sound pitched too high to be casual. "No. Nothing like that." Heat touched his cheeks, making his freckles glow. Oh, this was... interesting. Solo wet his lips, looking down, and Severn narrowed his eyes, picking up on the very real and potent scent of lust radiating off an angel who was not supposed to feel. What, by Haven, had happened in his absence? Were angels crushing on Mikhail now? Impossible. Solo had always been sensitive, but angels did not *feel*, at least not until Severn had become one. "Do you have something you want to confess?" he probed, adding a thin, authoritative note.

"What? No." Solo abruptly turned away, as though to leave, but hesitated. If he'd had his wings out, they'd have drooped like his shoulders. "We kissed."

It was a good thing Solo was turned away because there

wasn't a chance in Haven that Severn could have kept the shock from his face. *They fucking kissed?*

Solo turned back, and Severn froze his expression into cold detachment. "Well. That's..." he stammered, and Solo looked pained, like he needed someone to tell him he wasn't catching *emotions* from Mikhail. What the fuck was Severn supposed to say? Remiel would probably string Solo and Mikhail up by the wings and have them whipped. Severn cleared his throat. "Whiskey?"

Solo puffed out a sigh, having clearly expected the worst. "Whiskey?"

"Gin will do."

Fuck it. Severn needed a drink. He sauntered into the front room where humans sometimes kept their alcohol for entertaining and began to rummage through the cupboards either side of the fireplace. Mikhail and Solo had kissed. His Mikhail had kissed another angel. Who had instigated it, was it Solo? Did it matter? They'd fucking kissed, and shit, Severn knew jealousy. Hadn't felt it in a while, but it was sure burning him up now. Concubi didn't get jealous. But Mikhail wasn't concubi, and he was Severn's angel, despite their... disagreements. Major disagreements. Either-side-of-a-war disagreements. But Solo?

"Am I sick?" Solo asked behind him.

Severn snorted. Sick? Stupid angels. He found a bottle of Russian vodka and a few glasses, ripped off the top of the drink, and poured two drinks. One, he handed to Solo. Solo considered not taking it for a few seconds, and then snatched it from Severn's fingers and gulped it down, then spluttered and coughed in a way that had Severn smiling into his own glass.

"I think I might need to go to Haven," he wheezed.

Fuck Haven. The more he heard of it, the more he was sure it was a prison. "Who kissed whom?" Severn leaned back against the sideboard.

"What?"

"It's an important distinction. If Mikhail kissed you, well, then, it's nothing more than his continued madness. If you kissed him, then..." You're normal, and life goes on. "Maybe Haven would be for the best." Severn's heart thudded.

Solo swallowed and looked into his drink for the answer. "I don't think it matters."

"Then, you liked it?"

Solo sent his gaze out the window and stayed silent. His cheek flickering answered for him. He was hot for Mikhail.

"Was it just a kiss?" A part of Severn wanted them to have fucked because it would mean the allyanse was complete bullshit, as he'd suspected, and angels were a bunch of hypocrites who could do with some reality checks, but it also meant Mikhail had replaced Severn with Solo, and that thought made Severn want to drink the bottle of vodka dry.

"Just a kiss," he said softly. "I, er... I left him on the roof, afterward..." He winced. "He said it was wrong. He was sorry. I don't want to get him in trouble. This is as much my fault as his."

Severn rubbed at the bridge of his nose. Fucking angels. If he were Severn, he'd tell Solo to rub one off, or go get laid. Solo could visit what was left of the cauldron and find the more than eager nephilim who'd be very happy to suck angel cock. But he wasn't Severn. He was Remiel. And Remiel was a bastard.

"Finish your drink," he said. "And then don't speak of this again. To anyone."

Solo breathed a little too hard, no doubt worried he'd just gotten himself and Mikhail in more trouble than they already were. He nodded and downed the remaining vodka, grimacing afterward. "Will you tell him I told you?"

"I'll do what's necessary," Severn said, hating the fraught look on Solo's face. Someone needed to save these angels from themselves, and Severn wasn't sure that someone was him, given how he was lying to Solo with every breath. Maybe Mikhail would one day save them all, if he pulled his head out of his own ass in time.

Solo silently left after that, and Severn finished off the bottle, sinking into one of the chairs. He'd believed Mikhail had been so enraged on Tower Bridge because he loved Severn. Severn was counting on that love to save them both. But one question plagued him as he watched daylight wane: what if their love had died on that bridge?

evern

MIKHAIL HAD BEEN AVOIDING him all day, and with every hour that passed, the illusion tightened, becoming brittle, more liable to fail. He was running out of time.

He asked around and discovered Mikhail was in Aerie, so Severn rode the foundation-pillar elevator back up to the once-grand city above the clouds. The doors whispered open to reveal a hive of activity, most of it construction work. Aerie had lost its luster, but it was beginning to rise from its ashes. If angels knew anything, it was how to *heal*. It wouldn't be long before Aerie was once again the bustling city presiding over a cowering London. Severn hoped to be alive to see it. The chances of that largely depended on if he retrieved his wings.

He drifted through Aerie's vast glass hallways, seeking

Mikhail, and eventually found someone who pointed him in the direction of the training area.

High-level clouds seeped around Aerie, making the training disks appear to float inside the clouds. The half-obscured disks and shifting mist made training dangerous, hence why Mikhail was alone.

Severn approached the edge of the observation platform—not too close, London was a long way down—and watched the black-winged angel dance in the mist. The sweeping movements Mikhail performed were both striking and lethal. He spun and swept his blade down, wings spread or tucked or flared at an angle to balance himself. He hovered and dove and banked. He was a glorious vision of angel, the likes of which just didn't exist. Severn had never seen another like him.

His heart quickened. He stepped closer to the edge, aching to spread missing wings and fly with him. A foolish thought. Demons did not fly with angels. But he dreamed it all the same, like he'd dreamed of those soft feathers once again wrapped around him and the kiss they'd shared on a rooftop in the rain.

Mikhail suddenly stopped, wings holding him aloft, and looked over.

Severn swallowed his heart, which had somehow found its way into his throat, and stepped back from the edge. Mikhail couldn't see his rapt expression at that distance, could he? He took another step back as Mikhail flew in and fluttered to a landing on the platform. His damp hair —wet from the clouds—splayed about his shoulders, sticking to his glistening skin. His wings arched behind him, ragged and ruffled, like he'd ridden them to their last trembling muscle. He looked *wild*.

Shit, he was so fucking hot. Every nerve in Severn's body burned with savage desire.

Mikhail stared hard, expecting him to speak, to say something, anything. "A wonderful display," Severn finally growled out, butchering Remiel's voice while desperately trying to temper his rising cock. Thankfully, Mikhail appeared to be too caught up in his own head to notice.

Mikhail strode away, back into Aerie's hallways filled with the noise of construction. Severn cursed under his breath and shook out his hands, trying to wrestle his body back under control. It seemed like Mikhail's silent dismissal of Remiel was an affront to another guardian, but Severn had never seen two guardians in the same place to know how they should react around each other.

It had taken him ten years to perfect being an angel. He'd only been a guardian for three days. And one of those days he'd spent walking from demon territory to Whitechapel. Gods, this was a fucking disaster waiting to happen.

Body behaving, he strode after Mikhail, aware he drew many curious glances. On approaching Mikhail's chambers, he didn't slow, just pushed through the door inside. He was pretty sure guardians went where they pleased, considering all the times Mikhail had barged into his room without knocking.

His gaze slid to the wall, where he knew there to be a crack, hinting at another room. Were his wings behind there?

"What do you want from me, Remiel?" Mikhail demanded, throwing his sword down onto a dresser. Either he'd forgotten to hide the fact he was a beautiful disaster or he no longer cared. Severn wanted to throw his arms around him, pull him close, and whisper how everything was going to be all right, that together they'd make it so.

Instead, he clenched his hands into fists at his sides. Mikhail turned, immediately saw the gesture, and instantly misread it.

"Are you going to fight me, guardian?" he asked, voice flattening. "I'd advise against it. My emotions aren't the only things to have changed."

"I have no wish to fight you," Severn rumbled. "Tell me about Konstantin."

Mikhail's eyes widened, briefly revealing a chink in his armor before the barely restrained rage returned. "What is there to tell that you haven't already heard? He illusioned himself into the form of an angel and played the role to perfection for ten years. I believed every word of it. I..." he trailed off and raised his gaze to Severn again, softer this time. "I loved him. Even before the allyanse. I loved a liar with all my heart. That is the true horror of all this."

Severn's wretched heart thumped so loudly he was sure Mikhail could hear. He had to reply, and fast, but his racing thoughts had screeched to a halt. He'd known, or suspected, but to hear Mikhail say the words ripped his heart out anew. "Do you love him still?" he asked softly.

Mikhail growled and dragged a hand across his eyes. "What does it matter? Severn does not exist."

Oh, but he does, and I'm standing right in front of you, desperate to fix this, to fix us.

Mikhail plucked a feather from his own wing before illusioning them away and heading for the blank wall. "I have the truth of him right here." The wall cracked apart and rumbled open, and Mikhail strode right on through, into the long, narrow room. Exactly as the madam had said, his feathers were the key.

Severn stumbled forward a few steps and froze.

His wings.

They were right there.

Big and black and hung on the far wall like two grotesque trophies.

So big. He'd forgotten how big they were, forgotten they were even his. But there they were, as real as Mikhail now standing before them.

Gods, he couldn't breathe. His chest ached, right around his heart; it ached so much he wanted to drop to his knees and surrender. His heart pounded inside his ears. He tried to focus, to tell his body to calm, to breathe, to hold itself together, but his thoughts were in freefall, spiraling around and around. His enemy. His lover. His wings.

"I should burn them," Mikhail said, still facing the wings.

Severn reached for the dresser, missed, and stumbled against it. The illusion... he had to focus, to hold on to it. He looked up and caught sight of his reflection in the mirror. The face looking back at him was a stranger's. An angel he didn't know. Who was he now? Lies. More lies. What if he just let it all go, and when Mikhail turned around, he saw Severn again? Would that be so terrible a thing?

Mikhail, in his current state of mind, would kill him, and probably go on to kill every last demon in London.

He had to do this, for his kin, for Mikhail. Because there was a way out. But it was a carefully balanced one, and Mikhail wasn't ready. Nobody was ready.

Mikhail began to turn.

Severn whirled, quickly folded his arms, and plastered a bored expression on his face even as his heart continued to thump and ache and try to choke him.

"I intended to capture him for your arrival, but I failed in that too," Mikhail said. He returned to his chamber, and the gallery doors whispered closed, cutting Severn off from his wings once more.

Not seeing them was better. He could breathe again. He could pretend all of this was normal and his body wasn't warring with itself for things it couldn't have.

"I had my forces attack a healing center."

Severn's thoughts tripped again. "You *what*?"

"A hospital of sorts." Mikhail wasn't slowing. He strode right up to Severn. Severn rose from his slouched position to meet him eye-to-eye. "I killed them all."

Ice water spilled through Severn's veins. He'd killed wounded demons in their beds? "Mikhail, this has to stop." He wanted to touch his face, even as fury burned inside him. Maybe the heat of Mikhail's rage would consume them both.

"You're here to force me to retire to Haven." Black wings unfurled, filling the room with darkness.

This close, Severn tasted angel on his lips and tasted the bitterness of rage, too, so potent it roused a whisper of ether from Mikhail's skin, ether Severn missed with all his incubus heart. He needed this angel, needed to be close to him, to fix him, needed to love him. He was half himself without him.

But most of all, he needed to stop him.

Severn had half a mind to kiss him. He'd get himself killed for it, but it'd be worth it.

"I'll kill us both before leaving Aerie and London," Mikhail vowed. The passion in those words was undeniable.

Severn swallowed hard, with a click. Gods, this angel was everything. So fierce, so passionate, so thoroughly fucked up, and if Severn had any doubts about his own love, those were dashed now. He wanted to sweep him into his arms, wanted to kiss his breath away, make him moan and beg and turn that fury into wild, devastating lust. But when it happened, it had to be real. No more lies.

He blinked away. "Let's hope it doesn't come to that." And stepped from his trapped position between Mikhail and the dresser.

He walked away, wondering if these steps were the hardest he'd ever had to take.

CHAPTER 13

*M*ikhail

REMIEL WAS NOT the kind of guardian he'd expected.

Mikhail stared at the empty seats around the council table. The church was silent. Peaceful. Even though the demons depicted in the stained glass windows leered at him.

The guardian angel was more calculating than reports had made him out to be, more careful. Mikhail was well aware he was being watched, studied. Probably for his final judgment. And perhaps he should have bent the truth some, but it was not in his nature to lie. He could not change the things that had happened. But he would master his own fate and not have another guardian deliver it for him. Of course, he could not fight all the angels, but he would fight until his last breath to hold on to everything he loved.

He loved Aerie. He loved London too. And his angels. He'd been so afraid to love, like it was some mystical force he could not control, but love didn't ask to be controlled. It just was. And love was powerful. He was learning that now, albeit too late.

He wondered if perhaps love had given him six wings. Or at least, the loss of love.

Remiel had asked if he still loved Severn. It seemed like a simple question, but the guardian wouldn't have understood any answer. Remiel did not know love, so how could he be the judge of it?

"Your Grace."

Mikhail looked up from his musings and saw Solo standing in the church doorway, reluctant to enter. His wings were tucked away beneath illusion, and his face was set, chest gently rising and falling, as though he was making an effort to calm his breathing. Darkness had fallen on the street behind him. Mikhail must have been lost to his thoughts for hours.

"Yes?"

"The correctioners you asked me to report on..."

Ah, the tension stemmed from that order to visit the correctional facilities, not from the... other thing they weren't discussing. "What did you discover?"

Solo finally approached the table. "I visited the one near Harrow unannounced, as you suggested. What I found was disturbing."

"Go on."

Severn's words about how Mikhail truly thought the human correctioners did rehabilitate wayward cambion and nephilim came back to him now. Severn had implied more went on than Mikhail was aware of. It appeared as though Severn had been correct.

Solo's face was more than grim, it was as pale as milk in the church's flickering lights. His silence spoke for him. Whatever he'd seen, it had shaken him.

Mikhail rose to his feet. "Tell me."

"The captured cambion are killed with no efforts made to correct them, Your Grace."

Perhaps he should have been surprised, but a numbness was spreading through him. Because Severn had been right. Again. "And the nephilim?"

"I... I fear they are being exploited, put to work in ways that are degrading. Their trusting nature has left them vulnerable."

"You're sure of this?"

"I visited another facility and caught them in the midst of trying to conceal the evidence of their wrongdoing. I fear it is rife."

And Severn had known? Or suspected? "Take a rank of angels to each facility within a few hours flight of here and shut them all down. Bring the nephilim here, to our hospital, and see to it they are cared for. Report to me at dawn."

Solo nodded. "And any cambion we find?"

"Release them."

"Release them?"

"They do not control their heritage. Demons will take them in."

"Er... yes. And the human correctioners?"

"Relieve them of their duties—firmly. I will have the human ambassador brought to me to explain how this atrocity has come about."

"Of course." Solo thumped a fist to his chest, dismissing himself, but hesitated on the spot, a thought holding him back. The same thought that kept his head slightly turned away, his gaze shy of Mikhail's.

"Was there something else?" Mikhail studied the angel in profile. The soft light here softened him, too, like it had on the rooftop. Did he have someone, anyone in his life he could confide in? Anything outside of his duty? Mikhail knew so little about him. For as long as he could remember, the only thing that mattered had been war. Every day and night, he'd been consumed by his dedication as a guardian. So consumed, he'd forgotten to see those around him.

"I'm not sure, Your Grace. Perhaps now is not the time..." He turned to leave.

"Speak whatever is on your mind." Mikhail's pulse quickened as Solo faced him. This time his green eyes did not flinch away. "If it's about what happened, you have my sincerest apologies. Please, forget it."

"Yes, I would, but... I told Remiel."

Oh, by Haven, all Remiel needed was more evidence of Mikhail's insanity, and now his foolish actions had dragged Solo into this too. Remiel would absolutely consider Solo tainted. "I hope you told him it was all my doing."

"Well, no... not exactly."

"Solomon, you do not need to protect me." The way he frowned made it clear he had tried. "What did Remiel say?"

Solo tilted his head. "He offered me vodka."

"He did?" Drinking alcohol wasn't unheard of among angels, but it was unlikely. They didn't need the high or low from intoxication, and it took a great deal of alcohol to have any effect. For a guardian to drink vodka? Mikhail had never heard of such a thing.

"He told me not to tell anyone about the," Solo waved a hand, "kiss." Heat flushed his cheeks.

That didn't seem at all like Remiel. It was a wonder they both weren't already locked in a carriage on their way to Haven. "Well, thank you for telling me."

"He's not what I expected." Solo frowned. "His behavior is strange, don't you think?"

"Yes." Mikhail's brow pinched. "It is strange."

CHAPTER 14

S evern

THE ILLUSION HAD BEGUN to take its toll. He either needed to leave, before his grasp on it fell, or he needed a substantial kick of ether. Unfortunately, the madam wasn't on hand to offer her services, and as a guardian, he couldn't exactly invite an angel over for an evening of unbridled lust. Maybe he could find some besotted nephilim to feed from. But he disliked the idea of manipulating anyone unless they knew what they were signing up for, like Red— one of the madam's two pet nephilim Severn had routinely eye-fucked to get his hit.

He poured himself another top up of vodka and drank hard, barely tasting it. The alcohol wasn't having much impact and was probably the last thing he needed, but after seeing his wings, vodka seemed better than screaming at the night sky.

He was well on his way to finishing off a second bottle when something toppled to the floor in the house, a level above him. Grabbing his blade, he stumbled up the stairs and fell into the front bedroom.

"Caw!" A damned rayvern hopped about a dresser, pecking at the human homeowner's shiny shit. *"Caw-caw."* It accused Severn, but of what, he had no idea.

The window behind the dresser was slightly open, it must have flown in through there. "Get out of here." He opened the window some more. "Go."

The rayvern cocked its head, its beady black eye staring.

"Bird, get out of this room, or we're going to have a disagreement."

"Don' mind Jasper—"

Severn jumped and fell against the wall. "Fuck!" The rayvern cawed, echoing his curse in its own tongue. Amii sat on the side of the bed, their gray hair sticking out at all angles and their grin revealing gaps in their teeth.

He'd walked right by them.

"What..." Wait. "You." Why was Amii here? "You need to leave." The last time he'd seen them, they'd been wearing a Konstantin illusion at Tower Bridge. Severn had assumed they'd died there.

And now Amii was here? In *this* house?

He had to remember he wasn't Severn. He was a guardian, a partially drunk one, but still a guardian, and a concubi cambion in his house was absolutely unacceptable. Even if they were only half demon, if he believed them—which he was beginning to doubt—they couldn't be here. "Take your scrawny ass and your bird out of this house, demon." He added some guardian's loftiness to his voice.

They tutted, pushed to their feet, and stretched, like they were so terribly old and frail.

"Save the bullshit," Severn snapped. "I've seen it all before."

Their dark eyes sparkled. "I'm sure you 'ave, eh? But see, I was passing, an' I thought I'd drop by and see how my second favorite angel is doing."

Wait. Did Amii know Remiel? No, that was absurd. Then Amii had to be referring to Severn. Fuck. How did they know? "I don't know you." He gestured wildly between them. "We don't know each other. You've got the wrong house."

"Nah, I don't reckon I has." Amii straightened, their backache miraculously vanishing, and with a familiar shiver of concubi power, they shook themselves, spilling red hair around a familiar male face and stripping back the old woman act into a nephilim far more appetizing. "There we go. How's that? I remember yous like a bit of nephilim cock. Maybe more than a bit, eh?"

They sashayed closer. Severn pressed himself into the wall. "I'll not tell you again. Leave." He had an angelblade, and he would use it, if necessary.

"Pah, don' worry yahself. I ain't gonna touch you. Look a' you. All ugly self-righteousness. I'd rather touch myself." Their hand dropped to the impressive cock tenting their loose pants.

"Don't. Just leave." He bared his teeth in a demon snarl, giving up on the ruse. "If he fucking finds you here, it's over."

They huffed, and their pink nephilim tongue darted out, suggestively stroking their bottom lip as their hand stroked their own cock.

Red had been a delight. It was a fucking shame he'd died when half of Aerie fell, but now he was back, and this wretched demon—not a cambion, they were too powerful—was fucking with Severn's head. "What do you want?"

"Stop talking, angel. Yap, yap, yap—"

"Caw!"

"And feed," Amii-as-Red purred.

Ether rose off them, swirling about like an aura of sweetness Severn could tap into, and gods, he needed it. Whoever this demon really was, whatever their purpose, he was too drunk and too exhausted to fight them, not when they were willing to give him exactly what he craved.

They dropped their loose trousers and undergarments, taking themselves in hand, and Severn's mouth watered, his own cock hardening in earnest. He wouldn't need it. He couldn't touch Amii anyway. He just needed the ether hit.

Power poured over him, into his mouth, down his throat, heating and filling and fixing all the pain and hurt he'd been drowning in since returning to Mikhail. Gods, it was almost too much—and certainly too much coming from one demon. But he was too lost to its thrall to question it.

He fell to his numb knees. The ether high rode him hard, and when the demon came with a cry, the ether slammed into him so fast and hard that he barely clung to his consciousness. He gripped the dresser, desperately keeping himself afloat as his body burned under wave after wave of power. The rayvern cawed somewhere distantly, and Red grinned into Severn's face. "There you go. That'll do you. Get it done, eh? Your new face upsets my Jasper, don't it, Jasper... Yes, it does, that's right..."

His eyes fluttered closed, and the overload of ether dragged him down to the sounds of rayverns cawing.

HE WOKE stiff and aching in the exact same place he'd succumbed to the high. The only indication that he hadn't been alone was the open window, letting in wintery air. He slammed it shut and plodded to the shower, stripping off yesterday's clothes before standing under the pummeling jets.

Who in the ever-loving fuck was Amii, really? They just show up, jerk off like they somehow knew Severn was running on empty, and leave? Full demon. Definitely. The ether kick had been proof of that. Shit, not even Lux had drowned him in so much power, and the High Lord had unwittingly tried.

He toweled off, troubled by the encounter, and was about to brew some coffee when a knock at the door interrupted his wandering thoughts.

Solo stood on the step. Damp mist clung to his red hair. "Morning," he smiled.

Severn ran his fingers through his wet hair while trying to recall the exact pitch and tone of his new guardian angel voice. "Good morning, Solomon."

"I, er... can I come in?"

"If you don't mind that I'm wearing only a towel."

Predictably, the angel took in an eyeful of Severn-slash-Remiel's chest and the towel tucked around Severn's waist and blushed. Gods, he was adorable. He'd make someone a delightful lover someday. Or not, because angels were all in denial that their cocks were used for more than swinging in the wind.

Severn stepped aside, and Solo ventured into the front room.

Severn followed and winced at the sight of the empty vodka bottles. Apparently, Remiel had a drinking problem. Oh well, it wasn't like he was sticking around to deal with that fallout. With the amount of power running through him, he'd be fully charged all day and just needed to get into Mikhail's gallery. Today would be his last day in Aerie and this horribly uncomfortable illusion.

"About what I said," Solo blurted, turning suddenly on his heel.

"The kiss?"

"Yes. That. It was an experiment, for both of us—because of what Severn did—and it didn't mean anything."

"Wait," Severn laughed incredulously, "you're blaming Severn for you kissing Mikhail?" Severn folded his arms and adopted a stern expression, if only to mask how he wanted to grin and slap the fool on the shoulder. "How do you figure that when he's miles away and you had *your* hands down Mikhail's pants?"

"I didn't! That wasn't—"

Severn waved him off before he hurt himself. "It's fine. Really. You don't need to torture yourself. Look, between you and me, angels don't all abstain from sexual acts. I have it on good authority that some angels visited the cauldron here in London. I mean, clearly angels fucked humans in the past, hence the nephilim, so what's a kiss between friends?"

"They did?"

He nodded. "I mean, c'mon..." He half smiled. "You've never gotten hard thinking about touching another angel?"

"No." A flush crawled up his neck. "I have not done that." His pretty green eyes flicked down, roaming Remiel's sculpted chest again.

He had most definitely done that, and he might even be doing that right now too. And if Solo had desires, and others clearly had, too, then maybe angels weren't strangers to passion after all. Someone, somewhere, was lying to them all, but that was a problem for another day.

Solo pulled his collar away from his neck, and as he did, a soft black feather fluttered from inside his coat and settled gently on the carpet behind him. Severn tore his eyes from it. Had destiny delivered him the exact thing he needed to get into Mikhail's gallery? "Anyway, as I said. You're fine," he rushed. "We don't need to rehash it all." He headed back into the hallway, checking over his shoulder to see Solo following. "So, if that was all, I have important guardian duties to attend to." He opened the front door, and Solo jogged down the steps.

"Do you think Mikhail will be staying?" Solo asked, looking back, desperately not looking up Severn's towel.

"I think Mikhail will soon have a decision to make, and we'd all better hope he makes the right one." He closed the door on Solo and hurried back into the front room. Kneeling, he picked up the feather and cradled it in his palm. Solo spent time with Mikhail, like Severn had. He'd filled the void Severn had left behind, perhaps in more ways than one. Mikhail's stray feather had likely caught on his coat, and now it was here, in Severn's palm. The key to getting his wings back.

Now all he had to do was get back inside Mikhail's chambers without anyone stopping him.

His wings were close.

His back itched, their ghost haunting him.

Soon he'd be Konstantin again.

Soon it would all be over, one way or another.

CHAPTER 15

Severn

AERIE BUSTLED like it had before. Angels noted his passing, but none challenged him, and none would. He was the guardian angel Remiel; he went where he pleased, including Mikhail's chambers. Severn readied an excuse for why he was about to barge into Mikhail's room just in case Mikhail was inside, but he needn't have. The chamber was empty. The room smelled like sunshine, like Mikhail, and a stab of guilt tried to slow his stride. Yes, this was wrong, but it was also the only way. Mikhail would never return his wings, and thus, Severn would be stuck as an angel forever, stuck between two sides. He had to be Konstantin again to affect change. The truth had to be known.

He pulled a flare from a pocket, struck it, making it glow and hiss, and quickly tossed it from the balcony. There was no going back now. He just hoped Samiel saw the signal and caught his wings when Severn tossed them over the edge. If not, they'd likely shatter on a London street.

He pulled the feather from inside his trouser pocket and presented it to the bare wall. The hidden doors clunked and smoothly rolled open, revealing his wings. His breath caught. He hesitated. Long ago, his enemy had carved those wings from his back. What if he couldn't bear their weight again? What if he'd changed too much?

Didn't matter.

He was here. This had to be done.

He stopped beneath their great expanse. The right wing bore a vicious tear. Blood had dried on the wall and floor, left there like a scab. Only Mikhail could have mutilated them so. A sob tried to crawl up his throat. It had been war. Mikhail had taken the trophies ten years ago as a message, but to cut them now? Mikhail was so full of hate. It seemed impossible that love could exist surrounded by it. And Severn was not entirely blameless. He had betrayed Mikhail in the worst way.

He reached a hand up, hovering it away from the wing membrane. Gods, they were alive, warm and still, as though they'd been waiting all this time. He could feel their heat, *his* heat.

His fingertips brushed their leathery surface. Tiny veins flared, sparking outward, and a jolt of pain snapped up Severn's arm. He gasped, yanking his hand back, but it was too late. An unraveling power crackled up his arm, through his shoulder, into his chest—waves of lightning-like fractures—and to his horror, the Remiel illusion disintegrated piece by piece, turning to dust.

No, no, no... he wasn't ready. He wasn't done!

He clutched his arm and staggered backward, his whole body reverting—not to Konstantin's beautifully black skin—but to Severn's. "Dammit... no!"

This shouldn't be happening. He was brimming with power. The illusion had been solid enough to last for days. But it fell apart now, peeling off his torso, his thighs, *everywhere*.

Remiel lay in dust at his feet.

Gods, he was Severn again.

Severn, standing in Mikhail's gallery, staring at his fucking wings.

He had to get them down—now!

He reached for the wings.

"Stop!" Solo boomed.

Severn froze, a thousand scenarios running through his mind, and all of them ending in Solo dying. Why?! Why him, why here and now? Why was destiny so fucking intent on screwing with him? He lowered his hand and slowly turned. Solo approached, angelblade in his right hand. He had his wings hidden, but they'd be spread soon enough because the snarl on his lips was far from friendly.

Severn had his own blade hitched to his side. The illusion left him with his accessories, including clothing, but could he use the blade against Solo? He reached for the handle.

"Draw that blade and it ends with your death, *Severn*."

Dread sat cold and heavy in his gut. "Solo... wait."

Solo continued to approach. "I didn't think you'd be foolish enough to make the same mistake twice."

Severn held out his hands as though to slow him. "Solo... just listen. These wings... they belong to me. I have to have them back."

"You lied to us *again*!"

Severn winced. "Yes, and it's a fucking shitty thing to do, but I had no choice. Will you just listen before trying to kill me?"

"I listened to your lies for ten years. You're a *demon*." His mouth twisted in disgust. "You're the leech Konstantin!"

"Leech is harsh, but—"

Solo pressed the blade's tip to Severn's chest, his arm locked, face severe. Severn still held his hands aloft, but if Solo tensed to thrust the blade home, Severn had already mapped exactly how he'd knock the blade aside, grab the angel by the throat, and see to it only one of them walked out of the gallery alive. But it wouldn't come to that. He had to believe it.

"It began as lies," Severn said. "But it ended in love."

Solo slowly shook his head. "How could you, Severn? How could you do this to us? You were my friend. You were Mikhail's friend."

"I still am—" Solo pushed against the tip, and the blade dug in a notch, stealing his breath. Solo would kill him, if he didn't talk him down, but it couldn't get that far. "There is more at stake here than my betrayal. Mikhail must be stopped, for everyone's sake, not just the demons'. You see it, don't you? He's powerful and out of control. I want to help him."

"Help him?" A silvery tear wet Solo's cheek. "You broke his heart!"

Angels did not *cry*. But the rules had been rewritten. Change was happening. "Solo, please. I love him."

"Lies!"

"I lied, yes, in everything, but not in that. I am

Konstantin, Lost Lord of the Red Manor, and those wings behind me are mine. That's the truth, and so is my love. I didn't see it at first. I couldn't. But in all those years, I changed. We've all changed. You've changed... can't you feel it?" Severn reached down and touched his own chest, over his heart, next to where Solo's blade pushed in. "In here?"

Solo's face fell. He exhaled hard, spluttering out his pain. "Angels don't feel." But he lowered his blade.

"Of course they do. You've just been conditioned to ignore it. You love him, don't you? You all love him? Well, so do I, and I'm not here to hurt him, I'm here to save him."

"Save me?"

Severn jerked his head up. Mikhail entered the gallery, his wings revealed behind him and his face full of fury. Severn's heart sank. It was over. He saw the end on Mikhail's face too. He'd never let Severn leave alive.

The demons were right, he really had failed.

CHAPTER 16

M ikhail

SEVERN STOOD at the end of the gallery, his demon wings framed behind his angel form, creating a portrait of lies. Fury blurred Mikhail's vision.

Konstantin was here. He'd slithered his way inside his chambers, inside his gallery. And he'd worn the illusion of a guardian angel to do it.

It hadn't seemed likely that Severn would return. Not after the cataclysm at Tower Bridge, but with Solo's suspicions about Remiel's odd behavior, coupled with his own observations, he'd ordered Solo to discreetly leave a feather at Remiel's feet and to follow him.

Mikhail hadn't truly believed Remiel was a lie, or that Severn had dared trick him twice.

And here they were, the terrible truth revealed. For a second time.

"Konstantin," Mikhail growled, approaching slowly.

The enemy looked up. "Mikhail..." Severn's voice cracked, like he suffered, and so he should. He'd suffer a great deal more before this was over.

"You came for your wings." Not a question.

Severn's eyes widened. "Mikhail... wait."

Mikhail nodded, signaling to Solo. Solo lunged. His blade struck Severn's. Severn parried and shoved Solo back, the pair evenly matched. But as Mikhail reached up and grabbed the demon wings from the wall, tearing them down, Severn stumbled to watch, and Solo struck out, kicking the blade from Severn's hand. Even Mikhail could see Severn's heart wasn't in the fight.

Solo clutched Severn to his chest, blade pressed to his throat, and held him rigid, forcing him to watch Mikhail.

The demon wings lay crumpled on the floor at Mikhail's feet. He hated them more for his own mistake in keeping them. He should not have cut them from Konstantin. This horror had all begun with that terrible moment.

Mikhail knelt and pressed his hand to the arch of the right wing, the wing he'd recently sliced open.

This ended now.

"What are you doing?" Severn demanded. "Mikhail... Listen. I could have hurt you a thousand times. I chose not to."

Did he think having his heart ripped out hadn't hurt? Weren't demons supposed to know emotion?

Power thrummed through Mikhail's chest, down his arm, into his hand, his fingers.

Severn bucked against Solo's hold. "Mikhail, I love you. Don't do this."

Rage scorched his palm.

"I need them back. I want to show you the truth!"

Smoke rose from between his fingers, bringing with it the smell of burning flesh.

"Gods, Mikhail... Don't, please!" Severn slumped, Solo holding him up. *"I just wanted to show you who I really am!"*

"I know exactly who you are!" Blue flame burst from Mikhail's touch and roared across the wing.

"No!"

Blue flame leaped to the left wing, skipping across skin and bone, devouring flesh and blood and the mistake Mikhail had made all those years ago. The wings crumbled to ash, and the flame spluttered out, leaving only a shadowy imprint of wings on the floor.

Mikhail straightened. The breeze from his feathers stirred the ash, blurring the remains.

Severn stared at the remains. He didn't look up, didn't beg for forgiveness, just stared.

Now, perhaps, Severn understood exactly how Mikhail had felt on that damned bridge when his own angels had told him his first and only love was a lie.

"Lock him up." Mikhail turned away, hearing Severn's sob when his wings swept the ash away, destroying Konstantin's wings forever.

CHAPTER 17

evern

His wings were gone.

Solo had thrown him in a holding cell deep inside Aerie and left him there, in the dark and the cold and the silence.

He shivered on a wooden bench, hugging himself.

He'd believed Mikhail would see sense, that he'd listen. Severn had hoped, even as his wings burned, that Mikhail would stop the flame. But he'd been wrong. There was no love left in the angel, just hate. But even now, after witnessing Mikhail destroy all that was left of Konstantin, Severn couldn't return that hate. He wanted to. He wanted to rage and scream at the bars fencing him in, to damn all the angels, but where there should be rage, there was nothing.

He'd let everyone down.
Demons were going to die.
Angels would reign supreme.
And there was nothing Severn could do to stop it.

CHAPTER 18

*M*ikhail

FANFARE AND CHEERS from the London crowds met the real Remiel's grand arrival, as was befitting a guardian. He shone at the head of a formation hundreds of angels strong.

Mikhail could only watch from Whitechapel's main street, flanked by his own sizable force. Enough to warn Remiel that he wasn't about to roll over and let the guardian take his home.

Remiel descended, white wings tipped with gold. He looked just as Severn had made him out to look, although Severn hadn't crafted wings. It all seemed so obvious now.

Severn was nothing if not a master of lies.

Remiel landed in a walk and tucked his wings in, making that simple gesture so lethally graceful it made

Mikhail want to brandish his blade and toss the guardian out of Whitechapel.

"Mikhail," Remiel said. His voice was deeper than Severn's had made it out to be and carried a foreign accent. The guardian stopped before Mikhail and bowed his head. "It is an honor."

"Likewise."

They shook, just as Severn had, but this guardian did not wince, likely because he wasn't wearing a wretched illusion that could have been shattered by touch.

The guardian's rank of angels flew over Whitechapel. Some alighted on the surrounding rooftops like a large flock of doves coming home to roost. Severn's words about an invading force haunted Mikhail. For all his lies, Severn had always seen the things Mikhail missed.

Remiel's hand fell, and the angel lifted his chin. "You know why I'm here?"

"To relieve me of my duties as Aerie's guardian."

Remiel's gaze remained, unblinking. "If only it were that simple." Before Mikhail could ask him to elaborate, he added, "At least you captured the demon responsible for your downfall. Take me to him."

Mikhail's wings bristled at the scolding tone. He didn't appreciate being spoken to like a fledgling, but there were bigger battles to win against Remiel. He took to the skies, and the guardian followed close behind. Mikhail fought not to glance back. Remiel hadn't come to kill him, had he? If he had, it wouldn't be with a blade in the back. Subterfuge was not the angel way.

He'd ordered a pause on Aerie's reconstruction so Remiel's visit wasn't met with the sounds of chaos. A few angels and nephilim bustled about, but the towering spaces were quiet, getting darker and quieter as Mikhail led Remiel down into the hidden heart of the city.

He hadn't seen Severn since burning his wings two weeks ago. Solo checked in on him on a daily basis but only reported that he was still alive. Mikhail hadn't cared to ask any more.

The angel charged with the unfortunate task of guarding the way into the cells nodded at their approach and unlocked the door.

All the other cells were empty. They'd been built to hold demons but were rarely used as demons preferred to end their own lives than be captured. Severn occupied the cell at the end, in the darkest, coldest depths, with just a single, flickering torch chasing off the gloom.

Mikhail instinctively hid his wings to keep them from touching the chilling walls, and Remiel did the same.

Severn was seated on a bench, leaning forward, with his arms resting on his thighs. With his head down, his long, tangled hair screened his face.

A sharp, stabbing jolt of guilt struck at Mikhail's chest. He rubbed over his heart and cleared his throat. "Konstantin, Lost Lord of the Red Manor."

"No longer lost," Remiel's voice rumbled with amusement.

Severn slowly lifted his head. Shadows made his eyes hollow. That damned stab of guilt twisted harder in Mikhail's chest, like a blade in a wound. He shouldn't feel guilt. Severn deserved this.

"He persists in wearing that illusion?" Remiel clasped his hands behind his back and appraised Severn.

Mikhail was considering all the replies when Severn shoved to his feet and approached the bars. He wrapped his fingers around them and eyed Remiel. "Your bone structure is so fucking pretty. All that beauty in a dickless, emotionless drone. Such a shame."

"Hm," Remiel mused, unfazed. "And he fooled you for a decade, Mikhail?"

He wanted to defend himself but had no defense that didn't sound trite. "He did."

"It's not a lie," Severn said. "I'm as much an angel as you are."

Remiel snorted. "Deluded, too, I see." He turned away. "See to it he's executed."

Mikhail hesitated, the order holding him rigid. What had he expected, leniency from a guardian? Of course Severn would be killed for his crimes.

"Mikhail," Severn whispered, his face pressed to the bars. "You have no reason to ever trust me again, I know that, but please, hear this, if nothing else: Remiel wants Aerie. He wants everything that's yours, and if you don't hand it over, he'll kill you."

Mikhail had always trusted Severn's judgment. He'd stood beside him for years, turned to him for advice in times like these, but how could he ever trust his words again? Besides, it wasn't anything Mikhail didn't already know. He turned away from Severn and left the cells.

CHAPTER 19

S
evern

SOLO DELIVERED the tray of food, sliding it under the bars. From the bench, Severn eyed it quietly. The sandwich had all the crusts cut off, and that seemed like such a Solo thing to do that Severn couldn't help his smile.

"You love Mikhail." Severn lifted his head. "We both know it."

Solo glared back. Every day over the past few weeks, Solo came with food, and every day, Severn spoke to him. He never replied, but Solo couldn't unhear the truth. "He's in danger."

Solo turned to leave.

Severn shot from the bench and grabbed the bars. "Remiel is reading the scene. He's calculating where Mikhail is weakest, so that when he strikes, it will be quick and devastating."

Solo turned back, his russet brows pinched. "Mikhail has it in hand."

He'd finally spoken, and now Severn had a chance to really be heard. "Mikhail is a fucking mess. Somewhere in all that neurosis, he probably thinks he deserves to be killed for loving me. You have to help him."

"Whatever happens is none of your concern."

"Solo." Saying his name pulled him back each time. Solo wanted to stay, he wanted to believe Severn. "Don't leave his side."

Solo marched back to stand in front of Severn. "Your words are worthless. I look at you, and all I see is lies. And to think I admired you. I'm disgusted in myself."

"I care—"

"You don't get to care for him!"

"And I don't get to choose who I love, else I wouldn't have fallen in love with a fucking angel!"

Solo lifted his chin. "You are to be executed tomorrow at dawn."

Severn let go of the bars and stepped back, rocking on his feet. "How?"

When Solo turned his face away, his cheek fluttered. "The edge."

The edge was a terrible punishment. Spoken of among angels like a fledgling's nursery rhythm. It hadn't been used in decades. An angel's wings were tied near the shoulders, so they had no chance to writhe free, and the angel pushed from Aerie.

Ice filled Severn's veins. "For what crime?"

"You seriously just asked me that?" Solo snapped, green eyes flashing with wrath.

"For loving Mikhail?" He stepped back some more and

threw his arms up. "Gods, you're all so fucking hypocritical. *'Angels don't feel. Angels don't love.'* It's bullshit and always has been. You think I lie? You lie to yourselves every day. I don't know what the fuck they do to you in Haven, but whatever it is, it screws you up for life." He paced and then abruptly stopped. "I'm going to be killed for loving Mikhail. What part of that is right?"

"No, you're going to be killed because you're the demon lord Konstantin."

Severn grabbed a fistful of his own golden hair. "What's this, then? Huh?" He pinched his arm, feeling the sting. "Or this? I don't know how it happened, but I'm an angel. This illusion hasn't been an illusion for months. It's who I am now. My wings are gone. You saw him burn them. If this were an illusion, it would have come off. I didn't want this. No demon in their right mind wants to be an angel, but here I am. Konstantin is dead. He's been dead for years. If you push me over the edge, Solo, you prove you're nothing but a bunch of savage, self-righteous, hypocritical bastards."

"It doesn't matter," he said sadly. "It's over. Make peace with yourself... brother."

He hurried to leave. Severn grabbed the bars again and called after him, but the door slammed, the lock turned over, and silence flooded the cells.

Samiel would have seen his flare. He'd have flown in fast and true, keeping low, among the clouds, until the last moment, when he would have emerged to catch Severn's wings. That had been the plan. But with no wings having fallen from Mikhail's balcony, Samiel would have retreated again before any angels spotted him. He wouldn't have thought to stay to look for Severn. Besides, Samiel was just one demon, and one demon couldn't break into Aerie to break Severn out.

And nobody else cared enough to try.

Mikhail could stop the execution but wouldn't. Not even for love because he was so damn deep in denial he didn't know what way was up.

Severn was alone.

They were going to shove him from the edge, and there wouldn't be anyone to catch him.

When the door rattled, Severn rose to his feet to see who the new visitor might be, hoping Solo had returned, or even Mikhail, but Remiel stopped in front of his cell. The guardian was as big and brutish as angels could get. He'd probably never cracked a smile in his life.

Remiel studied him silently, so Severn studied him right back.

Severn had made a damn fine job of the illusion. The voice had been all wrong, but nobody was perfect. "My illusion of you had a tiny dick."

Remiel, predictably, just blinked.

Severn wrapped his fingers around the bars. "Don't kill him."

"You beg for his life, not yours?" The guardian folded his arms, settling in for a heart-to-heart.

"Firstly, I didn't fucking beg. Secondly, Mikhail is brilliant and strong and passionate, and he's worth a thousand of you."

Remiel tilted his head, his piercing eyes delving deep. "You thoroughly believe you're an angel, don't you?"

"It doesn't matter. I know you're going to kill him, and if this is my last conversation, then I'm asking you not to. Just send him away to Haven. Don't kill him."

"Love is truly a terrible thing."

Severn scowled at the bastard. Angels like him couldn't be reasoned with.

"There is only one way this ends," Remiel said.

Ugh, two stubborn guardian angels. He should have known neither would back down. They didn't have it in them. If he could just talk to Mikhail again, try and convince him to surrender for his own good. But Mikhail would never surrender. He'd fight. Fighting was his life, he didn't know any other way. Severn could have taught him to live, but now he'd run out of time.

"It's almost a shame to kill you. There are people who would be fascinated to dissect all..." he gestured at Severn, "that."

"Demons tried it."

"They did?"

"Like I said, this skin ain't coming off. Every cut healed right back up."

"But not your wings?"

"No..." Because they'd been alive on Mikhail's wall and now they were ash. "You can't heal something that's missing."

"True," the guardian agreed, his blue-eyed gaze still roaming Severn in an entirely uncomfortable way. "It's said Seraphim made angels from the skies and demons from the earth. Do you believe that?"

"I believe we're not as different as angels like to think. I believe Seraphim didn't make us to war. He made us to love. But because he's no more perfect than you are, he fucked up somewhere, and here we are, with bars between us."

Remiel stepped closer, his dark pupils widening, focusing. "What you suggest is blasphemy."

"Why? Because you don't like to hear it?" Severn laughed. "Maybe I won't be the one to change things, but change will come. I'm not the only angel with feelings. Neither is Mikhail. Word's getting out, angels are beginning to open their eyes. Someone is lying to you all, but those lies are unraveling, and I say that as someone who knows a bit about deception."

Remiel nodded slowly. "Yes, I think you're right. And that's exactly why it's time you're removed from this equation."

Wait. "What?"

A snarl twitched Remiel's mouth. "Tomorrow, you and Mikhail both die, and all of London becomes mine. I supposed I should thank you for making his fall so effortless."

"Wait... I'm right about which part exactly?"

"Doesn't matter, demon. Your part in all of this is over."

"Mikhail will stop you."

"Mikhail's time has come to an end."

Severn bared his teeth. "He'll fight you."

Remiel snorted. "*The Demon Lord Who Would be an Angel.* Your worthless life is almost over. You'll die forgotten alongside the truth."

Severn pressed his face to the bars. "What truth? Tell me. I'm dead anyway."

"As you are so fond of secrets and nobody is likely to believe yours, you should know..." Remiel's smile was the kind that haunted nightmares. "Secure in Haven, there are ancient texts supporting your claim."

Books? That seemed... unlikely. This angel was clearly baiting him, but Severn was in no position to argue. "My *claim*?"

Remiel approached the bars, confidently placing himself easily within reach of Severn's grasp. "Seraphim made demons to love, not fight."

Severn had never heard of such a thing, and as changed as he was, he struggled to believe it. The legends told of how Seraphim made demons after his angels began to suffocate humans with their overprotectiveness. Demons were meant to stop his angels from getting out of control, and he spectacularly failed there too.

"If that's true, why are we at war?" Severn asked.

Remiel appeared to genuinely consider the question. He drew in a breath, expanding his chest behind his folded arms, and slowly exhaled. "We're at war because love is the most powerful emotion of all. Powerful enough to topple civilizations. Eradicating it was the only way."

"Wait... just... let's be clear here. Angels killed love out of fear it would destroy them?"

Remiel held his gaze. "You're not the first demon to love an angel, and Mikhail is not the first angel to love a demon."

Severn's grip on the bars tightened as his heart raced. Angels had loved demons before? "Then why are you doing this? Why am I in this cell?"

"It has always been a guardian's sacred duty to protect humans from demons, and from themselves, if necessary. Love kills, therefore, we kill love."

This knowledge, if true, was revolutionary. It could

change everything. Demons had always loved angels? Angels and demons could love each other. Such things were... shocking, but if true, if there was proof in Haven... The proof could end the war.

"If we were made to love, what happened?" Severn asked.

Remiel cast his gaze to the prison ceiling and briefly wet his lips. When he faced Severn again, a cruel delight shone in his eyes. "Seraphim fell in love with a demon, the first demon, his own creation—the Rayvern King, Aerius. But the guardians witnessed their love and feared Seraphim would succumb to it, and as they were made to, they did what was necessary to protect angel and humankind."

Seraphim's mysterious disappearance. The myth that he was somewhere out there still, waiting for the right time to return. It sounded like angel bullshit to cover up their own mistakes because it was. "Guardians killed Seraphim?"

"Guardians will always do what is right. They tried to kill Aerius, believing on the demon's death Seraphim would forget his love. Seraphim stopped them, but at a huge cost."

"His life." Their love had been so true, Seraphim had sacrificed himself for it? Gods, the implications were huge. If Seraphim and Aerius had been truly, deeply in love, then this whole war was a terrible mistake. Severn was suddenly glad for the bars holding him up, else he might have sunk to his knees and sobbed. "Is this true?" But of course it was, at least a version of it that Remiel believed, because angels did not lie. "You've seen evidence?"

"As true as an old book penned by a demon can be."

Remiel stood closer now, although Severn had been so lost to his words, he hadn't noticed him move in. The angel reached between the bars. His soft knuckles brushed Severn's cheek. The urge to brush him off fought with the urge to pull him closer, and so Severn did nothing, letting the trickle of sizzling pleasure ripple down his spine. Remiel's lips parted and his pupils expanded some more, savoring the sensation that should have been abhorrent. "Your kind are so easy to love."

He withdrew his hand back through the bars. "Guardian's rewrote history, proclaiming demons the enemy, and emotions are forever stripped from angels."

"You can't know all this," Severn whispered.

"Not with certainty, but I do know your love—your *allyanse*—is the most honest thing about you both, and tomorrow, it dies with you."

Mikhail

SUNLIGHT MADE AERIE SHINE, and it should have been glorious, but a darkness consumed Mikhail, made worse when his own angels brought out Severn—bound and gagged—from the cells and marched him toward the edge of the vast platform.

After weeks in the dark, Severn squinted into the sunlight. His eyes widened at the sight greeting him.

Almost every angel in Aerie had gathered to watch his execution, including Vearn, who'd been increasingly distancing herself from Mikhail. She stood closer to Remiel now, too, her allegiance apparently decided.

Remiel's ranks hovered in the skies, ready to intervene should anything go awry.

Severn looked about him, scanning hundreds of his

friends, his ranks, angels he'd trained with, led into battle and returned, bloody and weary. Angels who had admired and revered him. He'd betrayed every single one.

He deserved this.

Severn's panicked eyes found Mikhail and locked on. He tripped, and the angels escorting him shoved him forward. The gag muffled his string of words, made them incomprehensible. Whatever he said, it would be lies.

Mikhail tucked his wings in tighter, holding them aloft but rigid, keeping everything about him detached and controlled. Remiel watched. The guardian stood close to the edge, too, his golden-fringed wings held aloft, each feather touched by sunlight. His wings were the light to Mikhail's ever-darkening feathers. Feathers he was sure the angels must have begun to notice were changing. He wished he didn't care about any of this, wished it didn't hurt to see Severn stumbling toward the edge, wished he didn't ache all over with the need to go to him and comfort him. This love would shatter Mikhail's mind. But until then, all he had to do was get through this.

Remiel would soon push Severn over the edge.

Mikhail swallowed under Severn's pleading gaze.

He could do this. He could watch it unfold, and when it was done, the madness would end.

Solo drew up alongside Mikhail, his red wings held loose and low. He stared ahead, careful not to look at Severn. "This is necessary, Your Grace." His words were so soft that the wind almost tore them away. But they held a note of regret. "He deserves this."

Mikhail stayed silent.

The angels maneuvered Severn toward the edge. He

tried to dig his heels in, but his boots slipped on Aerie's smooth floors. His muffled words grew louder. He struggled and fought against those holding his arms.

Mikhail had expected Severn to accept his fate and be honorable in his last moments. Fighting did nothing but weaken him in the eyes of everyone here and sully what honorable memory he had left.

Severn broke free of the angel to his right and stumbled to a knee. Sensing weakness in his captors, he tugged harder and somehow managed to free himself from his second guard. Suddenly unguarded, he bolted straight for Mikhail.

Mikhail's heart thudded. All the angels watched as Severn rushed in.

A shout rose, followed by another. Remiel's angels swooped.

Faster, he ran, hands bound behind him, mouth gagged. He'd surely plow into Mikhail, yet Mikhail couldn't bring himself to move.

Solo stepped forward, his blade out, abruptly ending Severn's charge at its tip.

Severn went down to his knees but kept his pleading gaze tilted upward, silently begging for something. Freedom? To be heard?

Mikhail breathed too hard through his nose. His damned heart thumped like it could change everything unfolding before him. Even his wings had opened a little, of their own accord. But he could not reach down, he could not take Severn's face in his hands and rage at him, demand to know if any of it had been real before the answer was lost forever. The hurt in Severn's eyes was real, the agony summoned by his own terrible actions. It was good demons felt emotions, because he'd know, in his final moments, exactly how Mikhail felt too.

Angels scooped Severn up by his bound arms and dragged him backward, toward Remiel, toward the edge. Still, he spewed words behind the gag, so desperate to have his lies heard. But that look in his eyes. That wasn't a lie. Terror. Regret. Pain. A plea to be heard.

Mikhail forced himself to hold Severn's gaze even as every instinct demanded he look away. How could one angel still have the power to hurt Mikhail so?

"We are here to witness the demise of the demon lord Konstantin." The wind flung Remiel's words around them, making them fill Aerie. "A heinous liar, a brutal warrior, and an insult to all angelkind."

Severn mumbled something likely derogatory and aimed a scathing glare at Remiel. A flicker of knowing passed between them in a beat, and Remiel's lips ticked. Mikhail might not have seen it had he not been so intently watching them.

"By Haven, this isn't right," Solo whispered and then stilled, realizing he'd spoken aloud.

Mikhail stiffened. "Severn is a lie. He is not your friend."

Remiel continued, naming all Konstantin's numerous crimes.

Solo lowered his gaze and then lifted it to Mikhail. "I do not think it was all lies, Your Grace."

I love you, that is no lie.

Mikhail clenched his teeth.

"He will die here. At the very least, he should not be gagged," Solo added firmly.

"He will only speak more lies."

"Then, does it matter? Let him speak them. He will still die."

Mikhail observed Remiel approach Severn. Severn lifted his chin and met the guardian's glare without blinking. There was something between them, something that made Severn furious, and it wasn't just because Remiel was the angel who held Severn's fate in his hands.

Mikhail broke from his statuesque state and stepped forward. "Remove the gag." And now he was moving again, he found each step easier, because allowing Severn to speak was the right thing.

Remiel narrowed his eyes at Mikhail's approach.

"Allow him to speak. Angels who are subjected to the edge are permitted to speak their final words."

Remiel threw a gesture at Severn. "He is no angel."

Mikhail approached, lifting his wings high, despite their changed, matte blackness. Let the other angels see. He didn't care how he'd changed and certainly had no wish to hide himself from anyone. "He is Konstantin, but he has also done more for Aerie than you have. Allow him to speak."

Remiel blinked. "Be very careful with your words, Mikhail."

Mikhail stopped in front of Remiel. Severn watched on at his left, now silent behind the gag, his emotive eyes suddenly curious.

Remiel glowed, every inch the guardian, from his golden wings to his platinum hair, and Mikhail found himself wishing he could shove him over the edge instead of Severn. "Aerie is still mine. You are not yet its commander. My word is law." Mikhail stepped behind Severn and quickly untied the gag. Remiel glared the entire time, but there was nothing the guardian could do to stop him.

Severn gasped as the gag came away and looked at Mikhail moving back to stand between him and Remiel.

Severn wet his cracked lips and wheezed, "Thank you, Your Grace."

Mikhail tossed the gag aside, using the motion to hide his wince at hearing those words upon Severn's lips. "Speak your final words, Konstantin, and let's have this spectacle over with."

He glanced between Mikhail and Remiel. And then at the hundreds of angels in the skies and poised all about Aerie. Mikhail could almost hear Severn's heart racing and feel his breathless panic, or perhaps the allyanse was reminding him of their bond.

"Mikhail," he spoke quietly, his words meant for privacy. "Remiel told me demons are meant to love angels, it's what Seraphim originally created them for. Not war."

Mikhail's thoughts stalled. He'd expected begging or accusations, not... this. "Nonsense." Now he regretted removing the gag. "Severn, this is your chance to regain some of your pride. Use this time for truth, not fantasy."

"I am, you stubborn fool. There is nothing more important than this. Don't you see? Our love, it's not wrong. It never was. Remiel told me himself. Our allyanse is true."

Mikhail lifted his gaze to Remiel.

"Obviously lies," the guardian said nonchalantly.

But why would Severn spend his last moments concocting such ridiculous nonsense?

"I'm ready to die," Severn said. "But before I do, you

must know the truth, Mikhail. There's a book, written by—"

Remiel's hand thrust out and grabbed Severn by the neck. He hauled him off his feet and turned, dangling Severn over the edge. A heartbeat, a second, Severn's eyes widened in true fear, and then Remiel let go.

Severn fell, mouth open in a silent plea.

A split second—that was all it took for Mikhail to know he could not allow Severn to die. He snatched at one of Severn's bound arms and swung him back onto the platform, then snapped the bindings at his wrists, freeing his arms. Severn dropped forward onto trembling hands. Their gazes met, Severn's blown wide, full of uncertainty and relief, but mostly love. And by Haven, it was real. It had always been real. Mikhail wasn't sure how or why or what it meant, but love was love, even after the betrayal, and his heart swelled to see it.

A sudden, breathtaking blow punched into Mikhail's lower back.

Red blood speckled Severn's pale face. Blood from where?

Thoughts fragmented.

Pain sparked through his chest.

What... was this?

"NO!" Severn roared, hands reaching for Mikhail.

Mikhail looked down, saw the end of an angelblade protruding from his gut, and instinctively tried to grasp at it, to pull it free. But his attacker pulled the blade back out from behind him, momentum yanking Mikhail off balance.

He staggered, breathless, and pressed his fingers to the bubbling wound.

An arm looped around his waist. "Your love dies with you," Remiel hissed in his ear, and then a second blow ripped all the light from his vision, plunging him into full darkness.

evern

REMIEL DEALT a blow to the back of Mikhail's head using the handle of the angelblade. Mikhail's eyes rolled, his body dropping into Remiel's grip. His wings sagged, limp and useless.

Severn had been falling, he'd been about to die—he'd lived a lifetime in a blink, when he'd known with absolutely certainty that it was all over—and then Mikhail had caught him. Saved him. Hauled him back to safety and pulled his bindings free. Impossible. Wonderful.

Then blood, and a blade, and Mikhail with a sword through his middle... It happened too fast.

Remiel twisted, lifted Mikhail's dead weight, and dropped him over the edge.

Mikhail's lifeless body pitched over the side. Black wings vanished.

No... No!

Remiel lunged for Severn, blade thrust out, wings ablaze in sunlight. Shouts rose, blades clashed, but it didn't matter because Mikhail was *falling*!

Severn ran, wedged his foot on the edge of the ledge, and leaped into the sky.

Momentum carried him so far, and then gravity grabbed hold of him and pulled. His gut lurched, and the wind rushed, tearing at his body, his hair, his clothes, tossing him over and under himself.

He desperately looked for black wings against blue skies. There. Limp wings—suddenly swallowed by cloud. Severn tucked his arms into his sides and dove. With no wings of his own, he flew light and free, plunging through the air so fast it stole his breath and burned his eyes. Wet clouds dashed his face, suddenly cold, blurring his vision. He only had one thought: get to Mikhail. Wake him, somehow. Before their bodies shattered against London's skyline.

There, just ahead, Mikhail tumbled, his enormous wings tipped at odd angles, twirling him. Severn reached out and grabbed a fistful of feathers. The shift in weight tipped them both over, Mikhail flipping on his back and Severn falling beneath him. Severn pulled on the wing, climbing along its arch. Wind howled, and his lungs screamed their agony at not being able to catch enough air. London spread far and wide in every direction. A hard landscape of gray.

"Mikhail..." Severn grasped at where the wing joined Mikhail's back and pulled himself in, clutching a hold around his waist so his mouth pressed to Mikhail's ear. "Wake up!" *Or we're both going to die.*

London's swathe of gray grew ever bigger.

Death would be quick.

Severn would die with Mikhail, and while he'd known he would die today, he couldn't allow Mikhail to die too. There was still too much for him to do. "I love you. I won't leave you. Wake up, Mikhail."

One of Mikhail's wings flipped, tipping them over, and Severn clung on, closing his eyes, breathing in the scent of sunshine and feathers. It would be all right. Maybe the demons would figure it all out without him. Maybe Solo would go on to kiss another angel. If demons were meant to love, then the truth would find a way. Eventually.

But he would not be a part of it. And neither would Mikhail.

An angel and a demon, their love shattered.

It wasn't right.

Gods, none of this was right.

It should not have been this way.

Had he told Mikhail the truth, had he found another way to reach him, all of this could have been prevented.

It wasn't right, and he couldn't do a damn thing to fix it, and damn destiny for leading him to this wretched moment. What had it all been for if it ended here? Rage and injustice scorched his veins.

London's spires and high-rises blurred into sight, so close now.

Damn you, Seraphim, you bastard, for making us love! Damn you to Haven and back. You deserved to die saving Aerius. Because he deserved better than an angel!

Pain tore down Severn's back. He arched away, hearing his own screams. A terrible weight slammed into him, and for a blinding second, he thought he'd hit the ground, but he was still falling, still had Mikhail clutched in his arms, the big angel's wings uselessly flailing, raining feathers in their wake.

But his wings weren't alone. Leathery demon wings curled in, encircling them both.

Demon wings?

His wings?

His wings!

Severn flung them open. Agony scorched his spine. He cried out but clutched control of the impossible appendages and tilted, twisted, rolling in the air so he had Mikhail tucked against his chest. London's unforgiving streets continued to rush up to greet them. Severn flapped his wings, inducing the kind of raging pain that almost blacked him out. He flapped again, but they still fell too fast. Locking his wings stretched outward, he finally caught the air. Gravity tried to yank Mikhail from his arms or snap his wings in two, but somehow Severn clung onto both.

He narrowly missed a high-rise apartment block by inches, then tucked his right wing in, banking around another sharp-edged building before soaring on to where the houses became smaller, scattered among greenery. He spied a field among the streets and tilted toward it, but the wings were ungainly, or his control of them was, and he already knew the landing was going to be a disaster.

He rolled at the last moment, tucking Mikhail against this chest. There was nothing he could do about the angel's limp wings—just hope they didn't shatter.

His back hit the ground. He skidded instead of tumbled, and while the friction tore flesh from bone,

Mikhail was safely tucked against his chest, his wings trailing behind them.

They came to rest in the long grass, Severn panting, his back and wings on fire from the impact.

Mikhail...

Severn probed at his neck, searching for a pulse, and found it beating strongly beneath his fingertips.

Alive.

They were both alive.

He gently rolled Mikhail to one side and, hissing, pulled his damaged demon wings out from under them both.

He staggered to his feet, dragging his bleeding wings behind him.

Wings.

He had wings again.

But gods, they were ablaze with pain and looked as though they'd been through a cheese grater. But fuck, he had wings...

They were back.

Or were they?

Demon wings on an angel body? That didn't seem right.

He staggered in the grass and tried to look for shelter, somewhere they could get away from prying eyes. If anyone had seen them fall, they'd tell the correctioners, or worse, the angels.

Pain throbbed so hard and so heavy, he went down to his knees in the grass. His heart thumped too heavily in his ears, and his head pounded.

He glanced over at the unconscious guardian angel. The wound in his gut had sealed itself shut. He'd wake soon, and he'd see Severn, and then what? Would he kill him?

Severn bowed his head and breathed around the agony, focusing on that instead of the clusterfuck that was everything else. Slowly, carefully, he drew the battered wings in, panting at their ache, until they were pinched in enough to illusion away. Then, with the dregs of strength he had left, he crawled back to Mikhail's side and collapsed beside him.

Let destiny make the next move, because he was too wrecked to go on.

A SPRIG of hay tickled his nose. More hay stabbed at sore skin. He blinked open gritty eyes and spied timber beams arched high above him. Why wasn't he in the damp, dark, cold space he always woke in now? He raised a hand and rubbed his eyes.

Memories poured in; the edge, the blazing sunlight, and Remiel throwing Mikhail over the side. Black wings tumbling against blue skies.

He jolted upright with a gasp. Gods, he was alive. He was in an old barn, its rusted tin roof peppered with pinpricks of light, and Mikhail was perched on a stack of bales, his face unreadable, his wings hidden. No, not unreadable... utterly flat, which meant he was hiding everything going on inside his head right now.

At least Mikhail hadn't killed him while he was out cold. Although, there was still time, and Severn was in no condition to defend himself.

His back burned where his landing had scraped off

layers of skin. He winced around the pain and shifted awkwardly on the straw bed.

"You're hurt." Instead of sounding sympathetic, Mikhail's words growled like an accusation.

He twisted his arm and frowned at the grated shirt and skin. "It'll heal. Not as fast as you, but..." Severn trailed off as his gaze found its way to Mikhail's bare middle, where Remiel's blade had protruded. Just a thin, pale line marked Remiel's attack.

The sight of Remiel shoving Mikhail over the edge would haunt him for the rest of his days—although he doubted there'd be many days left.

Word of his plunge from Aerie would soon reach the demons. Just one sighting of his dramatic rescue of Mikhail would be enough for them to mount a search, especially if they learned of his wings. The angels would similarly be looking for them.

Mikhail was watching in that unblinking way he did, trying to decide the best way to solve a problem—terminally. But he was alive. They were both alive. Which was more than Severn had predicted a few hours before.

"How long have we been here?" He draped his forearms over his knees.

"All night. I carried you in before sunset."

Mikhail had carried him, and he'd missed every second of it?

"This situation isn't amusing." Mikhail glowered from high up on his hay bale tower.

Severn kept his smile, maybe even widened it some. Had Mikhail contemplated leaving him out there in the field? He must have argued with himself over it. Leave the lying demon-angel in the dirt or carry him to safety so he could question him and discover what really happened for them both to land in a field somewhere outside London? He hadn't asked any questions, though. His pride probably wouldn't allow it.

Severn filled his lungs with air and sighed hard. "Well, I guess we're both outcasts now."

"I'm not an outcast. When I return to Aerie, I'll force Remiel aside."

"Just like that?"

"He'll have no choice."

"He stabbed you in the back and threw you off the edge. Your angels did nothing, and you want to go back?"

Mikhail's eyes widened before narrowing again. "They were afraid."

"Yes, of you."

Mikhail shoved off the bales suddenly, spread appearing wings, and landed a few feet from Severn, his wings still unveiling. "This was all your doing."

Severn stayed sitting on the floor and kept his smile as Mikhail loomed over him. If Mikhail was going to attack, there was little point in resisting. "Yes, I've lied since we met up until Tower Bridge, but I did not summon Remiel to deal with you, and I did not make you put demon heads on stakes to line the killing fields, and I did not ask you to kill people in your pursuit of me. For someone so full of shit, you sure do shine, Mikhail."

Mikhail's wings flared, but whatever he'd been about to do, the sound of the barn door creaking open had him turning instead.

An elderly man stood in the doorway, his threadbare coat bigger than him, and his trousers tucked into his wellington boots. He aimed a shotgun at Mikhail. "Mary!" he called. "There's angels in the barn!"

Severn heard a muffled reply from outside and glanced up at Mikhail's stoic face. He was not about to handle this well. Mikhail knew they were both at risk of being found if a single person misspoke. He just might be unhinged enough to threaten or hurt the farmer.

Climbing to his feet, Severn opened his hands. "We were just using your barn as shelter. We'll be on our way."

"Put the gun down," Mikhail growled.

Severn laughed lightly and placed himself between Mikhail and the man. "We've had a rough few days." He added again, for emphasis, "We'll just be on our way."

The door opened wider, and a short, well-rounded woman squinted into the barn. "You can't aim guns at angels, Barrie!" She grabbed the shotgun from Barrie's hands and cracked it open, disarming it with well-prac-ticed ease. "Sorry about that. You two look pretty beat up. How about you come have some tea and a bit of cake. A nice cuppa makes everything better."

Going with them wasn't the worst idea, and he could ensure they didn't call in the correctioners. He tilted his head and side-eyed Mikhail. "Cake?"

"I—"

"You'll have to put your wings away, mind. Our house ain't big now." She marched out with Barrie hanging back, holding the barn door open.

"Best c'mon," he said. "I'll never hear the end of it else."

Severn made for the door, and Mikhail followed, silently tucking his wings out of sight once more. The idea that Mikhail would even sit and drink tea with humans was such a novelty, Severn found his smile blooming. Until he felt the heat of Mikhail's glare on his back. He couldn't know about Severn's wings, could he? No, the illusion to hide them had held. He'd only reveal them when he was sure Mikhail wouldn't rip them off again. And right now, the chance of that was high.

CHAPTER 22

M ikhail

Brunch with the humans was a distraction from everything he should have been planning for, but he rather found he enjoyed their endless chitter, the sweet slice of chocolate cake, and the jam-filled biscuits.

Mary produced one of Barrie's shirts and insisted Mikhail wear it, saying his naked torso was *distracting*. He looked at the blue-checkered pattern, then at Severn's attempt to hide a smirk behind his mug, graciously thanked the woman for her kindness, and tugged the garment on.

When she asked Severn if he, too, would like a change of clothes, he hadn't heard and stared instead at Mikhail before blinking himself out of his reverie to accept her offer. So now they both wore patterned shirts. Severn's was green. It brought out the blue in his eyes.

When the conversation turned back around to why they weren't in Aerie, Severn masterfully spun a lie about their *vacation* that Mikhail was sure the humans wouldn't believe. But not only did they believe him, they offered the use of their rental cottage for a few nights.

Mikhail could have done without the reminder of how Severn used lies to win over the hearts and minds of everyone he met.

It had been easier to love him when he'd lain unconscious in Mikhail's arms in the barn. After waking in the field to find Severn's bloody and motionless body beside him, he'd almost spiraled into despair, but then he'd heard Severn's soft breathing and cursed him instead. He'd told him all the ways he hated him and why, while carrying him limp in his arms to the safety of the barn, where he'd tucked him close, listening for any stutter in his breathing or his heart. Only when Severn had begun to wake had Mikhail abandoned him for the top of the hay bales.

Then he'd woken, and there had been no bars between them, just a whole lot of emotional wreckage.

Mikhail mused over events as Severn offered to help the human couple fix their failing roof. Nobody asked Mikhail, so he used the time to silently observe Severn. The way his eyes laughed, even when his mouth did not. He carried a lightness about him, a joy in the simple things —like speaking with these humans on their level. And they loved him for it.

The day rushed by, and Mikhail considered those last moments in Aerie. He'd pulled Severn to safety, and Remiel had stabbed him in the back.

Deep in thought, he found himself content to deliver slate tiles to Severn on the farmhouse roof and, perhaps sensing his need for space, Severn didn't demand answers, just took each roof tile when it was needed so he could happily hammer and nail it home.

His joy had always been there, in his laughter, the sly way in which he'd read others and tell them what they needed to hear, in the coy looks and thoughtful silences. He'd always been demon, but Mikhail hadn't wanted to see it.

The day faded into early evening, and their gracious hosts gave them a tour of the tiny cottage. A renovation project, they said. It was warm and dry and smelled faintly of washing powder.

"It's lovely. Thank you. We're honored to stay," Severn gushed, making Mary blush. Even Barrie seemed smitten. They had no idea they had a demon lord in their midst.

They left, and Severn closed the door behind them, then pressed his forehead against it. "I know what you're going to say, but don't hurt them. They won't call the correctioners."

Mikhail stood back in the narrow hallway, feeling like the house was trying to envelop him in humanity. Severn's words pulled him back from his thoughts and into the moment. "I had no intention of hurting them." They might have been the first words he'd spoken all day.

Severn huffed and turned to lean back against the door. "And you call me the liar."

Thoughtlessly, Mikhail closed the distance between them in a few strides. Severn's breath hitched, he straightened, and then Mikhail braced an arm against the door beside him and... stopped.

Severn's parted lips were so close, he could already taste their tingling tease. Blue eyes searched Mikhail's, pupils full. He should kill him. End this here and now. But his ever-moving mouth held Mikhail briefly captivated. He desperately wanted to kiss him, but that was wrong, and so he did nothing, trapped instead between two terrible needs. Kiss or kill.

Severn's hand came up and touched Mikhail's cheek, and the agony on feeling that gentle caress nearly freed a moan from Mikhail's lips. He should not want this. But every restrained inch of him needed it.

Severn was Konstantin, and Konstantin was an incubus.

Mikhail tilted his head. Severn's lips were soft beneath his, but he didn't kiss them. They shared breaths, and Mikhail's heart thumped heavy and hot. His body knew its wants, even if his mind did not.

Demon. Angel. Did it matter anymore? His position in Aerie had been taken. The moment he'd saved Severn from falling, he'd sealed his own fate. And then... whatever Severn had done between Remiel stabbing him and waking in the field with Severn collapsed beside him, his back shredded down to bone.

Severn had saved him. That was true.

In the end, when they should have died, they'd saved each other.

But he hated this, hated himself for wanting this.

By Haven, he didn't know what was right anymore.

Mikhail gripped Severn's jaw, holding him still. Whatever the feelings were, he couldn't navigate them, not alone. For all the betrayal and lies and heartache, Mikhail needed Severn. And if Severn was Konstantin, so be it.

He kissed his soft lips, tasting their familiar tingle. Lust and need surged through his veins, making him want to throw open his wings and consume Severn in all ways, but the cottage hallway was too small and Severn so still, that the sudden rush of need had Mikhail pulling back before anything had really begun. A kiss, a brush of the lips—that was all, but it almost brought Mikhail to his knees. His body raged, demanding everything Severn could give, but they were strangers now, and Mikhail no longer knew how they fit together. If they fit at all.

Severn's hand clamped down on the back of Mikhail's neck, and Severn's mouth smothered his, tongue thrusting. The savage kiss ripped Mikhail's indecision and uncertainty aside, taking all of his thoughts with them. By Haven, he needed to touch—to taste—Severn, like some kind of madness had hijacked his soul.

Was that what incubi did? Was Severn manipulating him?

Mikhail jerked back, shoving so hard against Severn that the little cottage door behind him rattled its hinges.

Severn reached for him, the fear back in his face. "Mikhail?"

Breathless, he staggered back, bumping into the stair banister. This tiny house was too small, and Severn stood between him and the exit.

"Mikhail..." he said, softer now, approaching slowly, his hand out and head dipped, as though approaching a vicious animal.

The heels of Mikhail's boots struck the bottom step, and he dropped to the stairs, slumping over to bury his face in his hands. He couldn't hide from this, but all he really wanted to do was wrap his wings around himself and pretend he didn't exist, pretend Severn hadn't stolen his heart and Remiel hadn't stabbed him in the back.

He sensed Severn sit beside him but kept his face down and covered, and his eyes closed. "I don't understand anything," he whispered, mostly to himself, but then the words wouldn't stop. They gushed out of him like an open wound. "I don't understand why this happened. I don't understand why I still feel the way I do..." He looked up at the closed cottage door. "Without Aerie, I don't understand my purpose. Nothing makes any sense."

Severn didn't answer. Maybe he agreed. Or maybe he thought Mikhail insane too. He wanted to sob but bit the inside of his cheek instead, like he used to as a fledgling and he'd failed in training. He was coming undone here on this step, next to his enemy, and he did not know what should happen next.

Warm fingers slipped between Mikhail's, then Severn leaned against his arm, and the brittle tension he'd been feeling all day began to fade beneath Severn's warmth. He closed his eyes. His heart beat steadily, his body slowly back under control.

"For what it's worth, I don't understand any of it either," Severn finally said. "I just know that even with everything that's happened between us, even when I see the hate in your eyes, I'd still die for you."

Mikhail's heart hiccupped. "Why?"

"You're different. I mean... you have your moments of being a stubborn, self-centered prick, but then I see how much you've changed and how you could change *everything*, not just us, but the war too, and I know it has to be you. Destiny brought me here, to you, for a reason."

Mikhail looked down at their hands. Severn's were slightly smaller but no less capable. "Destiny?"

Severn's little smile seemed suddenly shy. "How else can an angel and a demon fall in love?"

His golden hair lay tossed about his shoulders, and the ridiculous shirt sat askew. Severn didn't look dangerous, but therein lay the danger.

"I can't ever trust you."

"I know," Severn sighed, "and I'll forever be sorry for that."

"I burned your wings." Shame made Mikhail want to turn his face away, but Severn reached up and caught his cheek again. "How do you not despise me?" He'd been beside himself with cold rage, and the wings had been an easy target, like all the other demons he'd destroyed in his search for vengeance. He'd been a monster. Was a worse monster now.

"The wings were part of the old me. I don't think I'm him anymore."

Mikhail pulled his head free and leaned against the banister. "I want to believe you."

"In time, maybe."

"But you're not all angel. Inside, you're demon still? I... I can taste it... when we..." He wet his lips, tasting the lingering heat of Severn still. He'd felt it before. Every time they'd touched, kissed, fucked, or made love, it had always been there, and he wanted to feel it again. He wanted to feel *demon* beneath his hands. "Gods, I deserve to be cast out of Aerie."

"No," Severn said firmly. "You did not deserve what was done to you. Remiel is a bastard. He told me some things, thinking I'd be too dead to pass them on. I want to tell you, but first, will you come to bed—not like that," he hastily added, seeing Mikhail's face fall. "Not for sex. Just...

it's better if I show you, and I'm fucking wrecked, and I need to be with you." He took Mikhail's hand, and when there was no resistance, asked, "Will you be with me?"

"I don't think I can—"

Severn smiled softly. "This is a friend thing, all right? Not an angel and demon thing." He stood and drew Mikhail to his feet, and it was all Mikhail could do to be led up the staircase and into one of the cottage's bedrooms with creaking floors and wonky windows.

Severn threw back the bed covers, then quickly unbuttoned his borrowed shirt and draped it over a nearby chair. Soft moonlight from the windows painted the smooth skin of his scratched back and shoulder, and then he turned, and the light played down his chest in a way Mikhail longed to follow with his mouth and tongue.

He crossed the small bedroom in two strides and reached for Mikhail's shirt buttons. "May I, Your Grace?"

He made efficient work of the buttons, and Mikhail shrugged the shirt off. Severn methodically took it and laid it next to his, then returned to take both of Mikhail's hands. He walked backward to the bed, climbed on, and slowly urged Mikhail onto the creaking bed so they both knelt, eye-to-eye, the mattress sagging under their weight. Mikhail wondered, absently, if their trousers might go next, and then what might happen, and if he'd even be able to without wondering if Severn was manipulating his body. But Severn merely let go of his hands and lay down on his side, implying Mikhail could do the same.

Moonlight lay over him, and he was exactly how Mikhail remembered him, but also a stranger.

"It's all right if you don't want to," Severn said, appearing to mean it.

Did Mikhail want to lay next to his enemy? He wasn't sure he trusted himself, or whatever this thing was between them.

"It's fine..." Severn said. "There's another room. You take this one—"

Mikhail lay down on his back and stared at the ceiling. "What happens now?"

Severn sighed in a way that suggested he was sorry, not frustrated. "I've hurt you, and that will take a long time to heal, if it ever does. So, for now, we lie here, like this, and rest."

The bed creaked as Severn made himself comfortable.

"Nothing else?" Mikhail asked the ceiling.

"Nothing else."

Mikhail sighed, too, surprised to find he'd been holding back some tension at what he might be expected to do here and how much it would hurt when he refused. Severn *had* hurt him, but Mikhail had hurt Severn too. He did not know much about love, but he was certain that wasn't how these things were meant to go.

Mikhail let his lashes fall. Yes, this was strange, but for the first time in a long time, he wasn't alone.

evern

HE WAS GOING to have to show him the wings and explain everything Remiel had said about demons and love and a book in Haven, but before all that, he just wanted to lay next to the sleeping Mikhail as the sunlight warmed the room and pretend it was just the two of them in a world that wouldn't destroy them both if it knew the depth of their love.

Gods, he was beautiful, sprawled on the bed, an arm flung behind his head and the other resting over his waist, below the vanishing scar. He wanted to touch. To kiss. The desire was almost unbearable. But Mikhail wasn't ready. Severn had abused his trust, abused him... Mikhail had opened up to Severn in all ways and been betrayed. He was a long way off from being ready to love physically, might never be with Severn, and that was something Severn would have to come to terms with.

He rolled from the bed without waking Mikhail and padded downstairs to brew coffee. Angels weren't the sort to have ever experienced breakfast made for them, the war was too important for frivolous fancies. So Severn making breakfast would be a treat. He dug out the eggs and bread and set the pan down on the heat when a rayvern cawed outside the window.

"You'd better not fuck this up," Amii grumbled.

Severn didn't jump, not this time, but only because the damn rayvern had been a warning. He braced both hands on the edge of the counter and bowed his head. "You need to leave." How had they even found him here? If Mikhail came down those stairs now—

"Me an' Jasper are a goin'... Just figured we'd drop in. How are them shiny new wings workin' out for yah, eh?"

He whirled.

The kitchen table, where he'd expected to find them sitting, was empty.

The rayvern cawed again at the windowsill and took off.

Maybe they hadn't even been here, and Severn's ragged mind was screwing with him.

After checking the locks were still bolted, he finished making breakfast in time for Mikhail to appear, hair a mess and eyes sleepy. He wore the borrowed shirt again, but now it was wrinkled, along with the trousers. He scratched at his chin and regarded the breakfast spread with widening eyes. Fuck, sleepy Mikhail was adorable.

"What is this?" His tone suggested he suspected Severn had poisoned the food.

Severn swept a hand over the display. "A chance to talk while we eat." One thing that had taken the most adjusting to was the angels' preference for eating on the fly. They ate when they were hungry and did so as quickly and efficiently as possible. It was not a social thing. Whereas demons feasted and reveled and often ate for hours, using the time to debrief from battles or catch up on news. This breakfast was a little of both. Too small to be a feast, but large enough to slow Mikhail down.

Severn pulled out a chair and sat first, hoping to encourage Mikhail to do the same, but Mikhail loomed, uncertain. "It's just food, all right? Not a bribe for... anything else." He regretted the words as soon as Mikhail's sharp glance cut to him. "Just sit and eat, will you. We can do that without trying to kill each other?"

Mikhail finally relented and selected his food. Severn poured the coffee. And lo and behold, they could sit across a table from one another without bloodshed. It felt like a victory, even if just a small one.

Severn let him eat, avoiding his glances in the hope it would convince him he was safe. But the happy little domestic scene couldn't last forever. "We need to talk."

"Firstly, I want your word," Mikhail said. "No more lies."

"No more lies. You have my word."

Mikhail's lips twisted. Words weren't enough.

"Ask me anything." Severn picked up his coffee. "Anything at all. I promise to reply truthfully."

Mikhail swallowed, and his fingers teased the handle of his cup. "Samiel. What is he to you?"

Fuck, he went straight for the jugular. Severn looked

him in the eyes. "He was my lover. I thought he'd died. His death set me on the path of vengeance—to you."

"But he's not dead?"

"No."

"And how do you feel about that?"

Severn set his cup back down and leaned forward. "It's... complicated." He lifted a hand to stop Mikhail's protest. "I'm getting there. Give me a second. It's something I haven't dealt with." He looked up at the kitchen's quaint ceiling beams, trying to organize his thoughts around Samiel. "Samiel pulled me out of the Tower Bridge rubble. Without him, I'd be dead." Severn hadn't said it to hurt him, but Mikhail flinched anyway—knowing he'd been the one to put Severn in that rubble. "He's a good demon. He's a friend. We matured together, fought together. I loved him, but things have changed. I've changed."

"Did you fuck when you returned to him?"

"Yes."

Mikhail flinched at that, too, and Severn sighed, suddenly feeling the weight of their differences. "I look like an angel, but I'm still an incubus inside," he said, keeping his tone soft. "I need ether to survive. I assume you know how it works?"

"I do." Mikhail folded his arms and sat back in his chair, beginning to close down. The topic was an uncomfortable one, but he'd asked, and in the spirit of this new alliance, Severn was going to lay all the truths on the table.

"Emotions produce ether, but there's a reason the concubi are known for their sexual appetites. Sex is the easiest way to harvest ether. We feed off the enjoyment of others." Severn held Mikhail's gaze. He wasn't going to be ashamed for what he was just because he'd lived with angel for much of his lifetime.

Mikhail's beautiful eyes flicked downward at his breakfast, untouched. "Did you use me for ether?"

Severn reached for a glass of water and drank quickly. "The first time in my chamber, when you came to me..." When Mikhail's cock had spilled its load down Severn's throat... His cock semi-hardened now at the memory. That first time, having Mikhail fuck his mouth, that had been so fucking hot and Mikhail had needed it—they both had. "I consumed ether then, yes."

Mikhail stood suddenly, bumping the table. The plates rattled, a knife fell with a loud clang, and Mikhail fled for the door.

Severn sighed. "Dammit." Chasing him down would do no good. He could leave if he wanted, and Severn wouldn't stop him. But every instinct demanded Severn go after him. They'd been talking, and as painful as the truth was, every word had been progress. If Mikhail left, it would all be for nothing.

What if he went back to Aerie and got himself killed trying to reclaim the city alone? He wouldn't... would he? Of course, he would. He was stubborn, ridiculously naïve, and hopelessly proud.

Shoving from the table, Severn stumbled out of the cottage's front door and found Mikhail standing in the front garden among the tall wildflowers and overgrown weeds.

"How many times did you feed from me?" the guardian asked, his voice strained.

"All the time, in the beginning." Guilt twisted Severn's insides. "And then one night, I showed you London from a rooftop, and everything changed. I think it all changed long before any of that, but I couldn't see it... Didn't want to see it, maybe." He mumbled the last part, but Mikhail heard and turned his head to peer over his shoulder.

Severn wandered to his side, cutting a path through the high grass. He hadn't flown off. That had to be progress. "I set out to hurt my enemy and fell in love with him instead."

"Not very demon-like," Mikhail grumbled, turning his face toward the sky. Was he thinking of taking flight?

"No." Severn snorted.

"What do the demons think of all this? Of you?"

"They repeatedly tried to carve angel off me, and when that didn't work, they had a trial, without me, to determine my guilt. It's pretty safe to assume they're real pissed about the whole thing."

"You talked your way off the hook," Mikhail said, and the smallest of smiles touched his lips.

"Something like that." He had no desire to tell Mikhail about Luxen—telling Mikhail he'd actually fucked his way off the hook was a bit much—but if he asked, he'd have to. "I am an incubus. I can't change that. Honestly, I've lost count of the people I've fucked. But with you, when I realized how I felt, the ether didn't matter."

Mikhail's cheek fluttered.

He wasn't explaining this right but had never had to explain it to anyone who wasn't a demon before, and definitely not an angel. He puffed out a breath. Might as well tell him everything. "There's sex for ether and sex for pleasure. Sex for pleasure is a different kind of need that two people, or three—"

Mikhail's eyes widened.

"Never mind. I'm screwing this up." Severn thrust his hands into his pockets, suddenly awkward in the harsh daylight. "Ether is a part of my life. If I don't get it, I'll eventually starve."

"That's why you went to the madam."

Severn had almost forgotten Mikhail had held the madam and shredded her wings. Given his out-of-control methods of late, it was a wonder she'd escaped with her life. "She helped me, yes. She isn't bad either, you know."

Mikhail lowered his gaze, darting his eyes about the field, seeing all the things Severn had done wrong, no doubt. "We have a human device on her," he finally said. "Solo knows the details. It's how we found your home and the medical center. I regret what happened there. I have not been... I regret many things of late. The madam, I fear I would have killed her if not for Solomon's intervention."

"I know I have no right to ask, but I'm going to anyway. What happened between you and Solo?"

"I kissed him. I wondered if it would feel the same as it had with you."

"Did it?" His heart unexpectedly raced. Of course, he had no claim to Mikhail exclusively, but still, that odd little curl of jealousy squirmed inside Severn's mind, making him uneasy. Jealousy was not a common incubus trait. Maybe it was an angel one?

"No," Mikhail replied after some thought. "It was not the same."

"Did you want it to be?" Severn asked, wishing again that he hadn't.

"Yes." Mikhail looked down and clasped his hands behind his back. "Another mistake. I likely scarred Solo for life."

"I think you woke him up, actually. And he's not the only one. Nobody talks about it, but clearly angels do feel a need for company, otherwise the nephilim wouldn't exist. And there's more... Before he tried to kill me, Remiel told me a story. There's a book in Haven, written by a demon, that proves Seraphim made demons to love, not war." Mikhail's eyebrow arched, making him look skeptical, but Severn plowed on. "Demons were supposed to diffuse the angels, not make everything worse. Aerius and Seraphim were a couple. But fearing they were losing their leader to love, the guardians attacked Aerius. Seraphim saved him and died doing so."

Mikhail's brow pinched. "A tale, nothing more."

"How many angels do you know who lie?"

Mikhail leveled him under a glare but then softened and huffed an unexpected laugh. "You sound as though you've been speaking with the crone. Seraphim and Aerius as lovers... It's all mythical nonsense."

"What crone?"

"A cauldron cambion." He waved his own words away. "She lived with a pet rayvern. She fixed my wings after I broke out of that cage. I thought it was you who fixed them. Ever since then, I've been... There have been changes in me."

"Change in your wings?" Severn kept his tone carefully level.

"I'm sure it's nothing related."

It was absolutely related. The crone from the cauldron had to be the meddling Amii. No doubt about it. And by the sounds of it, they'd been pulling his and Mikhail's strings for a long time. He'd have to have more than a word with that demon when he next saw them. If Mikhail discovered another demon had manipulated him, he would not react well.

This seemed like the right moment to mention *his* wings. But they were talking and not fighting, and the sun was shining, and the flowers swayed in the breeze, and if Severn fucked it all up by revealing demon wings attached to an angel too soon, Mikhail was liable to lose his shit, and there'd be no going back. Things were already on a knife-edge between them.

"But what if the myths are true?" he went on, opting for a different time to reveal that final piece of himself.

"Why would a book written by a demon be in Haven?" Mikhail half smiled, thinking the notion ridiculous.

"Do you even know what goes on in Haven?"

"Yes, I know." He sounded mildly offended.

"The same as you know what's going on with the correctioners?"

Mikhail winced. "That has been dealt with."

"Not what you thought, was it?" Severn's demon heart skipped a few beats to know Mikhail had listened to him, even after the betrayal. It was a good sign, a sign his angel hadn't completely given up on him. "So you admit you're not all-knowing?"

"I do not admit that."

"It certainly sounds like it, Your Grace."

His dark brows pinched. "Haven is a sanctuary for mated pairs. They produce offspring, and those offspring, once fledglings, are sent to Aerie and other cities to complete their training."

"So you're told. Do you remember any of it?"

"No." He hesitated. "Few do."

"Few or none?"

"I... don't know."

Severn fought a grin. "And once a pair go to Haven, they never return. Don't you find that strange? If it's so benign a place, why does nobody escape it?"

Mikhail dismissed his words with an incredulous laugh. "It's always been that way. There's nothing insidious about it."

Severn snorted. "Just because it's always been that way doesn't make it right. Gods, I love how naïve you are."

The word *love* lodged between them. "It's called focus," Mikhail replied. "I focus on the task at hand, not fanciful stories told by wayward cambion."

"No, it's called having your emotions conditioned out of you so you can all pretend to reign supreme while, deep down, you're emotional wrecks, just like the rest of us." Was he pushing too much? "Tell me I'm wrong."

The corners of Mikhail's soft mouth ticked. "You're wrong."

Severn beamed. "Liar."

Mikhail smiled, and Severn dug his heels in to keep from grabbing his wonderful face and kissing the fledgling smile right off his lips. It was a good thing his hands were already rammed into his pockets. This was progress. Finally. No more lies, and Mikhail was listening to his words, even knowing he was demon inside. This was... monumental. "We should go to Haven and find the book."

"They won't allow us entry," Mikhail replied, squinting at the sky and then bringing his gaze back down to earth, to Severn. "And word would have spread of our incident at Aerie."

Severn shrugged, keeping his hands in his pockets so he didn't do something foolish like act on the desire to kiss his angel's mouth. "We're the mated pair everyone is talking about. We're *supposed* to be in Haven. Things got a little complicated, but we're ready to go produce impossible offspring, if that's indeed what Haven helps angels do. They'll take us in."

Mikhail's charming smile had grown into something almost as bright as sunlight. That smile, it was real, and priceless, and did good things to Severn's insides he thought he'd never feel again after Tower Bridge. He'd seen that smile when they'd lain tangled on his bed, seen it on a sleepy Mikhail when he woke in the morning.

"I cannot abandon Aerie." The smile crumbled.

"Aerie abandoned you, Your Grace." Mikhail's gaze darkened, and Severn wished he hadn't mentioned Haven. They could have talked some more about demons and Aerius and Seraphim, but of course, none of that changed anything. "You think anything is going to change while Remiel reigns? The war will go on. Demons and angels will die. The only thing that can change things is the truth. And that's in Haven."

"The truth?"

"Yes."

Mikhail drew in a deep breath. "If this is the truth, and demons and angels were never meant to war, do you think this—*us*—is destiny?"

"It feels like it. Can't you feel it too?" He pulled a hand from his pocket and touched his fingers to his own chest. "In here." Closing the distance between them with a single step, he carefully touched Mikhail's shirt, over his heart. "In there?" The touch immediately tingled with warmth and familiarity.

Mikhail's breath caught, and for a moment, it seemed

as though he'd shove Severn back again, but then his hand covered Severn's, squeezed, and let go. Severn let his hand fall, too, and there they stood, enemies, toe-to-toe, but closer than angel and demon ever had been in recent times.

"To Haven then," Mikhail said. "Let us see what your destiny has planned for us."

"To Haven."

 evern

MARY AND BARRIE were quick to offer their services in anything Mikhail could want. Severn suspected they knew exactly who his companion was but were too afraid to come right out and acknowledge him as London's guardian. Mikhail had, at least, ceased snapping at them and appeared to have settled into familiarity of having humans close. He might even grow to like it.

They offered to drive them the few hours out of London toward the southwest coastal regions, which Severn agreed to before giving Mikhail a chance to refuse. Angels did not ride in cars. The reason why became painfully evident when Mikhail folded all of his impressive self into the back seat of a Fiat.

With his wings on display, it would have been impossible. Severn joined him, distracting himself from the closeness of Mikhail's knee and hip by chatting amiably with Mary. Barrie seemed as though he was dying to ask why they weren't flying but thankfully kept the question to himself.

After a while, they fell into a soft silence, and Severn watched the world flow past the car's grubby window, his mind drifting to what it would be like to fly again. Falling from Aerie didn't count. He'd barely done more than slow their rapid descent.

He hadn't flown in years, and these new wings, what he'd felt of them, were different, and not just because they were attached to an angel body. What he really wanted to do was head out of sight somewhere and stretch his wings out, give them some experimental flaps to judge their weight and density. But to do that, he'd have to tell Mikhail, and the thought of doing so still brought about a small spike of fear at the thought of having his wings taken a second time.

Mikhail probably wouldn't do that, but... he was still Mikhail, and although he appeared to be more controlled, the sight of new demon wings could easily set him off. If he snapped, Severn wouldn't be able to stop him, and then they'd be back on that battlefield, with Mikhail blazing over him, his blade coming down, slicing wing from body —history repeating.

The delightful human couple left them near the ancient town of Bath and bid their farewells. Severn promised to check in and fix their roof if they had any more trouble, and away they went, leaving Mikhail and Severn on a grassy verge, the occasional car rushing by. "We'd best get out of sight." Angels didn't hang around roadsides, and Mikhail was too distinctive to go unnoticed for long.

Severn vaulted a fence and strode into a field. Mikhail trailed in the flattened grass behind him. This could have been the perfect moment to mention his new additions. The field was large enough, with no houses in sight. Haven was a few days' walk away. But if they flew, they'd arrive in hours. Assuming Severn could fly. He hadn't been born with these wings or this body; trying to make both work together wasn't going to be intuitive.

"I've been thinking about what we say on arrival," Mikhail said.

Severn glanced behind him and slowed to allow Mikhail to walk beside him. "The truth?" Severn ventured.

"That you're Konstantin?"

"Not *that much* truth. We're bonded, we're emotional, Haven is our only hope at redemption, yadda yadda."

Mikhail mused over that for a few strides. "That is true."

Grass heads swayed around them, so high they reached Severn's waist. He stroked his hands over them. Flying over the fields would be so much easier. Just spread his wings and take to the air... "Mikhail... there's something—"

Mikhail jolted to a halt, his face tilted skyward. "Angels."

They looked like a distant flock of birds dotting up the sky, but their formation was too tight to be birds.

"Shit." Severn checked the hedge line running around the outside of the vast field. The only nearby cover was a copse, its huddle of trees breaking the smooth line of rolling hills. "There, the trees. Go." If they had to fight, the tightly packed trees would limit the angels' movements. Severn was used to fighting without wings, most angels were not.

They waded through the grass and dove inside the cool shadows beneath the trees. Mikhail leaned back against a tree, and Severn crouched, looking out. The angels were incoming, but there was still a chance they'd fly over. "It could just be a routine patrol." If the angels had seen Severn sprout wings, or if anyone had seen him glide out of London, they'd surely be looking.

Mikhail thumped his head back against the tree trunk with his eyes closed and his hands clenched into fists. Whatever was going on inside his head, he was controlling it. For now. But if he broke cover and tried to fight his angels, or talk with them, more would come, and their chances of getting to Haven with their story intact would be slim.

The sound of wings beating the air grew louder overhead.

Mikhail opened his eyes, his gaze far away. He was going to intercept them, because he was a damned stubborn guardian angel who hadn't yet realized most of his own forces wanted him gone.

Severn moved in front of him, blocking his view of whatever he saw inside his mind.

"Don't," he said.

"This isn't right," Mikhail ground out between his teeth.

"No, it's not. But we're going to make it right." Moving closer, he watched Mikhail's gaze track his face. Some of the icy madness melted from Mikhail's eyes. His soft, mildly confused frown returned, and Severn touched some of it at the corner of his lips. "I told you once, how we might end this war." Severn swallowed and stepped closer to his guardian. Heat throbbed from the angel—his rage, no doubt. Potent enough to give rise to a hint of ether. "I said it wouldn't be tomorrow, but it would happen. Together. I still believe it."

Mikhail's fingertips brushed Severn's cheek. He leaned in, hovering close as though to kiss, and whispered, "I wish I could believe you."

The sound of angel wings faded away until just the sound of the breeze disturbed the leaves above. Severn stayed close to Mikhail, fingers resting on his face, stroking downward, marveling at his warmth and strength, all wrapped up on the body designed to guard and protect. If Mikhail told him to drop to his knees now and suck him off, he'd do it. If he told him to leave, he'd do that too. He'd do anything this angel desired, just so long as it made him smile again. But all of this was too fragile, and they were about to go to Haven, to perhaps uncover truths that could change the future. This fledgling friendship they had somehow salvaged from the wreckage of what they'd had before was still new and so terribly fragile. The slightest thing might drive them apart again. Haven wasn't going to make any of that easier.

But the truth might.

"I have something to show you." Severn withdrew, and before he could lose his nerve, he strode out into the field again. "Don't lose your shit, okay? It doesn't change anything. It's just... well... they are what they are."

Mikhail emerged from the woods, bringing the shadows with him in his dark glances.

A cloud sailed across the sun, cooling the air. Severn frowned at its timing. Fine, it was now or never. He shook his fingers out, aware of Mikhail's penetrating glare. He could do this. He just had to trust that Mikhail wouldn't lose control. They were just wings. Though, Severn wasn't sure what they looked like. Hopefully, they weren't hideous.

He breathed in, held the breath, and carefully exhaled, relaxing the illusion holding the wings out of sight.

CHAPTER 25

Mikhail

SEVERN STOOD in the long grass, biting into his bottom lip.

Mikhail had been waiting for Severn's trick, his lie, his trap to be sprung. Perhaps this was the inevitable betrayal because Severn had never looked more terrified than he did in that moment.

And then the air behind him shimmered, darkened, and peeled apart, unveiling two great, arched demon wings.

Mikhail's breath snagged in his throat.

More of Severn's illusion fell away, and more of their expanse emerged. They were clamped closed, but that didn't lessen their impact. Half as high as Severn again, they rivaled the height of Mikhail's arches. And then they slowly stretched open, hinged arches flexing. Featherless, dark, and undeniably demon.

Severn, the blue-eyed, blond-haired devil that had caught Mikhail's heart, had demon wings. He almost laughed, but the look on Severn's face made the laugh lodge in his throat too. And then Mikhail realized why Severn looked so distraught. He was terrified he'd lose his wings again, to Mikhail.

But he'd still revealed them.

Because they'd agreed there would be no more lies between them.

For Severn to reveal them to Mikhail took great bravery.

Mikhail exhaled the breath he'd been holding.

He held himself back, filtering through the urges to go to Severn, forcing himself to visually examine the wings to keep from startling him. Had he moved forward, he wasn't sure what he'd have done—touched them, definitely. Embraced him, maybe.

These wings were different from Konstantin's. More vertical, more angel-like, but without a down of feathers to soften them. Where the membranes stretched, veins pulsed in time with Severn's demon heart.

"How do they look?" Severn asked hoarsely.

"You don't know?"

"No... I... They're, er..." he cleared his throat. "They're new."

Mikhail strode forward and circled around their expanse, focusing on the map of muscle and sinew, forcing himself to look at them analytically even as his heart raced. Their shadow fell over him, and Mikhail looked up, admiring their great height. "When did they appear?" He circled around to face Severn again and watched the hybrid angel's blue-eyed gaze dart away.

"After I leaped from Aerie and caught you."

Mikhail's feet jolted to a stop. "You did what?"

He reached for the memory of that moment after Remiel had stabbed him, but there was nothing between that and waking in a field. He'd suspected Severn had performed something to save them both, but had Severn genuinely jumped from Aerie with no wings to save him? "What happened exactly?"

"He, er..." The wings retracted a little, as though Severn ached to pull them close, to protect them. "Remiel threw you over the edge, and I went after you."

He had *jumped*. "And you didn't know you had these?" He'd thrown himself from Aerie after Mikhail without any means of surviving. That seemed... incredulous. Foolhardy. Outright insane.

"No, the wings were a surprise." He looked down.

By Haven. "Why did you do that?"

"Because..." Severn rolled his lips together, carefully forming the reply, "Because you would have died alone, and I couldn't let that happen."

His heart stuttered. "But we're enemies," Mikhail whispered. "You came to Aerie ten years ago to kill me."

Severn threw his hands up and stepped back. "Yeah, well, shit happens, and I didn't kill you. I don't pretend to know much of anything anymore. Just that you need to survive."

Out of the thousands of angels who had observed Remiel stab Mikhail in the back, Severn had been the one to save him. If he'd been the enemy, he would have wanted Mikhail's death. He'd have let him fall. Instead, he'd plunged from Aerie, assuming they'd both die. And he'd done it so Mikhail wouldn't die alone.

The shock and weight of that realization left him breathless. He suddenly ached to embrace him, to pull him close and tell him he was sorry for everything. If he were the Severn he'd fallen in love with, he would have, but nothing was as simple as it had been. This could still be a trick, some ploy to reel Mikhail in again. Angels didn't have demon wings. Severn was no angel, but he wasn't demon either. They were still strangers, and Mikhail could not allow his feelings for Severn to leave him vulnerable again.

"How did you get the wings back?" he asked, voice thick with emotion. He swallowed hard to clear the clog.

"I didn't." Severn looked up. "These aren't Konstantin's wings, they're all-new. Demons can't heal missing wings. Maybe angels can, but I'm not exactly that either." Severn filled his lungs, making his wings lift. "I'm both and neither."

He sounded regretful, perhaps even a little lost, and again Mikhail found himself desperate to believe it all. Stiffly, he stepped back. "I think it's best you keep them hidden. We'll walk to Haven." He turned away and headed in the general direction of Haven. The sanctuary should come into sight soon. Haven would take them in, and maybe Haven would have a solution for all the things he still felt for Severn.

THEY WALKED in silence across farmland, and by dusk, Haven's huge glass domes glinted in the distance, painted pink by dying daylight. Another barn provided shelter from a sudden rain shower. Severn sat alone against the barn wall, and Mikhail gave him room. He should probably say something but had no idea what. Everything he wanted to say sounded foolish in his head. He'd always found Severn's company to be the easiest of all his angels. Now the silence was suffocating.

He leaned against the open door and watched the skies, thinking of how they'd kissed on a rooftop and the hours after, exploring each other, discovering and learning what Severn liked, making him grin or laugh, and writhe and clutch at the sheets. Making him bite his lip, making him desperate.

"Can you fly?" Mikhail finally asked the next morning as they walked the final few miles toward Haven.

Severn walked the footpath ahead. "I don't think so. I mostly fell from Aerie and didn't stick the landing. It was a good thing you were out cold."

"Thank you... for saving me." It sounded wooden. He hadn't meant it to but didn't know how to express the terrible weight of emotion trying to choke him.

"You're welcome, Your Grace." Severn brushed his hand over the tall grasses alongside the path.

Haven loomed ahead, its glass domes so large their peaks touched the clouds. Unusually for an angel structure, there were no angels in the skies around it.

"How do you want to play this?" Severn asked, slowing up so Mikhail could fall into step alongside.

"I'll demand entry."

"That's it?"

"What else is there?"

Severn smiled again. "We need a story. They may have

heard about the commotion at Aerie. We'll tell them the rumors of our death are clearly false, and we're submitting ourselves into their care." Severn stared ahead at the structure. "Hopefully, they'll keep us together, seeing as we're infamously mated."

"Separating mated pairs would be pointless."

"Unless that pair consists of two males. Has that ever happened before... an allyanse between angels of the same sex?"

"If it has, I've not heard of it, but I have never paid much attention to mated pairs. Once they became emotional, they were of no use to me." He shook his head in dismay. "To separate a bonded pair would be cruel."

Severn's lips ticked. "Have you met angels?"

"I know some," Mikhail replied easily. "One in particular is especially taxing. He was always the rebel."

"Oh?" Severn's tone lightened. "Is he handsome?"

Very, especially with his borrowed shirt untucked and his hair an unruly mess about his brilliantly animated face. "He thinks he is."

"Funny, too, am I right?"

"And delusional most of the time."

Severn's sudden laugh startled a bird from a nearby tree. "You do know you're describing yourself?"

"I was speaking of you, actually."

His laughter faded but stayed as warmth in his eyes. "If we weren't enemies, we'd be perfect for each other."

"We were perfect—" He cut himself off. What they'd had, Severn and him, it had been a wonderful thing, a thing of feeling. Impossible to reason with but utterly wholesome.

"Until I fucked it up." Severn frowned and looked down. "I still hope to fix it—us."

"If we're fixable," Mikhail replied quietly, unsure if Severn heard.

A whistle sounded, and a pair of angels took flight ahead, soaring toward them.

"Here we go," Severn mumbled.

Mikhail freed his wings—instinctively wanting to shield Severn within them. Instead, he let them droop, so as not to appear threatening.

"Drop any weapons!" the guards demanded.

Severn raised his hands. "We're unarmed."

"Names?" The lead guard landed in front of them, gleaming in silver armor.

"Mikhail and Severn," Mikhail replied. The guard's audible intake of breath instantly gave his knowledge of them away. "We're surrendering ourselves to Haven. We have no wish to cause trouble."

"Severn and the guardian angel Mikhail?" the guard queried, disbelievingly.

"Yes."

The second angel landed, ready to back the first up. Mikhail regarded them coolly. Frankly, he could render both helpless with little effort and didn't need an angel-blade to do it, but fighting them wasn't the point of this exercise. They'd walk willingly into Haven. Getting out again would no doubt be far harder.

"We'd heard you were both dead. Fallen from Aerie?"

Mikhail sighed and glanced at Severn, who shrugged, content to let him continue. "Clearly, we're alive. Whatever you may have heard doesn't change the fact we're here, and we're now your responsibility, so I suggest you escort us inside."

"Yes, of course, Your Grace." The guard thumped a fist to his chest, and Mikhail caught a glimpse of Severn's smirk, and together they were led toward the towering glass doors.

Mikhail

PROCESSING WAS TORTURE. It began well. Mikhail was escorted alongside Severn through several entrance chambers, where a startling array of human technology catalogued their irises, and more alarmingly, Mikhail's wings. Only one guard asked Severn to reveal his wings and was met with a, "My nickname *Severn the Wingless* isn't obvious enough for you?" If they knew he was Konstantin, they didn't show it. Perhaps the angels of Haven didn't care who an angel is, just that they're withdrawn from society.

Then began the questions. How long had the allyanse been active, had either of them experienced uncontrollable emotion, how many times had they physically *coupled*... That last one, Severn had laughed at and dryly asked if an angel counted the times he flew each day. From Severn's tone, it was clear he wasn't enjoying the scrutiny.

Mikhail considered the process necessary. Hundreds of angels surely lived in Haven, and all had to be processed so they might be cared for and managed effectively.

Their answers were recorded on more human technology, and finally, they were escorted from the processing center, through a sprawling park, to a neighborhood of large pod-like structures called habitats. They'd seen only a handful of angels throughout the experience, and only a few had been present in the park, speaking in small groups while Mikhail and Severn passed them by.

Inside the habitat was pleasant enough. A single room with a bathroom area on one side and kitchen on the other. The bed was the main focus. It reminded him of his own chamber in Aerie, but without the endless blue-sky view.

The door clunked closed, and Severn's glare cut into Mikhail. "Still think this is some angel utopia where angels fuck and pop out babes for the war? I assume they think we're capable of exactly that, hence shutting us both in here." He turned on the spot, sneering at the inoffensive room. "Try the door. It's probably locked."

Seeing Severn so thoroughly unnerved was... interesting. During all the years he'd known Severn, he'd rarely seen him so flustered. "I suspect they don't know what to do with us." Mikhail tried the door. It swung open, revealing a view of the park and the angels strolling by, enjoying the outdoor space. Nothing overtly insidious had presented itself, and they clearly weren't locked in. Really, it was all quite satisfactory.

By the time Mikhail closed the door and faced Severn again, he was rooting through cupboards, pulling out the white and gray loose-fitting clothes they'd seen others wearing. He sneered at those too and tossed them on the bed. "It's a prison."

"There's no evidence of that."

His smile was shallow and sharp. "How about the enormous glass dome and the three gates we had to pass through to get inside?"

"To protect those outside from volatile angels."

Severn pursed his lips. "I'm taking a shower." He stormed into the bathroom, and moments later, the shower hissed behind the smoked glass screen, offering a tantalizing glimpse of Severn's outline. Mikhail tore his gaze away and wandered the room, finding everything in order.

Severn soon reappeared, towel tucked around his waist, his scowl cutting deeper into his face. He ran a hand through his wet hair, gathered it behind him, and bundled it all into a loose bun, and all the while his rack of damp muscles rippled. He knew exactly how Severn tasted and how that body stretched, so very tight beneath Mikhail's lips and hands.

Mikhail folded his arms and watched Severn snatch the trousers off the bed. Clearly, the shower had done nothing to ease his restlessness.

"We can't stay long. We find the book and leave—if they let us." Severn dropped his towel, absolutely unconcerned by his nakedness in Mikhail's presence. Mikhail's breath skipped, cinching his lungs. Severn's powerful thighs had, in the past, trapped Mikhail between them. He'd slapped his own thighs against the backs of Severn's, his stiff member buried deep, so lost to pleasure the lines between them had blurred.

His body began to wake in wanting. He strode by

Severn, snatched up a fresh towel, and ventured into the hot bathroom. "We will explore Haven. At the very least, it will settle your mind."

"Very well, Your Grace," Severn said, tightly.

Mikhail showered, pinning his thoughts on how they'd find this mysterious book and away from how Severn could see him through the smoked glass and was no doubt watching him, the same as Mikhail had.

Dried off and dressed in the provided white and gray loose-fitting clothing, he emerged to find Severn peering out the habitat's small window at the parkland outside. "Gods, give me strength," he said. "I did not expect to feel like this."

"And how exactly are you feeling?" Mikhail asked.

"This place is a cage. They won't let us leave, Mikhail. Angels don't leave Haven. They tag you and bag you and keep you controlled under all that glass, like you're a specimen to be studied. You don't see that?"

"No." But Severn had always been able to see things differently. "You wanted this."

"I know... I just..."

More investigation was necessary.

"Come." Mikhail opened the door and strolled outside into the afternoon light. He shielded his eyes, fighting the glare from the domes, and scanned the beautiful grounds. Tropical flowers towered, topped with splashes of color. Fountains burbled. Pairs of angels wandered by, all dressed in the same clothing. Some nodded respectfully toward Mikhail. In all, it seemed harmless. Peaceful, in fact, considering most angels here were supposed to be bonded and emotional.

"Let's find the evidence we need and get out of here,"

Severn mumbled, glancing behind him as they walked the winding path away from the habitat.

Mikhail lifted his chin. "No harm will come to you under my protection."

Severn tripped over something on the path. Mikhail caught his arm, preventing him from falling, and met Severn's wide eyes.

Despite the pledge to protect his enemy, the words had felt right. At least with all these emotions, he was beginning to understand what *right* actually felt like. Severn let go of his arm, muttered a thanks, and straightened his clothes, then silently fell into step beside Mikhail.

They walked Haven's meandering parklands and above ground buildings, orientating themselves with the food court, administration centers, and more. There were other levels, below ground, that the general population didn't have access to. Mikhail made a mental note to try and use his guardianship to gain access, but the light was fading, the footpath lamps flickering to life, guiding them back toward the residential zone.

Mikhail had spoken little, and Severn seemed content to observe his surroundings. His eyes told of the many thoughts he'd probably share later. It was clear he didn't trust anything they'd seen, and while it all seemed perfectly acceptable on the surface, Mikhail couldn't deny his own gut feeling—a new experience for him—was warning him that something was wrong with Haven.

Severn came to a sudden stop in the path ahead. Mikhail almost plowed into him, then saw he was staring upward and followed his gaze. Above them, two angels silently danced beneath the glass dome, their light wings softly lit from below. They swooped and soared and spun in the air, their dance so perfectly synchronized that it didn't seem possible.

They were beautiful.

Severn watched them intently, the soft light illuminating the awe in his eyes. He hadn't flown in years. He clearly craved it.

Mikhail's damaged heart ached for Severn's loss, knowing he'd been the one to take his freedom. And then he'd burned his original wings as Severn had watched on. What kind of creature did such a terrible thing to the only soul he'd ever loved?

Severn glanced over. His brow creased, and he sauntered on, retreating to their habitat without waiting for Mikhail. Despite his words about redemption, did Severn despise him, as he rightfully should?

Was the damage between them too great to be salvaged? Mikhail wasn't even sure it should be saved. He could not forgive himself. So where did that leave them?

He returned to the habitat to find Severn seated on the end of the bed, hands on his knees, head bowed, illuminated by a single lamp in the corner of the room.

Mikhail hesitated as the door swung closed. Severn lifted his head, and before Mikhail's own thoughts could sabotage his desires, he crossed the floor in two strides and kissed him, enjoying the shocked silence of Severn's mouth against his.

Severn wavered, his mouth pliable, but then broke free of whatever thought was holding him back and returned the kiss with a desperate hardness that instantly ignited the spark of Mikhail's restrained passion.

Severn pushed against Mikhail, his tongue sliding in, and Mikhail pushed back, tasting the sweetness of angel and sizzling heat of demon and everything uniquely Severn —everything he'd missed for months. Gods, he wanted him, and there was no controlling it.

Mikhail's hands fit perfectly against Severn's hips. He eased his touch around, behind Severn, to the tempting curve of his back, and drew him closer still. Severn surrendered against him, all of the tension melting away. Mikhail dug his fingers into the tight rise of Severn's ass and jerked Severn against him. Severn moaned into the kiss and then broke away, slipping his wet tongue down Mikhail's neck.

It was too much, and everything, and not enough.

Severn's fingers found the hard evidence of Mikhail's need and rubbed him through his clothes. Mikhail's breath hitched with every stroke. This was all kinds of wrong. Severn was an incubus. But Mikhail's mind had shattered, leaving a single thought: he didn't care what Severn was, he needed this.

Severn's hands tore at Mikhail's shirt, tugging in his haste to find skin, and when he did, Mikhail threw his head back and relished the feel of Severn's soft lips closing around a nipple. His teeth nipped lower, and then he was on his knees, his fingers at Mikhail's trouser fly. Mikhail's cock twitched at the thought of what was to come.

"I haven't stopped thinking of this, of you." Severn had barely finished speaking before his lips closed over Mikhail's sensitive member and sucked him deep.

Mikhail sank his fingers into Severn's hair, dislodging the loose knot holding it up, spilling his golden locks free. He plunged his cock deep into the tight, heated feel of Severn's mouth, hearing and feeling Severn hum his pleasure.

Suddenly, the warm pressure of his mouth slid free,

gone, but before Mikhail could protest, Severn drew the sack between his lips and teeth and gently sucked.

Oh, by Haven. In his long life, he'd never known pleasure like this. Words abandoned him.

He dragged Severn to his feet. His swollen, glistening lips smiled, and Mikhail could think of little more he wanted to do than fuck his mouth until he came, crying Severn's name. But there was something more he'd missed —the way it had felt when Severn took control. How easy Severn made it to surrender to desire. How perfect it was to bend beneath him.

"Where do you want me, Your Grace?" Severn's eyes sparkled.

Mikhail closed his fingers around Severn's throat tight enough to make Severn's lashes flutter. He nipped at his mouth, letting his lip spring back. "In me."

His pink tongue stroked Mikhail's bottom lip.

"Now."

Mikhail loosened his grip and turned them both, guiding Severn with him until the backs of his legs bumped the bed. Severn's gaze stuttered downward to Mikhail's exposed and glistening member.

Mikhail slid his hand inside Severn's waistband and found his smooth rod, its soft tip slick enough for him to slide his palm over it. "Do you want to fuck me?"

Severn grabbed Mikhail's head and slammed his mouth into his so hard, a hint of blood tainted the kiss. He shoved Mikhail back, who fell, unresisting, to the bed. Severn's hands scorched his hips and jerked Mikhail downward. The rough demands in his gestures stuttered Mikhail's breaths and made his member ache. Severn bared his teeth in a wild grin and flipped Mikhail over, facedown on the sheets.

Mikhail's breaths came fast now. He gripped the sheets as Severn's hands tore his trousers down his thighs, exposing his ass. Fingers spread him. Probed. Mikhail clenched, and a wet finger slid in.

"Mm, so tight." Severn leaned over him, his chest against Mikhail's back, and whispered, "You want this, Your Grace?" He slid the finger in again, deeper this time, and a shudder revealed exactly how much he did want this. "You want it *hard*, Your Grace?" In, out, brushing that toe-curling spot that made Mikhail lose his thoughts.

A pulse of lust danced down his cock. It leaked against the sheets and arched his hips, seeking friction.

"You like that?" Severn removed his finger, shifted slightly, kicked Mikhail's legs apart, and then spread his ass again. A flick of warm, wet tongue against his sensitive opening tore a groan from Mikhail. The tongue flicked again, quicker, and Mikhail moaned his need. The touch was too light, too quick. He wanted heat and hardness and Severn thrusting deep, so he didn't have to think about anything anymore.

"Show me your wings," Severn ordered.

He let them spill open and fall over either side of the bed until the leading feathers fell against the floor. Facedown, exposed and vulnerable, he'd never experienced such racing desire.

Severn's hand stroked down his spine. "So fucking beautiful, Your Grace."

Severn's hard, silken cock pushed against his hole. Fingers stretched him, working him, and then that hardness eased in, friction caressing the hole, filling him up. Haven, yes... Mikhail panted, pleasure drowning him.

Severn shifted again, pulled out, and carefully drove back in, inch by inch. By Haven, it was everything, pain and pleasure a tantalizing mix, each heightening the other. Faster, Severn found his rhythm, and Mikhail gave himself to the mindless sensation.

Severn's fingers dug into Mikhail's hips, thighs slapping. Foul words spilled from Severn's luscious mouth. Then he slowed and withdrew, and Mikhail bit into the sheet to keep from whimpering like a scalded fledgling. Severn's steady, warm hand sank beneath his waist and hitched Mikhail's hips up at a different angle, giving him access to Mikhail's cock.

"I'm going to suck you off, Your Grace," the words brushed Mikhail's neck.

Mikhail moaned his need, incapable of anything else.

"Sit up for me."

Mikhail wedged his trembling knees on the bed and let himself be turned in Severn's arms. Stunning demon wings framed his impossible angel. Vast, dark, lethally beautiful wings.

He looked in Severn's brilliant, honest eyes. There were no lies there now, just open desire, and Mikhail almost sobbed.

Severn lay him down again, this time on his back, and with their gazes locked, Severn's hard length reentered, his passage impossibly slick. Severn bit into his own lip and groaned as his cock filled Mikhail to his balls. Gods, he was the torturous vision of a male, of everything Mikhail had come to realize he loved, despite the terrible price of that love.

Severn's masterful fingers stroked Mikhail's arousal erect between them, rhythmically rocking into Mikhail, and the pleasure doubled, stuttering through Mikhail, effortlessly stimulating him toward climax.

Mikhail was at his mercy, and that seemed as though that should be wrong, but in those moments, nothing had felt more right. Severn's hand brought him to the edge of the peak until he crested in that final, blinding, breathless moment. At that thought, as though he could read Mikhail's mind, Severn suddenly withdrew his cock from Mikhail's passage, replacing it with two fingers at the same time as Severn's hot mouth swallowed his painfully peaked member. Severn's fingers pounded inside Mikhail and his mouth expertly sucked, suddenly thrusting Mikhail into thoughtless ecstasy. His member pulsed and spent down Severn's throat.

Severn grinned, peering up his body, Mikhail's cock still snug between his lips.

Regret, shame, guilt—tried to unpick Mikhail's pleasure. With the help of Severn's blue-eyed gaze, he denied the emotions purchase. All but one. *Love.* His heart soared with that.

He caught Severn's arm and hauled him up, then kissed him slowly, tasting his own saltiness on Severn's tongue. He kissed deeper, more desperately, claiming his devilish angel. Mikhail palmed Severn's slick cock and pumped. Severn mumbled a hopeless plea, swearing that he couldn't last, then his back arched. Mikhail grabbed him, pulling him close, and hot and creamy seed dashed Mikhail's belly.

Breathing too hard, with Severn clutched against him, he feared what would happen when they parted. Because ending brought thoughts, and thoughts brought doubts—made him distrust all of this.

Severn pried himself from Mikhail's grip with a knowing smile and left the bed, returning moments later with a damp cloth to softly wipe Mikhail down. Again, Mikhail surrendered in silence once more, enjoying even these soft moments of aftercare. Once Severn was done, he folded Severn and his demon wings into a feathered cocoon and fell asleep with Severn in his arms.

evern

HE HADN'T INTENDED for this to happen, but when Mikhail had demanded to be fucked, he'd been helpless to resist the guardian's order. The sex hadn't begun as love, nothing as perfect as that. Mikhail still raged inside—hurt, insecure, vulnerable—but the fact he'd allowed Severn to fuck him meant everything. And then, sometime in all of the heat and lust and raw need, the rage in Mikhail's eyes had faded, replaced by a softness Severn had rarely seen in any angel, and certainly not a guardian. Maybe it had happened when Mikhail had seen the wings Severn hadn't realized he'd exposed. Whatever the reason, when they were both lying spent, with Severn tucked inside Mikhail's wings, he'd never experienced peace like it.

He wasn't as naïve as to think their problems had

miraculously been solved by sex, but things had changed, and hopefully for the better.

The morning came, and with it, the harsh light of day. Severn would have preferred to spend the next few days revisiting Mikhail's body and dozing, wrapped in black feathers, but Mikhail had left the bed and showered before sunup.

He'd spoken little, and he was quiet now, too, looming by the window. Distracted, he buttoned his loose, white, linen shirt.

Severn opened his mouth to ask if he wanted to visit the park for breakfast when Mikhail said, "We should split up today. We'll cover more of Haven that way. I'll try and access the subground levels."

The words were spoken with an angel's typically cold efficiency.

If he was going to distance himself from last night, Severn had no intention of calling him out on it. He could wait for Mikhail to unpack everything going on in his head. Gods knew they both had enough shit to work out.

He agreed to split up, told Mikhail he'd take the north and east sections of Haven's domes, and headed for the shower. Mikhail was gone when he emerged.

It was fine. The wings, the whole Konstantin betrayal, losing Aerie, getting stabbed in the back by the very people he'd spent his life protecting. All of that would be hard enough for anyone to deal with. And Mikhail still had to navigate his emotions around all of it too.

Severn just had to make himself available for whatever Mikhail needed to heal. They'd get through this. He believed it. They hadn't come this far and overcome so much to fail now.

Diffused sunlight dappled all of Haven. The enormous domes sheltered different islands, and each island dealt with a different aspect of running Haven, from residential to administrative, and it all looked so fucking perfect that it made Severn's teeth ache. Angels nodded politely as he passed them by, fountains trickled, and palms swayed in the air stirred by vast fans mounted on slim, white poles. The more Severn wandered, the more unsettling the apparent utopia became. Few angels laughed. They talked and smiled and gestured, but compared to the ruckus of a demon neighborhood, Haven felt hollow.

Maybe just the two of them coming to Haven unarmed hadn't been such a good idea. He'd hoped to play at being obedient, poke around, find the book, steal it or whatever information was in it, and leave. Now the itch between his shoulders was growing, his instincts ringing alarm bells. He was beginning to wonder if he should get Mikhail away from Haven before it swallowed them both whole.

He hadn't found the book, or any books. Looking for a library—the normal place to store books—yielded puzzled expressions from the pairs of angels he'd asked.

He returned to the large park and sat by one of the sparkling fountains. Mikhail may have had more luck. As a guardian, every angel naturally listened when he spoke. He'd find the book because he succeeded in everything he put his mind to.

Unless he hadn't come to Haven to find the book.

Severn squinted into the flowing water, following his thoughts into its depths.

What if Mikhail had only agreed to come here to have the allyanse dealt with? He had hardly argued, agreeing to

Severn's idea to find this book. A book he didn't believe existed.

What if Mikhail came here, to Haven, to surrender?

No, he wouldn't.

Severn frowned at the direction of his thoughts and glanced about the park, skimming small groups of angels, their wings touched by sunlight. So pretty, like lovebirds in a cage.

So wrong.

Severn stood and strode toward the nearest section Mikhail had agreed to search. It was all probably fine, and this unsettled itch beneath his skin was nothing more than demon instincts playing tricks on him. But just in case it wasn't, he had to find Mikhail. Now.

*M*ikhail

"YOU'RE capable of eradicating these emotions?" Mikhail asked the guardian Tien. She was seated across the table from him, straight-backed and professional.

"Indeed," she replied. She tapped a fingernail on an electronic information pad, a similar pad to the one used to consume all Severn's and Mikhail's details on arrival. Human technology. It unsettled him to see it so comfortably in the hands of a guardian. Haven appeared to have much of the same technology strewn about. The presence of it grated on his pride. Tien's presence grated, too, but he couldn't fathom why exactly. Silver hair framed a pleasant, aged face. She radiated power, the kind of ancient power Mikhail had always strived to evolve into.

Gold glittered in Tien's irises, making them entrancing. He'd not heard of a guardian with her name, but when he'd asked to be brought to an official, he'd found himself escorted inside one of the administration buildings, to her.

"But first, we must ascertain exactly the emotions we're dealing with." She leaned forward and rested both forearms on the tabletop, clasping her hands together pensively.

"Anger," he replied.

"Yes, we've heard about your outbursts. Go on."

He pulled away from her intense gaze. This was harder than he'd expected. He'd only spoken of his feelings to Saphia, and only then because he'd had no choice. Admitting his failures to another guardian brought with it its own landslide of emotion. Guilt, shame, and of course, more anger, because part of him believed he shouldn't feel shame or guilt for loving Severn. That love, for all its faults, was the only true thing in his world right now. Everything else was a disaster. But last night, being with Severn—even knowing what he truly was—that had felt so right.

"Love?" Tien softly prompted after he'd been silent for too long.

"How do I know what is love and what is infatuation or obsession or something else?" he asked, hearing the hardness in his tone and not knowing how to soften it.

"You tell me, Mikhail. How do you know?"

The last few days with Severn, walking across fields, being in the moment without the war, without angels and demons, they might have been the most peaceful few days of his life. He could not deny how Severn made his heart and soul swell. He could not deny he felt strongly for the angel-demon, but that was why he'd agreed to come here. To finally have himself *corrected*.

"Love?" He tested the weight of the word on his tongue. "Love was watching him die on the battlefield," he said, "and not accepting that as his end. Love was sacrificing anything to bring him back, including part of my myself." Yes, he loved Severn, even with the ugly truths between them. Love had crept up on him long ago. He'd loved him from afar for years, not understanding why he was so afraid that Severn may one day not return from battle. Or mistaking the skitter of breathlessness in his chest for a sickness whenever Severn used to carelessly throw a smile his way.

"The allyanse." Tien's irises shrank behind expanding pupils, and Mikhail had the distinct impression he was being studied. "Tell me about that."

"I'm sure you know how it works."

"I do, but of course, I've never experienced it, nor have I heard of a guardian experiencing it. I'd like to hear it in your words."

"When he died..." Mikhail's voice cracked. He coughed lightly to clear it. "It was as though all of the light in the world had been extinguished." That terrible moment still woke him at night, clutching for Severn as though he could physically snatch him from the hands of death. "I've devoted my life to Aerie and my angels, but when Severn fell, I would have sacrificed it all to save him." Haven, it was the truth. And it was terrifying. "I took his broken body into my arms." The slippery blood, he remembered the metallic smell of it. "I pulled him close. And I told him he could not die, that I would not permit it, and that I... I loved him. I told him then, and whatever power is bestowed upon us as guardians, I gave it to him. More than I should have, perhaps."

"In hindsight," Tien agreed.

"Yes."

Tien looked away as though disgusted by his behavior, and the wild sense of anger was back, lashing through him, demanding to be set free. She thought him weak, thought him distracted and broken by emotion because she didn't know what it felt like to love, and as horrible as it had been, there had been moments of light and laughter and warmth. Moments Mikhail wished had never happened because it made what was about to happen all the more painful.

"And you still love him?" she asked, swiping her fingers across her information pad.

Last night, with Severn pulled close, he'd wished they hadn't come to Haven, he'd wished they'd carried on walking, right to the ends of the earth if necessary. He'd wished he were not a guardian, that the war didn't need to be fought, and that the angels did not rely on him for a victory over an enemy he was no longer sure he hated.

"Mikhail?" Tien looked up. "You still love him, after everything you know? You love a demon?"

Love a demon? He supposed he did. "Yes."

"And you want us to remove that feeling so that you might become Aerie's guardian again?"

Mikhail stared her in the eye. "Yes." His heart fluttered, like a butterfly with just days to live. "But... give me another day?"

Tien frowned. "Why?"

"I want to..." He looked down at his hands on the table, hands that had burned Severn's wings. "...to say goodbye."

"All right. We'll collect you tomorrow evening for the procedure."

"What will happen to Severn?"

"We have facilities for jilted lovers like him. He'll be cared for."

They surely knew who he really was. Konstantin. "Even knowing his origins?"

"You don't need to worry." Tien stood and tucked the information pad under her arm. "Haven is the best place for you both. It always was. You're doing the right thing."

She escorted him back through the administration building to the marble steps. "I'm looking forward to welcoming you back into the fold, Mikhail. A guardian such as yourself has a bright future ahead of him."

He smiled at her words, wishing he could find some warmth in them. She was turning back toward the doors when a thought occurred to him.

"Tien... A library? Is there one here?"

"A library?" she asked, eyes narrowing. "Whatever do you want with a library?"

"Books, naturally?"

She huffed. "No, there's no library. All of our written works were transcribed into data years ago. Only administrators have access. If there's some information you seek, I'm sure I can find it for you."

"Thank you." But how could he go about asking after Aerius and Seraphim without raising suspicion? He dipped his chin, bidding her a silent and respectful farewell, and watched her disappear inside the building.

Bright morning light warmed him through, amplified by Haven's domes, but guilt twisted, eel-like inside Mikhail's chest. This did not feel right, but his emotions would always get in the way of the necessary. As a guardian, he had no room in his life for such things. He'd been distracted, he'd killed angels and people, he'd brought devastation upon Tower Bridge, and that power was growing, not receding. He had to do this. He had to stop himself, just as Severn had said. Severn would understand. Maybe not initially, but eventually, he'd see reason.

In a day, these wretched emotions would be gone.

In a day, his love would be gone too.

He had twenty-four hours left to love Severn.

As though summoning him by thought alone, Severn hastily jogged down one of the interconnecting paths toward him. He seemed flustered, his hair loose and face hot.

"Mikhail, I... Are you all right?" Severn asked, out of breath.

"Fine." He descended the remaining steps and captured Severn's hands in his. "It's a beautiful day. Spend it with me?"

Uncertainty pinched Severn's brow. "What about the book?"

Mikhail drew Severn close and peered down into his uncertain eyes. "There's no library. All information is electronic. I've spoken with a guardian. She'll help me find what we need, but I can't press her too quickly, or she'll grow suspicious."

"All right..." he agreed warily. But then Mikhail bowed his head, and Severn immediately lifted his, the promise of a kiss suddenly between them. Gods, Mikhail loved the way Severn responded to his closeness. He wanted to see his wings again, to feel their heat, but of course, Severn could not reveal them here.

"Mikhail, are you sure you're all right?"

Ah, his face was revealing too much. Severn had always watched him closely.

He freed Severn's hands and stepped back. "Are you hungry?"

"I... Yes?"

"Then let's eat." He started forward, taking the path that would eventually lead them to the food court. Severn followed. Mikhail couldn't spoil these last few hours by rousing Severn's suspicions. It had to be the perfect good-bye. There would not be another chance to get it right.

evern

MIKHAIL WAS NOT HIMSELF. Maybe it was Haven because the more time they spent in the damn place, the creepier it became, and now Mikhail was acting... nice. He'd never been nice. Powerful, stubborn, commanding, but not nice.

They'd taken a table at Haven's only eatery and ordered a lavish dinner. Haven's nightlights illuminated the gardens around them. Angels occasionally glanced their way. At least their table was set aside, keeping their conversation private.

The meal of fresh fish and an exotic salad had to be one of the finest things Severn had ever eaten, although he could have devoured three more plates.

"Tell me about your family," Mikhail asked, and Severn almost choked on his mouthful.

He spluttered and gulped water. "I..." No one nearby

was paying them any attention, but even so. Was Mikhail really asking him about demons? "My *real* family?"

"Well, yes." Mikhail raised an eyebrow. "Angels don't have families."

Pushing his plate aside, he picked up the glass of water again and leaned in. "All right. So... I was raised in Red Manor. Do you know what a manor is?"

"A territory," Mikhail replied with confidence. He set his own half-eaten dinner aside and leaned an elbow on the table, casually scanning the small crowd while glancing back at Severn.

"Yes, but it's more than land. A manor is a family. Each family can trace its roots back to the first er... demons," he whispered the last word. "Red Manor was one of the oldest, believed to be linked to Aerius." The name simmered in the silence between them.

Mikhail's gaze drifted back to Severn and stayed. "You were their lord."

"By default more than anything. Most of Red Manor was killed..." Severn glanced down. "They—we consist mostly of concubi, so..."

"So I killed them."

"Yes."

Mikhail swallowed, but his gaze stayed, brows pinching.

"It's war," Severn added, feeling the need to explain how he did not blame Mikhail for performing his duties.

"Is there... love in the manors?" the angel carefully asked.

"Yes. We protect our own first. The Manor is every-thing. We love our siblings, our sires—parents. Though mine are long dead."

"I see." His cheek fluttered. "We don't have that sense of family among angels."

"No." Severn sipped his water. The loneliness of being an angel had been one of the hardest aspects of becoming one of them. It had never felt right.

He felt his mood souring and steered his mind toward happier times. "As a pup, I had a brother or sister around every corner." He fondly remembered the games of chase through abandoned streets, bounding off the burned-out shells of buildings and diving through gaping windows.

"Djall is all that remained of my siblings." He glanced up, checking for Mikhail's response to the name, expecting a flinch or a snarl, but Mikhail merely nodded and stroked his fingers down his glass, gathering droplets of condensation.

Severn wanted to tell him everything and anything. He hadn't yet flipped the table or vowed to kill all demons. The old Mikhail would not have listened to a demon about their home, their life. This felt like monumental progress, but also a fragile one, as though this change came with a cost Severn didn't fully understand.

Mikhail seemed to notice the quiet, and with a soft smile, he began to speak of his time as a fledgling, and of how he had *"grown into his wings,"* meaning he'd been a small youth. The thought of a young Mikhail, all feathers and fire, made Severn's heart swell.

It was late by the time they returned to the habitat. Mikhail went inside first, but Severn hung back, turning to face the open park. The grounds glowed, lit by footpath lights, like strings of fairy lights leading into the dark.

He thrust his hands into his pockets.

Maybe he was overthinking this place.

Maybe it was just a sanctuary.

Maybe his skin crawled at the sight of the domes because he wasn't an angel inside.

He looked up. The domes weren't as obvious in the night. Stars were still visible, maybe even brighter somehow, as though the glass amplified their twinkle. He caught sight of shadowy wings and spotted the pair of sky-dancing angels again. Perhaps not the same pair as he'd seen in daylight, but it didn't matter. Their aerial display was a silent display of agility and stamina, and it made Severn's wings ache with the need to spread them.

A soft, soulful music began to play from inside the habitat behind him. Severn frowned. Surely Mikhail hadn't deliberately put some music on? He pushed open the door. The single lamp in the corner barely illuminated the room, but the shadows it painted across Mikhail were the soft kind. Mikhail approached and wordlessly handed him a glass of... wine?

As Mikhail turned away, Severn sniffed it, checking for poison. "All right, what's going on with you?" He tasted the wine, finding it strong and sweet and exactly what he needed to settle the strange sense of being unbalanced by this new Mikhail.

"Nothing is *going on*. I'm trying to make things right between us."

Severn let the front door swing closed and sauntered across the room to place his wine on the small kitchen countertop. "You being *nice* is unnerving."

He'd meant the words to be a joke, but when Mikhail looked up, his gaze was briefly full of hurt, and Severn's grin fell away. Severn leaned against the counter because if he didn't use it to hold him up, he'd pull Mikhail into his arms and kiss that sadness from his lips.

The music played on, soft and soothing in the background, coming from concealed speakers somewhere. Human music, Severn guessed, although he couldn't be sure. Humans were full of creativity like this. It was kind on the ear and warm in the soul. He liked it.

On a whim, he took Mikhail's glass from his hand, placed it beside his, and took Mikhail's hand in his, then led him to the middle of the room. The fact he allowed himself to be led along tugged on Severn's heart. He placed Mikhail's hand on his hip and the other on his shoulder, and then mirrored the gesture, and began to sway in time to the music.

"What are we doing?" Mikhail asked softly, his breath tickling Severn's forehead.

"Dancing." Severn winced at the roughness of his voice. "We can't in the sky, so this will have to be enough." It started out awkwardly, but Mikhail's fingers tightened at Severn's words, and he pulled Severn close. His body, his strength, Severn wanted to wrap himself up in it all. He leaned close, chest-to-chest, and fell into a rhythmic sway.

This.

This moment was everything.

No lies, no battle, no spilled blood. Just him and Mikhail, in each other's arms.

Mikhail's hand roamed from Severn's shoulder, down to mirror the other at Severn's waist, and Mikhail's breaths tickled his ear. The warm, tingling sensation simmered where they touched, and Severn smiled into Mikhail's shoulder. They'd fought and fucked, but never just stood together in a single moment.

"I'm afraid of love," Mikhail whispered. "Of us."

Severn tilted his head back and peered into Mikhail's dark eyes. A guardian's love was a powerful thing. Severn had abused it before, and he might never forgive himself for that. "That's how you know it's real." The angel's gaze burned with a new fervor. Severn rested his head against his shoulder again, savoring the moment while he could, because it wouldn't last. This world wouldn't allow a demon and an angel to love, not without divine intervention.

Mikhail shifted his hips, probably adjusting for the impressive erection pressing into Severn's hip. Severn smiled, breathing in the smell of sunshine and Mikhail. His big, naïve angel.

"I have no control over my member," Mikhail grumbled. "It used to do as I commanded, now it does as it pleases."

Severn barked a free and sudden laugh. Only Mikhail would refer to his own cock with disdain. He rose onto the tips of his toes and gently molded his fingers around the trickster in question in Mikhail's loose trousers, instantly making Mikhail still. "I'm glad," he said against Mikhail's lips. "Because I'm very fond of its free will."

"Hm." Mikhail turned his head a little and brushed his cheek alongside Severn's. His warm mouth suckled at Severn's neck, and he began to sway with the music again. Severn let his head fall back, relishing the feel of Mikhail's lips gliding over his skin. He kept his hand where it was, absorbing each pulse from Mikhail's betraying member. Gods, he was so very precious.

"Do you think Seraphim ever danced with Aerius?" Mikhail asked, so softly Severn almost didn't hear.

What a thought... the Rayvern King and the god Seraphim, dancing in the skies. "It would have been wonderful." Demons would have loved it, once they got over the angels-are-assholes hang-up. Angels would have despised it.

"I would dance with you." Mikhail's words brushed Severn's collarbone, pouring pleasurable shivers down his spine.

"Knowing who I really am?" Severn whispered back, the thought so fragile it might shatter if spoken any louder.

"Knowing who you really are."

A jagged, painful knot tightened Severn's throat. Gods, Mikhail was right, love was fucking terrifying. He had no idea where all this brutal honesty was coming from or why now, but he needed to hear it, if only to know Mikhail's feelings cut as deeply as his own.

Severn savagely gripped Mikhail's face, holding him back. His eyes widened, briefly alarmed. Severn wanted to kiss him, to devour him, to cherish him, to protect him from the war that would surely soon consume them both. His terrible angel. His mouth twisted around words that wouldn't come. He didn't know how to voice everything in his head, and so he pulled him down and kissed him with everything he had, hoping that Mikhail would feel all the things he couldn't seem to speak.

Mikhail's arm looped around his back and hauled him so close Severn felt the shudder run through him. His tongue thrust in, and Severn tore himself free with a gasp, mindless with lust. Gods, yes, this. He needed this, needed Mikhail to fill his world. Mikhail marched him backward. Severn's ass hit the kitchen countertop. Black feathered wings suddenly burst open, crowding Mikhail, and Severn fought his laugh all over again.

"No control," Mikhail mumbled against his neck, and Severn laughed into Mikhail's chest. He twisted his fingers in Mikhail's shirt, tore the thin fabric open, and drew one of Mikhail's nipples between his teeth, loosing a growl from his world-ending angel.

Thick fingers gripped Severn's chin, holding his head aside as Mikhail nipped at Severn's neck.

A glass shattered on the floor, carelessly knocked aside, either by Mikhail or Severn, Severn couldn't tell and didn't care. Just when he believed he couldn't desire Mikhail more, the guardian proved him wrong. Mikhail's grip found his hips again, but this time, gripped and lifted, dumping Severn firmly on the countertop. Severn parted his legs, inviting Mikhail between them, which he quickly took advantage of. And now they were eye-to-eye. Severn pressed a hand to the side of Mikhail's face, instantly freezing him. He brushed a thumb lightly over his angel's lashes. So soft. Like his feathers.

Mikhail blinked quickly, then took Severn's hand from his cheek and placed a kiss on the backs of his fingers, gaze flicking up in question. Severn didn't know the answer, unless it was *yes, gods yes*. Mikhail turned Severn's hand over and placed a kiss on his wrist, where the blood pulsed beneath thin skin. Need had Severn's hard cock twitching inside his loose pants.

Ether swirled, too, but Severn ignored it, reaching instead for the feel of Mikhail solid and real beneath his hands. He'd been so long starved of touch that to have it now with Mikhail was a blissful treat.

Mikhail's mouth owned his once more. Lips soft and

hot. Fingers brushed Severn's cock, stealing his breath. Or maybe the kiss did that? He didn't know, couldn't keep it all straight in his head. His trousers loosened from his waist, and those warm, strong fingers encircled Severn's cock. Mikhail's tongue teased Severn's as his hand stroked him. Severn heard himself asking for more, heard himself say Mikhail's name, but it was all wrapped up in a blur of ecstasy.

Then Mikhail's hand vanished.

Severn fluttered his eyes open and looked down.

Mikhail bowed forward, hands spread either side of Severn's thighs on the countertop. His dark eyes looked up as his mouth took Severn's jutting cock, and a dart of exquisite lust tore a gasp from Severn's lips. He plunged his hands into Mikhail's hair, knotting the perfect locks around his fingers, and Mikhail's wicked tongue rode Severn's hard length. Soft, warm, wet, and tight. Gods, this had to be a sin because it felt too good to be right.

Severn's lashes had fallen closed, but the sweet chase of climax was approaching, and he needed to see.

Mikhail.

Between Severn's knees. Wings spread. Gaze lifted, mouth sucking him off.

And all at once, it was too much.

Severn gripped the counter, pleasure snapped down his back, his eyes rolled, his wings snapped from their illusion, and he came so fucking hard he couldn't keep from crying out. Pulses wrung his seed from his cock, and Mikhail took it all, the angel's dark eyes alight with forbidden desire.

Nothing—*nobody* was like Mikhail.

And Severn knew, in that moment, he'd never touch

another for pleasure. It had to be Mikhail. Always and forever.

He grabbed the angel by the hair and yanked him into a kiss that tasted of saltiness and sunshine. Mikhail moaned into his mouth.

"The bed," Severn growled. What he wanted to do next, he couldn't from the countertop. He gently shoved Mikhail on the chest, and the angel went, his lopsided smile and erect cock tenting his loose trousers a beautiful and mouthwatering sight to behold.

He hopped off the counter, kicked his trousers off, and quickly searched in the drawers for oil, finding a bottle of extra virgin olive oil. Smirking at the irony, he carried the bottle to Mikhail at the bed, who arched an inquiring eyebrow, then shoved him back.

Loose-limbed, Mikhail fell, pillowing himself on his wings. "Lubricant? We've not needed it before?"

A few splashes of oil in his palms and Severn knelt astride Mikhail's thighs. "We've never needed it because I'm a concubi incubus and I..." He trailed off, wondering how much to explain and how much was too much. Concubi all self-lubricated but a lesson in a concubi's lesser-known traits might ruin the mood. "Lubricant isn't a problem when I enter you, but for this, we'll need some help." Keeping himself raised over Mikhail, he fingered the oil around his own tight hole, taking a moment to enjoy the thrill of Mikhail watching, and then freed and stroked over Mikhail's disobedient cock. Mikhail's hips jumped, cock jutting.

"Eager, *Your Grace?*" Severn purred, fingers running down the veined shaft.

Mikhail's throat moved. Was his mouth dry? Oh, how his eyes burned with anxious anticipation.

Severn shifted forward slightly, riding Mikhail's cock up the valley of his ass a few times, teasing him with penetration until Mikhail bared his teeth in wordless demand. Severn smirked and lowered himself over Mikhail's oiled rod, and gods, its hard length immediately stretched him, filling and sliding deeper until Severn fully seated himself.

Mikhail lay back, chest heaving, hair fanned about him, spilling into the inky blackness of his wings. His fingers dug into Severn's knees, clutching hold as Severn rocked a steady rhythm. He had him, his terrible angel, pinned and at the mercy of the pleasure Severn was more than willing to give. Mikhail liked to surrender, to be fucked, and the thrill of it made Severn breathless and hard all over again. He rode him slowly, watching his face tense, his eyes narrow and blow wide again as the tingling need to spill his load crept ever closer. Severn scrutinized the way Mikhail's mouth tightened, then fell open in a gasp. His back arched, and there... Severn propped himself on his knees as Mikhail's cock spilled its hot seed inside him. Then slowly, so slowly, he shifted his hips, wringing the last, shuddering drops from Mikhail.

"Fuck," Mikhail gasped.

Severn chuckled dirtily and fell forward, fencing Mikhail between braced arms. His golden hair curtained them off from the world so he saw only Mikhail's, proud, beautiful face and his big eyes dilated with pleasure. Severn bit at Mikhail's lip and let it spring back. Mikhail's hand stroked over Severn's wing, summoning a very demon-sounding growl from Severn.

"You burn as brightly as one of those stars you pulled

from the sky." Severn teased his mouth, nudging his smile bigger.

Mikhail's lips brushed his but didn't seal the kiss. "I'd pull them all down for you."

"Would you really?" Severn clenched around Mikhail's cock, summoning a hiss from his angel.

"Yes." A flicker of something like concern, or maybe even fear, crossed his face, but then Mikhail grabbed him by the back of the neck and pulled him into so savage a kiss that the flicker of fear Severn thought he'd seen quickly vanished from his thoughts.

CHAPTER 30

M ikhail

DAWNLIGHT CREPT through the glass domes above, but lamps still lit the way ahead, leading Mikhail toward the administration building.

He couldn't surrender his love. As messy and uncontrollable as his emotions were, and as much as he needed them gone so he could reclaim his rightful place in Aerie, he couldn't let them go because he couldn't stand the thought of abandoning Severn.

Yes, it was love telling him this. And without love, he wouldn't feel anything again, but during the last day—the last few days, really— he'd learned a great deal about himself. He didn't want to be the cold, hollow guardian from his past. He did not want to be empty again, and Severn filled him up, made him bright, and warmed him down to his very soul. Sometime in the night, with Severn folded into his arms, the idea of giving it all up had filled him with icy horror.

In saying goodbye for a day, he'd allowed himself to finally love, and by Haven, loving Severn was glorious. It was wanting to spend every minute with him, wanting to watch him watching the dancing angels and see the beauty through Severn's awe-filled eyes. It was dancing together, bodies close, and it was the feel of Severn clutching him, of crying his name, the taste of him on Mikhail's lips.

No, he could not give that up. Not even for Aerie.

He'd fought to keep Severn alive. He'd shared half himself with him. And while they'd had their vast differences, it didn't matter who Severn was inside, Mikhail loved all of him. Always had. He'd done terrible things. Both of them had. But Mikhail was beginning to understand how love forgave the unforgivable.

He could not betray Severn or the allyanse or himself. If it cost him Aerie and his guardianship, so be it.

He strode up the steps. It was still early. He'd left Severn sleeping. He'd tell Tien he'd changed his mind, and they'd have to manage the allyanse instead of destroying it. And if they refused, then Mikhail would take Severn, and they'd leave. Book and the past be damned. They'd leave and go back to the cottage a while. After that, Severn would know where to go.

"Ah, Mikhail." Tien smiled from behind the reception desk. "You're early. Follow me, we'll talk somewhere more private."

She led him down the same corridors, turned into a stairwell, and descended, where cold lights were the only illumination.

Tien opened a door to a windowless room and stepped

aside to allow Mikhail entry. He stopped at the empty table but didn't sit. "I've changed my mind."

Tien circled around him to take her position behind the desk. She placed her information pad on the table and took her seat. "Please, sit. Let's discuss this."

He regarded the chair, and something in his chest flickered inside, briefly shortening his breath. It couldn't be fear because there was nothing here to be afraid of. He didn't need to loom over her like some emotional beast. Mikhail obligingly sat as she settled in the chair across the desk.

"So," she sighed, "you've convinced yourself you love the demon." Her mouth twisted around the word *love*, her distaste clear.

Her tone grated, but it would. She was a guardian. She'd take some convincing, but she'd listen to him. "It's more complicated than that."

"I don't think that it is." She opened her pad and turned it to face Mikhail.

On-screen, Mikhail recognized a still image of his own wings spread wide, and Severn, his demon wings flung apart, his back arched, as he fucked Mikhail into the habitat's bed.

Icy shock stole his breath.

The image was frozen still, but he heard the memories of Severn's moans. The words they'd shared, bodies combined as one. It was beautiful. And they'd been observed the whole time? Tien had witnessed *everything*?

"How does seeing that image make you feel?" Tien asked.

She wanted him to be disgusted at himself, and not so long ago, he would have been, but Severn's face was caught in a precise moment of rapture. His powerful body gleamed. Tight and hard curves were a vision of temptation, and his wings—magnificent. It was not the image that disgusted Mikhail. No. The angel opposite him did that. "You watched us?"

"We observed your coupling both during this time and last night." She placed the pad down. "Of course, we suspected something along those lines might occur. He is clearly demon of concubi origin, and you—a guardian of Aerie—prostrated yourself before him. He feeds from sex. With this *act*, you're making the enemy stronger." She leaned back, her case rested. "It is not uncommon for the allyanse to go awry. Our procedure will vanquish all of these faults and return you to your original flawless being. You have done the right thing by coming to me. You can still be salvaged, Mikhail."

The sound of the door lock flicking closed punctuated her words.

Severn's suspicions were correct. This was not a place of consent, but he had to be certain. "And if I refuse?"

Tien's smile was as thin as ice. "There are no choices in Haven."

He let those words settle. Severn had been right about many, many things. Mikhail just didn't want to hear him. He didn't want to hear the great institution of Haven was a prison. He'd wanted to believe Haven was the pinnacle of angel care and control. But Haven was no voluntary center helping paired mates produce offspring. He'd seen the shallow smiles of the angels in the parks. He'd witnessed their hushed voices. And that was only what was observable, a thin veneer over the ugly. An insidious thread wove beneath Haven and its inhabitants. One of those threads sat opposite him.

"What of Severn?" he asked, warily eyeing the room in a new light. No windows. One door, now locked. A room or a cell?

Tien stood and picked up her pad. "You need not concern yourself with him any longer. He will shortly be in our custody. We will care for him."

A lie. He heard it as plain as day. They'd kill Severn. And Mikhail had brought him here, to his executioners.

Mikhail rose to his feet too. He'd come to Haven seeking an escape from the terrible emotions, but all it had done was remind him why he cared so deeply for Severn when everything about this world demanded he shouldn't. He'd had doubts. He'd feared his own mind and body were out of control, but Severn had banished those fears. He knew, with absolute certainty, that their love was right. And he would not allow anyone to take it from them.

"Unlock the door. Allow Severn and I to leave Haven." He pressed his fingers to the tabletop, pushing against the tingle of power beginning at their tips.

Tien sighed. "Your name was spoken of with the highest regards. To see how far you have fallen is truly disappointing."

"Is there a book?" he asked.

"A book?"

"Demons and angels, together. Love, not war."

Tien came out from behind the desk. "Ah, Aerius's book. It was destroyed long ago." She dared pity him with a look. "If it's evidence you seek, you need only look in a mirror. You are the evidence of Seraphim and Aerius's crime, as were the thousands of demons who visited the correctional facilities, fearing they loved angels, or those angels who came to Haven before you, so distraught by their own emotions they could no longer function. Angels and demons were made to love. It is our greatest weakness. Unfortunately, love is the only emotion to have a habit of unraveling all the hard work undertaken here at Haven."

Then it was true. Remiel and now Tien confirmed it. The old guardians knew demons were made to love; they knew war was not inevitable and were covering it up—had been covering it up ever since the ancient guardians had tried to murder Aerius to keep Seraphim theirs. Guardians, like Tien, continued to hide the truth today. He hadn't known. None of the angels knew. All this time, all the dead left on the killing fields... Demons and angels, needlessly warring.

It was a travesty.

"What happens to those who love?" he asked quietly.

She sighed. "Are you really that naïve that you don't already know? Some can be saved. The others, well, love is destructive. They're euthanized in the kindest way." She faced him. "Fortunately, we're certain you can be saved. Angels are shaped from birth to fledgling, as were you. It would be a terrible blow to lose an angel of your caliber to preventable emotions." She touched his shoulder, delivering an instant prick of pain.

He flinched away and touched his shoulder. *Euthanasia?!* Guardians *killing* their own kind out of fear of love? A heavy, numbing throb consumed his arm and chest. He hissed and stumbled back from Tien. Whatever drug she'd administered began to ravage his veins and thump through his body. The room spun, the walls tilted.

No... he had to return to Severn.

"Soon, this will all be over, and you will once again be the guardian you were designed to be, for your own good and the good of angelkind."

He stumbled against the table. Lies. His whole world, his entire life, had all been one terrible lie. And not just his life. Every angel who had left Haven had been manipulated by the guardians. Guardians should protect the truth, not deny it.

Heat raced through his veins, fighting the poison Tien had administered. Rage. He'd feared it, shied from it, hated it, but right now, he embraced it. This guardian, reaching for him now, to guide him away and make him forget everything he was supposed to be—she had failed angelkind. She'd failed Seraphim, who in his last moments had protected the demon Aerius. For love.

Mikhail knocked the guardian's hand aside, thrust a hand beneath her chin, and drove her against the wall. The terrible weight of too many wings bore down on his shoulders. Her wide, fear-filled eyes reflected his six wings.

And it felt right.

He leaned into the guardian's throat, ignoring how her fingers tried to pry his off. "This is not the way of angels."

Tien dared smile. "This has always been our way."

CHAPTER 31

evern

THE SOUND of the door latch rattling roused him. Mikhail must have left early and returned. Gods, what time was it? Harsh light spilled into the habitat. Severn raised a hand to shield his eyes. Two figures filled the doorway.

Angels.

His heart lodged in his throat.

"Get dressed, *demon*." One of the guards tore the sheet from the bed, exposing Severn's nakedness, complete with demon wings he hadn't been awake enough to hide. The angels loomed closer, angelblades glinting in their hands. He scrambled for the opposite side of the bed and tumbled off the edge—damned wings flapping uselessly.

Hands gripped his arm and hauled him to his feet. The guard roughly threw him back against the bed and sneered. "Disgusting."

He raised his hands. "All right... okay..." Unarmed, naked, and outnumbered, there was little he could do but keep them from killing him by staying low and compliant.

"Cover yourself," the other guard barked, bigger than the one crowding Severn, with wild dark chestnut hair and hard eyes. Severn would get no sympathy from them.

Where was Mikhail?

The dark-haired guard threw Severn's clothes at him. Severn gathered them up and hastily stepped into the trousers. The smaller angel—still a match for Severn—lifted his angelblade, making sure Severn saw it hovering inches from his face.

Why wasn't Mikhail here? He must have left... Had these guards waited for him to leave? Had Mikhail known they'd be here...?

Had Mikhail deliberately left Severn alone?

No, he was too honest for that. Their love was too true for fresh betrayal...

"Hurry!"

Severn folded his wings away and illusioned them from sight, then tossed on the shirt, focusing on the collar laces as his thoughts raced.

Mikhail's behavior yesterday had been... odd. He'd been kind, and nice, and things that Mikhail wasn't known for. Severn had doubted it, but then relished it, and now... Now, he wondered if Mikhail had been that way because he'd known yesterday would be their last day together. Had *he* sent the guards?

"Where's Mikhail?"

The dark angel chuckled. "Right now? Having his emotions ripped from him."

Severn's fingers stilled at the shirt laces.

The lighter angel snickered. "Oh, he went sniveling to Tien, begging to be free of you. Didn't you know, *demon*?"

No... Mikhail wouldn't.

Severn straightened, and the light angel stepped back, his blade raised, tip dangerously close to Severn's chin.

But angels didn't lie.

And yesterday had been so good, so special. Severn had known then that he didn't deserve it, and now he knew why. Mikhail *had* abandoned him. The realization almost choked him. But he couldn't listen to these guards. They had their own motives. He had to hear the truth from Mikhail.

Severn batted the blade aside. "Get that blade out of my face and take me to Mikhail." The light angel lunged. Severn ducked his blade's slash, but the dark angel slammed into him, captured his arms, and swung Severn around, kicking out the backs of Severn's knees, causing them to strike the floor. He pulled on the angel's grip, trying to free his arms, but the bastard held on.

"The Mikhail you knew is gone," Dark hissed against his cheek.

Cold metal touched Severn's wrists.

No, this couldn't happen. Without Mikhail, they'd kill him. Or perhaps because of Mikhail? He moaned out the hurt. Would Mikhail betray him so? Wasn't it all Severn deserved for breaking his heart? It might even be justice. But angels did not lie. And Mikhail was righteous. But he'd changed. They both had.

And now Mikhail had surrendered his love to become the cold-hearted creature Severn feared.

Severn flung his head back. His skull smacked into Dark's face. The angel barked, and the pressure on

Severn's wrists loosened. He unleashed his wings and flapped them wildly, buying him space and time to climb to his feet and turn on the guards.

The lighter angel launched himself forward. Severn ducked and delivered an uppercut into the angel's gut, instantly winding him. He shoved him aside.

Pain tore down his left wing. Blood scented the air.

Severn whirled with a roar and tackled Dark low in the chest, slamming him into the wall. He plastered a hand over his face, pinning him still. "Cut my wings, you feathered fucker, an' I'll rip yours off."

He sensed more than saw the lighter angel dart back in. Twisting, Severn backhanded him, but not before the edge of his blade sliced through Severn's waist, zipping open a stinging wound.

Fuck these freaks—all of them—he needed to find Mikhail.

He fled the habitat and hastily illusioned his wings away again. Mikhail had said he'd spoken to an angel at the administration building. He'd go there for them to remove his emotions.

"Halt, demon!"

He glanced down the path behind him. The guards sprinted after him.

His unruly wings sprang from their illusion. "*Fuck.*" Severn turned and raised his hands. "Fellas, clearly we're not gonna get along, so if you want to die, keep coming at me. I'm happy to oblige."

Their wings flew open and launched them off the ground, then they bolted toward him.

He launched off his back foot, burst forward, and sprang at the dark one, catching hold of his right wing and dragging him to the ground in a blast of white feathers. A punch to his jaw stunned him enough for Severn to snatch the blade from his hand. He could have stabbed it into his heart, but despite what they thought, he hadn't come here to kill angels. He thrust the blade into the guard's thigh. The angel cried out, his wail echoing across the park. Gods, they'd all be on him soon.

His back prickled. He whirled, lifting his wings, and shied sideways, avoiding a blade's incoming slash by a hairsbreadth. Oh, that light bastard was fast.

"You are to come with us!" the angel announced, as though his words alone could tie Severn up.

"That's not going to happen."

Dark hobbled to his feet, clutching his bleeding thigh. He'd be healed in minutes.

Movement above caught Severn's eye. Two more angels were inbound. He couldn't fight four. And in minutes, more would descend on him. Haven wasn't short on guards. So that left running. Or flying. Which was easier said than done. He spread his wings, rolling his shoulders to balance his wings' extended weight down his back and through his shoulders. Shit, it was like he was a pup again, trying to make the leathery extensions work together instead of flapping about like sheets in the wind.

He beat them once, pushing air downward to lift him off his feet. Simple. In theory. In practice, one of his wings wasn't as strong as the other, or he was just out of practice, because the right wing provided too much lift, shifting him sideways. He staggered to his feet and ducked Dark's sudden right hook, then rebounded and punched Dark across the face. Angels rarely expected to be met with fists when their opponent wielded a blade. The guard pirouetted, and Severn landed a heavy blow on the back of his neck, dropping him facedown into the dirt.

The light-footed angel suddenly rushed him.

Severn tried his wings again, flapping them haphazardly into the air. Fingers wrapped around his ankle and yanked. He kicked out. The light angel recoiled, and his kick went wide.

Severn hit the dirt in a mass of hands and wings and feathers. He slashed wildly with the stolen blade, keeping the angel at arm's length, but then his wings snagged a bush or tree or something behind him, and the angel thrust his blade in. Sudden, breath-stealing pressure in his chest jerked Severn back. He grunted, swung wildly, and punched the bastard in the jaw, then kicked him off, but the heated throb up his left side confirmed the angel's blade had gotten through and found its target.

He couldn't afford to look. If he looked, it'd be bad.

Two more angels landed on the path, freeing their blades just like the others.

Severn clutched at his side and tugged at his damn wings, still snagged in the bush. One sprang free, but the other wing was stuck fast, surrounded by branches.

The guards grinned, their prey caught.

"Shit."

He yanked again on his stuck wing. "Four on one is hardly fair, boys." His wing twitched, finally pulling free. The shift in weight stumbled him forward. The cool, smooth kiss of a blade lay beneath his chin, freezing him rigid. One wrong move, and he'd lose his head.

Severn blinked into the guard's cold, hard eyes. They both knew what came next. Ultimately, it would end with Severn broken at their feet.

"Did you think you could infiltrate our most sacred of places and survive?" the guard at the end of the blade asked.

He wet his lips, considering a witty reply that could very well be his last words. He did not want to die here. He'd always thought he'd die in battle for demonkind. He'd die fighting for what was right, not because he'd gotten caught fucking a guardian angel in Haven.

Destiny was hilarious. Until she wasn't.

More angels appeared in the skies.

Severn bared his teeth. "Kill me then. You'll not get another chance."

He just wished Mikhail were here, so Severn could see if he'd given him up. Was their love as real as Severn had hoped, or had Mikhail turned the ruse back on Severn as punishment? It would be the demon thing to do.

The ground rumbled.

He almost missed it beneath the thump of his racing heart and the loud beat of a dozen angel wings.

A strange, thundering noise shook the air.

Angels took flight from all over Haven, scattering like a startled flock of birds. But the guard with his blade propping up Severn's chin didn't move. Severn couldn't afford to look away. This one would cut his throat.

A chill fell over his skin. Haven's startling bright light dulled, as though clouds had smothered the sun on a summer's day. Darkness covered the domes. A storm had arrived.

Severn lifted his face.

He'd have liked to have felt the rain on his wings, just one last time.

"Seraphim?" One of the guards murmured in awe, before suddenly taking to the air.

Severn held the guard's glare. He knew hundreds of angels like this one. He'd trained them, led them into battle, and taught them how to kill demons just like Severn. He'd kill Severn and wouldn't bat an eye. It was his duty, his life, his single purpose, because Haven had created him that way.

Lightning flashed—a brief golden crack in the domes.

Severn's gaze slid over the guard's shoulder to where a star appeared to shine against the darkness. A blink revealed it wasn't an out of place star, but an angel clad in shining armor, framed by six enormous black wings. Seraphim. Light rippled around the god, warping the air, warping reality itself.

His heart raced harder, his mouth fell open, and for a second, he dared not breathe.

He was magnificent.

The guard's eyes narrowed. No longer able to ignore the commotion, he stepped back, kept his blade high and aimed at Severn's throat, and then glanced into the sky, where their god hovered like a vengeful, second sun.

Lightning flashed again, suddenly striking the dome. Glass exploded. Steel moaned and crumpled as though it were no stronger than paper straws. Metal screamed, and Seraphim raised his shining blade, his judgment and power tainting the air with an acrid bite.

CHAPTER 32

Mikhail

AT TOWER BRIDGE, the power blazing through him had been chaotic and misdirected. But now, lit from inside by pure righteousness, Mikhail held its reins. It scorched his veins, set him ablaze, and made the world tremble. Somewhere, distantly, he became aware of another's touch, another's guiding hand, and that other was full of pain and horror and anguish. It had power, and now that power was Mikhail's.

The war was a lie.

The guardians were the real enemy.

The time for truth had come.

Mikhail would be its harbinger.

He had a blade in his hand, taken from the angels who had already tried to stop him and fallen in his path. Lifting the sword focused the monumental power to a single point, and through it, he commanded the ageless energy of a god long dead. He had no voice, the god, but he had a name.

Seraphim. The god who sacrificed everything for love.

Lightning snapped and danced, striking Haven's domes again and again, stabbing at the glass like superheated blades from above. Angels cried, their horror and fear palpable.

Angels converged on Mikhail, each one a guardian's puppet, each one a victim of lies. Mikhail would not kill them. Only the guardians needed to die. Tien had been the first to fall after she'd tried to poison his blood. The rest would follow.

More glass and steel rained from above. Angels scattered mid-flight. Some fled, some looked at Mikhail with murder in their eyes. None could stop him. The truth was too powerful, and it was overdue its freedom.

Angels who attacked, he swept aside. Some blades got through, striking his shining armor. It didn't matter. He was untouchable. Unbeatable. He was Seraphim.

But then, far below, he saw the angel with demon wings set upon by guards.

His enemy, no more, this demon who had opened his heart and made him see a better world, one full of feeling.

Konstantin.

A blade twanged against his chestplate. Mikhail knocked the angel aside with a roar and plunged toward the ground.

The guard had Severn pinned, and somewhere distantly, at the back of Mikhail's mind, he remembered a fear that wasn't his, the fear of seeing his love threatened. Guardians had come for Aerius too. Guardians of Seraphim's own creation had attempted to kill his Rayvern King. And Mikhail knew, with absolute certainty, that Seraphim had not meant for it to end that way.

It must not end like that again.

Mikhail landed behind the guard, grabbed his wing, and tore him from Severn, who lay sprawled on the ground, hand clutched at his side, covering a wound.

The angel wasn't a guardian, so he didn't have to die, but Mikhail lusted after his death with a passion capable of destroying worlds.

The pathetic guard scrabbled to his feet in the dirt and dared brandish his blade. "Seraphim?"

Mikhail flared his wings. Long ago, Seraphim had protected his demon against guardians. He'd prevailed, but at a terrible cost. This guard was no threat, but the past warned Mikhail of what was to come.

"The truth must be known," Mikhail said, his voice doubled up, mirrored with another's. *"Do you understand, my child?"*

The guard stumbled backward, tears spilling down his cheeks. He took to the air.

Angels dotted the broken skies above Haven. Glass and steel continued to rain in upon the crumbling institution, but it wasn't enough.

Weariness tugged on Mikhail's strength, unraveling the power and his control of it. Poison thumped at his mind, trying to pull him back to earth.

Severn lay on his back, propped on his elbows, in the dirt, his wings pinned beneath him at odd angles. Demon wings. Beautiful wings. Gods, Mikhail had been so wrong about him, about everything.

"*M-Mikhail?*" Severn stammered, eyes wide in disbelief.

Mikhail offered his hand.

Severn's warm fingers wrapped around his. Mikhail pulled him into his arms. Severn's wings folded closed, and Mikhail hugged him close as he spread his six wings and carried him into the sky.

Haven's domes collapsed around them, but Mikhail tucked his demon safe against him. Lightning cut the dark, thunder growled, steel cried, and glass shattered, and Mikhail smiled into Severn's soft golden hair, allowing himself the freedom to love without restraint or doubt or fear.

"My terrible angel," Severn whispered, his blue eyes bright in the shadow of Mikhail's wings.

"*My impossible demon.*"

He clutched Severn close and used the wings not wrapped around Severn to carry them beyond the shattered Haven, into the storm of Mikhail's making.

THE TERRIBLE POWER waned a few miles from Haven, and the drug Tien had infected him with reasserted itself, forcing Mikhail to land on a city rooftop. He wasn't sure which city they'd found, but with Severn in his arms, he didn't care. As soon as they touched down, Mikhail's armor faded and his wings shuddered, the two extra pairs retracting, leaving him gasping and spent. Tien's attempt at poisoning continued to numb his body. Hopefully, its numbing effect was temporary.

"Are you all right?" Severn reached for him.

Mikhail took his hand and plastered himself close, needing to feel the beat of Severn's heart against his own. His hot and needful mouth found Mikhail's, and Mikhail tumbled into the kiss, relishing the spark of passion he'd so long denied. The urge to fall into the pleasure of Severn's touch almost overcame him, but a city rooftop was too open. Angels and demons would be looking for them.

Severn eased off, wincing, and Mikhail noticed the blood. Instinct drove him to slip his hand beneath Severn's shirt and press his palm to the clean cut. Heat poured into the touch, making Severn gasp and lift his shirt, finding the wound sealed.

Healing him cost Mikhail the last of his power. A wave of weakness rippled through him, but then Severn's touch trailed down Mikhail's cheek and jaw, and the look on his face spoke of awe.

"There is much to be done," Mikhail said, grateful his voice was his own again. Angels still remained in Haven—their minds manipulated—and that could not be allowed to continue. The war was a lie. Thousands were dying. "I do not know how to do it all," he added, wishing he had the answers. *Any* answers.

Severn clutched Mikhail's face. "We'll do it together."

He wanted to believe it, and he did, but love did not conquer all. Aerius and Seraphim were proof of that. The power inside—Seraphim's power— had told him so. "It's true. All of it, Aerius and Seraphim. The guardians killed Seraphim for protecting Aerius. The wrongness began then, so long ago. I have to make it right."

"*We* will." Severn kissed him softly, the taste of demon

so right on Mikhail's lips. "Trust me. *Trust us.* Destiny knows."

He smelled of warmth and spice and demon, and it wasn't wrong. It was fated. Their love, it was always meant to be this way. Mikhail folded an arm around Severn and buried his face against his neck. Severn stroked his hair. He sighed, so thoroughly spent, but his soul had never felt so light. He could stay like this, in his demon's arms, forever. But it was not over, and the guardians would stop at nothing to see them separated—to see Severn killed. Mikhail tightened his hold, suddenly fearful that Seraphim and Aerius's story might repeat itself in them.

"I am sorry," Mikhail whispered against his neck, "for the horrors myself and my angels have inflicted upon you and your people. We were wrong. We've been wrong through all of it."

Severn's grip tightened. "I know, but demons are not without blame. *I* am not without blame." Severn looked him in the eyes, and by the great god, Seraphim, Severn had never looked more beautiful. "Can we begin again? Here, now, on this rooftop? Angel and demon?"

The raw desperation in his eyes made Mikhail's heart ache. "Here and now."

Severn's mouth smothered Mikhail's, and Mikhail welcomed it, relishing the kiss, effortlessly falling into it with all he had.

Severn broke free first and bumped his forehead against Mikhail's. "I love you so hard it hurts."

It was true. Love did hurt, in all ways. He was beginning to understand a lot of things now he'd given himself permission to love. But convincing two sides of an endless war to love would be far more difficult.

"They destroyed the book, Severn. We are all the proof there is." Even with the borrowed power, how could they convince the world that love was the way forward?

Severn threaded his fingers with Mikhail's and smiled his lopsided, knowing smile. "Not all the proof..."

CHAPTER 33

Severn

HE COULDN'T STOP SMILING. It was absurd. A grown demon, not a pup, and he grinned every time he laid eyes on Mikhail, or when he recalled precisely how the avenging guardian angel had saved his ass instead of trying to kill it. Or how they'd left Haven in ruins. That place had long been overdue a revolution, and it was so fucking ironic that the one thing it was built to eradicate had brought it down: Love.

He half expected Mikhail to turn around, admit it had all been a joke, and take Severn's head with his stolen blade. A demon might have, but not Mikhail. Every word, every touch, every hand in his, every tiny little smile—barely lifting the lips but real—was true. As true as their destined love.

Destiny had been right all along.

They left the rooftop in the human city of Bristol and returned to the little cottage, much to the delight of Mary and Barrie. On seeing their Haven clothing, Barrie had immediately offered Mikhail one of his tropical-themed shirts, this one patterned with pineapples. The yellow surprisingly complimented Mikhail's black hair.

No sooner was he in the shirt than Severn imagined him out of it, but Mikhail was weary, his eyes tired, so they retired to the cottage.

A red sunset blazed across the grass fields. Severn checked there was nobody in the fields and freed his wings with a sigh, spreading them wide to soak up the sun's fading light. It felt good to have them stretched out and on display. The cut to his waist stung as his body bore the wings, but Mikhail's miraculous touch had healed the worst of it.

The soft flap of feathers drew his eye, and Mikhail landed gently in the grass beside him, tucking his now-normal wings in to keep them from gathering grass seed.

Mikhail reached for the tip of Severn's right wing. "May I?"

Severn nodded, afraid his voice might crack if he spoke, and then Mikhail's hand stroked over the trailing edge and up, toward the joint. "Remarkable."

Severn's knees weakened. He *liked* the wings. More than liked, if his expression was true, which of course it was because this was Mikhail.

Color rushed to Severn's face. He winced at his sudden attack of shyness and bowed his head. He did not get shy. Or, at least, he hadn't in years. But having Mikhail admire his wings was a whole kind of personal mixed with fear because of their past, and pride because his new wings, what he'd seen of them, were stunning and they were his, and he still couldn't believe he had wings again.

Mikhail's hand stroked over the right wing, venturing more toward the joint at Severn's back. Severn lifted his head, tilted it back, and sighed softly. There was an intimacy in having another touch your wings, especially when the other was an angel as dangerous as Mikhail. A spike of fear tried to trip his thought, but he snuffed it out. This was the new them. A place where fear did not belong.

"They have angel musculature but demon skin. I..." His hand stroked some more. "I hope you know how beautiful they are."

His hand roamed the left wing now, fingertips trailing, the touch beginning to meander and tease in a way that had moved on from the practical to something more sensual, and Severn's body was waking accordingly. Mikhail circled all the way around, not easy in the long grass and given the generous expanse of the wings. He faced Severn, his expression hungry.

Heat still touched Severn's cheeks. He maybe breathed a bit fast too. And he was as hard as a fucking stair rod. But besides all that, all of this—Mikhail admiring his demon wings—was perfectly normal.

Mikhail's deep blue eyes looked down and lingered. His lips parted. His gaze flicked back up. Questioning. Delaying. Like he knew this long, quiet, pause between moments was slowly killing Severn. Severn desperately wanted to kiss him, and taste him, and fuck him, and remember what it had been like before Tower Bridge, when they'd spent nights together. But it would be better now because the secrets were all gone. Would Mikhail cry the name Konstantin as he came?

Gods, his cock twitched at the thought, and Mikhail's eyebrow arched.

"You're killing me here," Severn grumbled.

"I can see that."

But he still didn't move, and now his mouth was tilting sideways, adopting a sly smile rarely seen on Mikhail's face. Bastard. Two could play that game.

"I'm going to rip that pineapple shirt off you and lick every inch of your body... Your Grace."

Mikhail leaned to one side and narrowed his eyes. "Then why haven't you begun?"

"Because of what I am, it has to be you who begins, or..."

"Or you fear I'll think I'm being manipulated?" His voice. Had it always held such a delicious cadence?

"Yes."

Mikhail considered it as Severn squirmed some more. "What if I want you to make the first move?" He sauntered closer, and Severn's heart thumped harder, driving hot blood through his veins. "What if..." Mikhail was close now, his body and wings filling Severn's vision. "I want you to hold me against that wall, grip my wings and," he leaned in, his mouth a tease against Severn's, "fuck me so hard I'll be feeling your touch for days?"

"Sounds fucking delightful!" a familiar but sudden female voice piped up.

Mikhail sprang back, wings thrown open, snarl on his lips. But his snarl quickly died.

"But you two aren't finished, and there's much to be done, isn't there, Jasper?"

"*Caw!*"

The crone hobbled down the cottage path, a hand on

her back like it troubled her, her rayvern on her shoulder. The rayvern locked gazes with Mikhail and squawked. Mikhail stood still, wings balanced, caught between attack and surprise.

Severn let the old demon wander into the cottage and sighed. Honestly, he was not surprised to see them but had hoped Amii would give them a little time. Still, they had arrived, as he'd suspected they might, and no doubt they knew a great deal more than they'd previously let on. "Just... try not to kill Amii?" he told Mikhail and reluctantly folded his wings away to follow Amii inside the cottage, hoping Mikhail would follow.

Amii found a threadbare armchair by the cold fireplace and eased their old bones into it, making Severn roll his eyes. He hung back, taking up a spot leaning against the wall, and glanced at Mikhail as the angel joined them— wings gone, but his face was guarded again.

"Before you pass judgment," Severn said to Mikhail, "Amii used us both."

"Why is the crone here?" He didn't sound angry, more carefully curious.

"Aye!" Amii exclaimed. "Why am I here, interrupting your"—she waved a hand—"testosterone-fueled fuck-fest? Nice shirt, angel. Pineapples. Very you."

Oh gods. Severn thumped his head back against the cottage wall. This wasn't going to go well. Mikhail would lose his shit, which was totally understandable given his past experience with lying demons, but Severn would have to protect Amii because they clearly needed answers, and Mikhail would read that as Severn protecting a demon, and—

Mikhail casually poured himself into the armchair

opposite Amii's and leaned forward. "Seraphim and the Rayvern King, Aerius," he said. "You told me a story about them. Why?"

They leveled their glare at Mikhail. "Finally ready for some truths, are you? It's about bloody time." They glanced at Severn. "Angels, amiright? Pretty to look at but lacking up here." They tapped their head. "Make us some tea, darling."

Their bird squawked, hopped off their shoulder and onto a mantelpiece over the fireplace, and stared at Mikhail like it wanted to peck out his eyes.

Severn presumed the tea comment was aimed at him and would have laughed if he wasn't utterly transfixed by the scene unfolding in front of him: Mikhail sitting opposite a demon, having a conversation. Talking. Not so long ago, such a thing would have been impossible.

"What changed your mind?" Amii asked Mikhail.

"The guardians told me the truth."

"Pah... guardians. Assholes, the lot of them." Amii waved their hand, startling their rayvern into a flap. "Worst thing Seraphim ever did, makin' guardians. Uber angels with god complexes."

Mikhail glanced toward Severn, his puzzled expression almost comical. Severn could only shrug. He knew no more than Mikhail. In fact, it sounded as though Mikhail knew more than Severn. Just how many times had Amii intervened during the past few months? Severn no more liked being lied to than Mikhail did, but he sensed no ill-will from Amii.

"Self-righteous, single-minded, jealous fools."

Mikhail wisely let them rant until they fell silent and looked around the small lounge, remembering where they were and their audience. "Anyway," they sniffed, "where were we?"

"You told me about Seraphim... you said he and Aerius had a relationship. I was less than kind, but in Haven, I thought I heard him, and I... my wings and my power. It's changing."

Amii nodded and adjusted the thick layers of long skirts covering their legs. "Yes, well. You had a lot of learning to do and not a lot of time to do it. That may have partly been something to do with my intervention."

"Your what?" Severn asked.

They waved a hand at him. "Hush now, can't you see an angel and a demon are talkin'? Where's my tea and biscuits? Are there custard creams? Or some Jammie Dodgers." They licked their lips. "Gotta lick the jam right out the middle, right?" Their eyebrows waggled suggestively.

"Make your own damn tea." Severn shoved off the wall and stalked closer. "You inserted yourself into our lives. You made out you didn't know Mikhail."

"Now," they waggled a finger, "I never lied. You both made assumptions. Your assumptions ain't my fault, is they?"

"You lied by omission."

Amii pulled a face. "Ain't you the pot calling the kettle black? Are you trying to climb up on some kinda high horse, Lord Konstantin? Cos the view up there on that there high horse must be mighty grand, seeing as you're wearing a big ol' fat lie right now."

Mikhail leaned back in his chair, almost smirking, which for him was basically an outright laugh. "Amii has a point," he said.

Oh, so he was on Amii's side now? What was even happening here? "Who are you, really?" Severn asked. "You said you had many names. You're clearly not just a cambion I dragged off the street to pretend to be Konstantin—nice work, by the way."

"I was rather proud of my Konstantin." They puffed up their ample chest at Mikhail. "He was a good likeness, no?"

"Hm." Mikhail's brow pinched.

"Pfft, illusion like that is a masterpiece," Amii grumbled. "An angel wouldn't know."

"Who *are* you?" Severn asked again, and this time, Mikhail leaned forward again, invested in the answer.

"Someone who wants the truth told, like you. And now we're all on the same page. So let's get to it. Angels and demons were made to love. Seraphim loved his demon, and Aerius loved his angel, and the two sides were supposed to be at peace. Peace is... relative, when it comes to demons and angels, as you've both discovered. But Seraphim and Aerius were a sign everything could be saved. Everything was right with the world, until them bastard guardians got jealous—"

"Why did you not explain this to me before?" Mikhail asked.

"I tried. You didn't listen." They fell silent, waiting for Mikhail to argue, but of course, he couldn't. "The second their love was destroyed, and Seraphim along with it, the world went to shit. Guardians set angels upon demons, and the demons had no choice but to fight back, and that's where we've been ever since. Stuck in a never-ending battle made from lies. The guardians knew love was dangerous, so they created Haven, where they conditioned love out of every single angel. It was deemed that no angel would ever again love a demon." They sniffed and leaned back. "That's where you two come in."

Severn threw his hands wide. "What, exactly, are we supposed to do? Go to Aerie and tell all the angels to stop fighting because we're in love?" He laughed and thrust a hand into his hair, cutting off the laughter's mad ring. "Remiel stabbed Mikhail in the back and shoved him off Aerie!"

"Oh yes, I heard about that. So very dramatic for an angel. You're welcome, by the way."

"For what?" Severn snapped.

"The wings. They saved you both, yes?"

"Yes," he replied stiffly. So his wings had been Amii's work? But when had they gotten their claws into him... Ah, in Whitechapel... when they'd delivered a massive hit of ether that had knocked Severn out cold.

"And you," they nodded at Mikhail, "I hear Haven just witnessed your latest manifestation of some god-like powers, hm?"

Mikhail's eyes narrowed. "Your serum?"

"Of course, my serum. Fucking hells, if I'd left it up to you two, you'd both be dead months ago. So the words you are looking for are, *'Thank you, Amii, for saving our beautiful angel asses.'"*

"You maneuvered both of us to suit your plan," Severn said, slightly surprised Mikhail hadn't cut in to rant at them. "So where's the rest of that plan? What are we supposed to do now?"

"Well, I don't know," they threw their hands up, exasperated. "I'm not doing it all for you. Frankly, getting you this far was exhausting."

"Our love," Mikhail said pointedly. "Is it real, or is that your fabrication too?"

Amii sighed. "Oh, Seraphim, give me strength with these two."

"It's a valid question," Severn said. "You've been watching us for months."

"Years actually, but okay, whatever, just assume the worst—"

"How do we know you didn't somehow make us love each other?"

Amii rolled their eyes. "Konstantin, dearest... You're young, but even you know emotions don't lie. You love that big oaf of an angel, and he loves you. There's a whole lot of other baggage tied up with you two, but if you didn't love each other, I wouldn't be here. So can we just get past the whole me helping you along bit and figure out what we do next?"

"We?" Mikhail asked.

"By all means, blunder along without me, but as you've mentioned, Remiel will stab you in the back, Mikhail, and he'll gleefully cut pieces off Konstantin. Plus, there's Luxen—the demon High Lord." She puffed. "Luxen is a problem."

Mikhail's gaze slid to Severn. "I've not heard of Luxen. Should I have?"

Severn winced. He'd hoped to have this conversation much, much later. "When I left the demons, and after you killed Argothun, it created a power vacuum among demons. Luxen is not a leader, but he was clearly waiting for an opportunity to grab power. He's now the High Lord, and a concubi. We engaged in sex—I needed his ether to wear the Remiel illusion. I didn't know he had a thing for angel."

Mikhail blinked.

"Darling..." Amii leaned an arm on the chair and raised their eyebrows. "Every single demon has a *thing* for angel. It was written into their creation."

"Are you suggesting they don't have a choice?" Severn asked, keeping Mikhail in the corner of his eye. "We're born to love angels?"

They waggled their finger. "No, that ain't what I said. We can choose not to love, same as we can choose not to fight. Fucking and fighting aren't so different. Y'all just got confused along the way when the creatures you're supposed to love weren't capable of reciprocating."

"All right, so maybe Lux getting hard for angel is a good thing?" He could hope? Mikhail's frown had gathered more shadows.

"The issue is more that Remiel is mobilizing your ranks, Mikhail, and Luxen isn't capable of efficiently retaliating. We need to stop the coming battle before Remiel slaughters the remaining demons."

"How?" Mikhail asked.

"Well, there's really only one way." Amii fixed their gaze on Mikhail. "You fight for demons."

A laugh almost choked Severn.

"I won't kill angels," Mikhail refused. "They're innocent. It's the guardians who need to be stopped."

Amii clicked their tongue. "A sudden attack of morals? Pfft, please."

All of this was moot anyway because Mikhail could not just command demons. "Demons will never accept him," Severn added, his voice pitched too high. "Most of them want him dead, preferably a long, painful death, ending with his head on a spike. They'll not follow an angel."

"No," Amii sighed, "but they'll follow you, Konstantin."

"No, they won't. Wings aside, I'm an angel."

"Well, that ain't strictly true, now is it?"

"What? It is."

Amii gave him a pitying look. "You gave up a powerful memory to wear that skin. It will take something equally powerful to remove it. Something you two have in swathes, if you'd get your heads out of your own asses."

Panic caged his heart in ice. "I don't—I don't want to remove it. I'm not Konstantin."

"But you are."

"No... This is me now. I'm Severn." *I'm the angel Mikhail loves.* Gods, he couldn't go back to being Konstantin. Not now. Not after Mikhail had finally accepted him, and he'd accepted himself this way. "If this is about love, as you say it is, you can't ask me to change again."

"Who and what you are is the final truth. It must be told."

"No." He looked to Mikhail and wished he hadn't because the sadness in his eyes already felt like a goodbye. If he lost his angelness, Mikhail wouldn't love him. Of that, he was certain.

Amii rose to their feet, old bones creaking. They approached Severn and cupped his face in their soft, wrinkled hands. "Love is not fed with the eyes," they said softly. "It comes from within, and you are the same within now as you've always been. A demon with a proud, honorable heart, full of love. Mikhail loves you, not your illusion."

Severn closed his eyes. Amii's touch fell away, and he found himself afraid to open his eyes, to *see*. When he did, Mikhail was there, in place of Amii, searching Severn's face, his expression soft.

"I'll give you two some time, but the final battle is brewing. Do not delay too long, Severn. Demonkind hinges on your bravery and sacrifice."

He turned his face away, half watching the mysterious demon leave, mostly to keep from seeing Mikhail. It didn't matter. He couldn't be Konstantin. He'd tried. Everyone had tried. Amii was wrong. The angel in him was not coming off.

CHAPTER 34

Mikhail

SEVERN SUFFERED. It wasn't a physical suffering, but a suffering of the heart, and Mikhail felt what must have been a similar pain inside of himself. He touched Severn's cheek, making him look up. "If I could take your hurt away, I would."

Severn's pale lashes fluttered closed. He leaned into Mikhail's hand and covered it with his own. "What Amii is asking is impossible." Pale blue eyes looked up again, wide and bright, and full of hurt. He was afraid. Mikhail had seen Severn afraid a thousand times before plunging into battle, but not like this. Real fear.

He moved closer, leaving no room between them, and tilted Severn's chin up. "You were always the impossible angel."

Severn turned his head away and moved back. He

thrust his hands into his hair and paced the small room in a few strides. "I've..." He glanced up.

"Say it."

"We've just found each other, for real this time. A miracle all of its own. If I let go of this illusion, everything will be different. I'll be different." He dropped his hands and swore. "I can't. I don't even know how." Back and forth, he marched. "The memory I gave up, it was from the final battle, the one where... where you took my wings. Clearly it was powerful. Even if I wanted to let go of this, what power can match that?"

Mikhail stepped into his path, abruptly halting him in place. The angel who looked at him was the most marvelous angel he'd ever known, and that would never change. But the crone was right, Severn was a lie. The final lie.

"I have not been the most understanding," Mikhail admitted, making Severn smile. "I have much to learn, and I am trying to find my way. Everything I thought I knew was a lie, including you." Severn opened his mouth to interrupt, but Mikhail plowed on. "But the crone, Amii, is right. Inside, you are you. The only lie, which remains, is on the outside. In there"—he touched Severn's chest, over his heart, and Severn looked down—"you're who I learned to love. You stood at my side for years. You're who I turned to when I could not find the answers. You were my guiding light when I was lost."

Severn wrapped his fingers around Mikhail's and lowered his hand. "But I betrayed all that," he said, sadly.

"You told me you loved me. You said that was no lie. I believe you."

"I do love you. I love your strength, your sense of righteousness, I love how you'll always do the right thing, even if it takes you a while to figure out what that is. But Mikhail... you love Severn."

"Perhaps." He moved closer again, and when Severn looked up, Mikhail pulled his hand to his chest, holding it against his heart. "I do not know the answer, but I do know the lies must end."

Severn swallowed. "I won't be able to stand it if I lose you again. I don't want this... any of it. The war, us in the middle of it. We could just leave?"

"You answered destiny's call, and it brought you here. Neither of us can argue with that."

He looked so hopeful and so young all at once that Mikhail's heart ached for him.

"Suddenly you believe in destiny?"

"I believe in you," Mikhail said. "I always have, which was why Tower Bridge broke my heart."

Severn grimaced. "Gods, I'm so, so sorry."

"So am I," Mikhail whispered across his lips, and when Severn opened, he sealed the kiss, making it achingly gentle, as though Severn might break apart in his hands.

The brush of Severn's lips, the softness of his mouth, accompanied by how Severn trembled in Mikhail's hands, it was true and real, and wasn't that all that mattered?

Mikhail broke away and whispered against his cheek, "I am a mess, and hopeless and riddled with flaws, but I'm trying to find my way. Please don't ever give up on us, on me."

"Never." Severn's hands clutched at Mikhail's shirt.

"I love you," Mikhail breathed the words against Severn's neck. Severn groaned and pulled him in for a second, hungrier kiss. His tongue and mouth plundered

Mikhail's, the kiss devastating. He threw his arms over Mikhail's shoulders and hitched his legs around Mikhail's waist, and Mikhail suddenly, desperately, needed to feel Severn's skin against his own. They staggered, and Mikhail backed Severn against a wall, holding him so close the lines between them blurred. Severn's teeth nipped Mikhail's neck. His fingers tore open the borrowed shirt, and his suckling mouth trailed over Mikhail's revealed shoulder.

He wanted this angel beneath him, inside of him, everywhere all at once. He wanted to spread his wings wide and have Severn kneeling at his feet, his beautiful mouth around Mikhail's erect member. The tiny cottage suddenly felt too small to contain them.

Severn still had his thighs locked around Mikhail's waist. Mikhail carried him out the door, through the small garden, and into the long grass fields, and there, under silent starlight, he let his wings open in all their glory.

At Severn's gasp, Mikhail caught sight of the wings in the corner of his eyes, finding three pairs instead of one. There was no denying destiny now. The evidence was right there.

Severn's wings revealed themselves—dark and demon, broad and powerful—and a potent rush of lust tore all the doubts from Mikhail's mind. He gritted his teeth, pressed his forehead to Severn's, clutching the back of his neck, and locked their gazes. This moment, this was it. There could be no more lies. "Be true," he demanded. "Be Konstantin." He didn't know if this was right, if it was even what he wanted and not some product of his body's unchained desire, but it felt right. Like they'd come full circle, but this was a battle of love, not hate.

Severn's breaths heaved through his gritted teeth. He stared into Mikhail's eyes, and then placed his boots back on the ground, took three steps away, spread his wings, flung his head back, clutched his fists at his sides and... *changed*.

The angel in front of Mikhail blurred at his edges. Pale skin darkened, absorbing the shadows, crafting form from night. His height grew, his body filled out, and two horns sprouted from his head, arching backward, and there stood the monster Mikhail had beaten on the battlefield ten years ago.

Powerful.

Undeniable.

The demon lord Konstantin.

He staggered, wings adjusting to counterbalance his new weight, and then he dropped to a knee, gasping. Long, sharp nails dug into the ground as he clutched at the earth, as though needing to hold on to it.

The truth.

Finally.

The last time Konstantin had been on his knees in front of Mikhail, Mikhail had butchered him, crippled him, and taken his wings.

Konstantin looked up. Pain etched deep lines into his face. A face not unlike Severn's but sharper, harder, with eyes so full of hurt, it made Mikhail want to tear out his own heart and hand it to him.

Mikhail's knees thumped against the ground. He clutched Konstantin's wrought face in his hands. His heart thumped against his ribs, his body flushed and hot and riddled with emotion. Fear. Fear that he'd asked too much of them both. But Severn was still inside Konstantin's beautiful eyes. Because Severn was Konstantin, and always had been.

Love swelled Mikhail's heart, unbidden and limitless, stronger than ever.

He eased his grip, careful not to force this, and leaned so close that his mouth hovered over Konstantin's. A moment passed, another, and it seemed as though the world held its breath along with Mikhail.

Konstantin's warm lips brushed Mikhail's, his tongue teased across Mikhail's bottom lip, and then Mikhail fell into the kiss, savoring the true taste of the impossible demon he loved. His enemy. His lover. The only true thing in a world made of lies.

He kissed his demon in a starlit field and knew nothing would ever be the same again.

CHAPTER 35

 jall

WHEN LUXEN HAD TOLD her Konstantin had fallen from
Aerie with Mikhail in his arms, she didn't believe him.
When he'd said a pair of mated humans had blabbered to
their neighbors, boasting they had two angels staying
inside their quaint little cottage outside London, she
refused to consider one of those angels was her brother.
But what other angel would lodge with humans?

Then a natural disaster had befallen the stronghold of
Haven—a storm so full of rage it had shattered their glass
sanctuary—rattling the feathered assholes from Aerie to
investigate, and Djall wondered again about the two angels
in a cottage in a field.

Now, hunkered in the grass outside the cottage,
cloaked by night, she witnessed the horrifying truth.

Konstantin—wings restored—on his knees, embracing

the butcher Mikhail in love, not hate. There was no blade in his hand, no intent to kill. The intent was obvious, and it had nothing to do with killing and everything to do with a different passion.

Her brother, in all his demon glory, looked at the enemy with love in his eyes.

She'd come to reason with him, but when she'd first approached the cottage, a third demon had stood outside the little building with Mikhail and Konstantin. Djall had silently landed out of sight and crept through the high grass. When the unknown demon left, Djall had moved in, staying low and silent. If she could just get Konstantin alone...

And then she'd witnessed the impossible, Konstantin shedding his wretched angel-skin in front of the guardian.

He'd lied about not being able to shake off the illusion, and he'd lied about wanting to stop Mikhail. The abundance of sexual ether smoking off the pair did not lie. Konstantin was hopelessly in love.

He was the traitor they'd all feared him to be.

Djall lowered her gaze, unable to watch any more.

Luxen would not be pleased. Konstantin had convinced him he was thoroughly on the side of the demonkind. He'd lied to the High Lord in the worst possible way—with sex. For Luxen to have missed the ruse was a slight against his concubi prowess. He would not stand for it. If he saw Konstantin with Mikhail, he'd kill Konstantin.

And her stupid brother, so deeply distracted by the guardian, wouldn't see the attack coming.

She had to separate them, by any means, for Konstantin's own good. He'd thank her eventually, when this ridiculous infatuation with the guardian had passed. Get him away from the angels, and he'd retake his place as Lost Lord of the Red Manor. Red Manor would be strong again, strong enough to snatch control from Luxen. And Konstantin would lead all demons to victory.

She melted back into the shadows and sent a silent prayer to the demon lord Aerius, asking for guidance. As she did, silent movement in the night sky caught her eye. Stars blinked, and briefly, starlight framed the unmistakable silhouette of Luxen's wings.

No!

How had he known...?

That sly bastard had followed her.

And he wasn't alone.

She had to act now. Before Luxen witnessed the same of Konstantin as she had. She had to protect Red Manor and her last remaining blood-brother.

Freeing the whip from her hip, she spied Mikhail through the swaying grass, his wings a vast, feathered target for her whip's vicious spike.

Konstantin would hate her, but one day he'd understand and thank her for destroying this forbidden love before it destroyed him.

Konstantin and Mikhail's journey continues in the final book, Infernal Sin.
Pre-order today.

If you enjoyed reading Eternal Sin, please leave a review.
Every review helps readers like you find new books.

Please sign up to Ariana's newsletter so you don't miss all the news.

www.ariananashbooks.com

Also by Ariana Nash

Silk & Steel Series

When Eroan, one of the last elf assassins, is captured trying to kill the dragon queen, he knows his death imminent. Until the queen's youngest son, Prince Lysander, inexplicably lets him go.

Eroan expected death, but in the darkest of places, when all hope is lost, love finds him instead.

This epic fantasy adventure topped the Amazon charts for months. Discover the darkly delicious world of Silk & Steel today.

Click here to start the adventure with Silk & Steel, Silk & Steel #1

Prince's Assassin Series

Soldier, Nikolas Yazdan, survived a brutal eight year war, but can he survive the wicked and cruel Prince Vasili Caville and the lies within the Caville palace?

Read King of the Dark, Prince's Assassin #1, today to find out!

ABOUT THE AUTHOR

Born to wolves, Rainbow Award winner Ariana Nash only ventures from the Cornish moors when the moon is fat and the night alive with myths and legends. She captures those myths in glass jars and returning home, weaves them into stories filled with forbidden desires, fantasy realms, and wicked delights.

Sign up to her newsletter and get a free ebook here: https://www.subscribepage.com/silk-steel

www.ingramcontent.com/pod-product-compliance
Lightning Source LLC
Chambersburg PA
CBHW060906190726
48286CB00002B/393